A stowaway. B ___ **to deal with s** ___ **now, when his** ___ **Bianca.**

"Mendoza!" he shouted. "Turn back to Santo Domingo. We have a knave to set ashore."

Balthazar reached down to grasp the lad by the collar of his doublet, knocking his cap askew. One long, dark brown curl escaped, falling along a startlingly graceful neck.

The stowaway shoved Balthazar's hand away, standing up straight as he/she pulled off the cap. Bianca glared up at him, shaking her hair free over her shoulders.

"You cannot turn back, Captain Grattiano," she said. "The wind is against you."

As Balthazar stared at her in utter astonishment, he heard someone roar with laughter. "Looks like we have a new crew member, captain."

"I can swab a deck or mend a rigging rope with the best of them," Bianca declared. Her words were bold, but her eyes – her eyes still held that deep caution. That distance.

A distance that had suddenly grown much narrower.

Balthazar caught her against him, his lips coming down hungrily on hers as his crew broke into raucous cheers.

HIGH SEAS STOWAWAY

"Smell the salt spray, feel the deck beneath your feet and hoist the Jolly Roger as McCabe takes you on an entertaining, romantic ride."

—*RT BOOKreviews*

A NOTORIOUS WOMAN

"Court intrigue, poison and murders fill this Renaissance romance. The setting is beautiful…"

—*RT BOOKreviews*

A SINFUL ALLIANCE

"Scandal, seduction, spies, counter-spies, murder, love and loyalty are skilfully woven into the tapestry of the Tudor court. Richly detailed and brimming with historical events and personages, McCabe's tale weaves together history and passion perfectly."

—*RT BOOKreviews*

HIGH SEAS STOWAWAY

BY
AMANDA McCABE

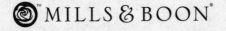

All the characters in this book have no existence outside the imagination of the author, and have no relation whatsoever to anyone bearing the same name or names. They are not even distantly inspired by any individual known or unknown to the author, and all the incidents are pure invention.

First published in Great Britain 2010
Harlequin Mills & Boon Limited,
Eton House, 18-24 Paradise Road, Richmond, Surrey TW9 1SR

High Seas Stowaway © Ammanda McCabe 2009
Shipwrecked & Seduced © Ammanda McCabe 2008

ISBN: 978 0 263 88303 9

04-0610

Harlequin Mills & Boon policy is to use papers that are natural, renewable and recyclable products and made from wood grown in sustainable forests. The logging and manufacturing processes conform to the legal environmental regulations of the country of origin.

Printed and bound in Spain
by Litografia Rosés S.A., Barcelona

Amanda McCabe wrote her first romance at the age of sixteen – a vast epic, starring all her friends as the characters, written secretly during algebra class.

She's never since used algebra, but her books have been nominated for many awards, including the RITA®, *Romantic Times* Reviewers' Choice Award, the Booksellers Best, the National Readers' Choice Award, and the Holt Medallion. She lives in Oklahoma, with a menagerie of two cats, a pug and a bossy miniature poodle, and loves dance classes, collecting cheesy travel souvenirs, and watching the Food Network – even though she doesn't cook. Visit her at http://ammandamccabe. tripod.com and http://www.riskyregencies.blogspot.com

Prologue

Venice—1525

He *was there*.

Bianca Simonetti stared down from her narrow bedroom window, peeking through the merest crack in her curtain to the young man who stood on the narrow walkway far below. Though she could see little but his pearl-trimmed red velvet cap, the glossy fall of his dark hair on his shoulders, she knew it had to be him. Balthazar Grattiano.

For no one else in all her fifteen years had ever made her heart beat as *he* did. It pounded now in her breast, the rush of nervous blood loud in her ears. Her very fingertips and toes tingled with hot, nervous life whenever she just looked at him!

She knew that she was far from the only female in Venice he affected this way. His dark green-gold eyes, muscled shoulders and elaborate codpieces were the subject of many whispered, blushing confidences from patrician salons to two *scudi* brothels all over the city. Bianca heard much of it, for all those women, countesses and whores alike, came to her mother with their secret desires.

Maria Simonetti, long a widow with her own household, was the most gifted fortune-teller and tarot-card reader in Venice. She could not practise her trade openly, of course; Venice was not the strictly religious enclave Madrid was, but no one wanted to court charges of witchcraft. So, the lower stories of their house were let to a dressmaker and a wigmaker, while Maria told her fortunes in a back room, discreetly draped and curtained.

But everyone in the city knew, in their own unstated way, of Maria's gifts. The women especially. They came seeking a glimpse of their future, assurances about their husbands or lovers or businesses. They came in tears, in hope, even sometimes in elation. And, very often, they came with anxious questions about Balthazar Grattiano. They never noticed Bianca, sitting so quietly in the shadows, and she heard them all.

Balthazar was handsome, one of the most handsome men in Venice. That was obvious just to look at him, of course. He was rich, the only son of the fabulously wealthy and powerful Ermano Grattiano. He was also now nineteen, of an age to marry, to take on the responsibilities of a patrician gentleman. Yet he did not seem inclined to do any such thing, preferring to spend his time with courtesans, gambling, drinking, or, most shocking of all, watching the ships being built at the Arsenal.

Bianca heard all this, heard the whispers of his great "inventiveness" in bed, his mystery and elusiveness. Heard the blushing pleas—would he one day marry her? Make her his exclusive mistress?

But Bianca knew more than his good looks, his riches, his sexual prowess. She looked into his luminous dark green eyes and saw a longing to match her own. A deep, endless pool of vast sadness.

She did not have her mother's gifts. The cards were just painted pasteboard to her, the future a blank. But from her infancy she had been taught about people. Had seen them come and go in her mother's house, heard their deepest fears and wishes, their goodness and their malevolence. She could read them, in her own prosaic way. When she first saw Balthazar, first looked into his beautiful eyes, she saw not the smug satisfaction expected of such a privileged young man. She saw only that sadness—and that swirling pool of anger.

In her everyday life, she would not expect to meet anyone like Balthazar Grattiano. They were not of the same status, and their lives did not overlap. Her mother did not mind Bianca listening to fortune-telling sessions. Maria was open about the realities of life, but she was also protective. Bianca was not allowed to go dancing with young men, or even to leave the house at night. Especially during this season of Carnival. She heard only about the masked, wine-fuelled parties from her mother's visitors.

But Balthazar's father, the powerful and fearsome Ermano Grattiano, had recently begun coming to the house, seeking card readings from her mother. Maria sent Bianca away when he was there, but she heard from the maidservant that Ermano, who had buried three wives, wished to marry again. He was passion-ately desirous to have more children, and was con-vinced Maria could tell him the right lady to bear those babes, convinced the cards would reveal his wife, his destiny.

Balthazar sometimes came with his father to these sessions, always waiting outside on the walkway. That was when Bianca first saw him, one day as she came home from the market. He leaned against the peeling stucco wall, wrapped in a rich fur-trimmed cloak, a book open in his hands.

Bianca, too, loved to read, a strange accomplish-ment for a young woman. She also learned languages, English and Spanish, and account-keeping, to run her own business one day. A bookseller on the Rialto sometimes loaned her volumes, yet never enough to satisfy her vast desire for knowledge. Her curiosity as to what such a handsome, well-dressed man was doing reading outside her house overcame her usual shyness, and she asked what the book was.

He glanced up at her, and that was when she saw

it—that great sadness, that barely leashed fury against she knew not what. He never seemed to turn that anger on to her, though. Instead, he smiled, and showed her his volume on navigation, surprised she could read the Spanish words. After that, whenever Ermano would come to discover more about his destined bride, Bianca would slip down to talk to Balthazar, to see what he was reading, to talk about the strange glories of the world outside Venice. The wonders of England, Spain, France, Turkey—even the new islands beyond the seas.

Bianca had never heard anyone speak of such things, and she was fascinated by this new vista of great lands. Fascinated by Balthazar himself, by this tiny glimpse of wishes and dreams hidden so deep beneath a glittering and careless façade. By this burning desire to run away, to soar free into some unknown fate.

But it frightened her, too, this view outside her narrow existence. This strange, wondrous young man.

"Why," she asked him once, "would you want to leave Venice? You have everything here." She could not imagine then that anyone could desire more than riches and fame, an old family name, which Balthazar possessed in abundance. Could not imagine someone would desire more than Venice, which was all the world and more, a sparkling golden place on the water. She herself would surely one day marry and raise a family, help run her husband's business, and be bound to her home and duties. Her only consolation was that it would be *here*, in Venice.

Balthazar—he had no need really to go out and seek his fortune, as those who travelled to the New World did. It lay at his very feet, wherever he walked. Money, glory, love. How could he want to leave it all?

But he merely smiled at her, that sweet, sad smile, his beautiful eyes old. So very old. "Come with me, Bianca," he said, taking her hand. It was the first time he had touched her, his fingers cool and strong over hers. She shivered at the sudden rush of pleasure, the joy even such a casual, innocent caress had on her senses. She held so tightly to him, not caring where he led her. She would surely walk into the very flames of hell, if it was with him.

But he led her not into brimstone, only to the edge of the nearest canal, where his father's gondola waited. People hurried past them: maids with their market baskets; serious patricians in their black robes, intent on affairs of state; satin-clad courtesans who smiled and giggled at Balthazar. Bianca saw, heard, none of them. It was as if she was wrapped in a silent, sun-drenched spell. In the presence of Balthazar, his warmth, his clean, seawater scent, that blocked out the noise and fury of the everyday world.

"You see this water?" he said, gesturing to the canal below them.

Bianca nodded absently. Of course she saw the water! She walked past it every day on her errands. It was like every other canal in Venice. Smelly, perhaps, but unremarkable. A way to get around.

"No, really look at it," Balthazar said, tugging on her hand, and she glanced down. The water was still with no gondolas passing to churn its waves, an iridescent swirl of blue, purple, green, a greasy black. A few bits of flotsam bobbed about, bottles, scraps of vegetables, a dead rat or two. Winter was coming on swiftly, and the usual sweet-sick smell was muted.

"What am I looking at?" Bianca whispered, making him laugh.

"We see here only the surface of the city," he said. "The beautiful churches and palazzos, the jewels and silks, the riches that are the envy of the world. But beneath that beauty…"

Bianca watched the slow swirl of the water, the blend of dark rainbow colours that concealed garbage and decay deep beneath. "Dead bodies? Chamber pots?"

Balthazar glanced at her, his brow raised. The sunlight caught on the fine emerald in his ear, dazzling green-yellow set in elaborate filigree. The jewel was also a concealment. Balthazar, too, was like the waters of Venice, like the city itself—beauty masking dark depths.

"Exactly, Bianca," he said quietly. "Death and decay. Dishonesty at every turn."

"But can you really run from such things?" she asked, thinking of his books of travel and adventure, of new lands. "They are surely always with us. We are only ourselves, no matter where we go."

"True enough," he said. "We can only try to make

amends, to find truth. To purify our own souls. Only then can we be free of what lies beneath, what we never dare reveal to the world. We can only seek the truth, at any price."

The truth at any price. Balthazar fascinated her more than ever at that moment, but also scared her. For an instant it was as if she glimpsed his very soul, so dark and labyrinthine, as hidden as the waters' depths. It was only a glimpse, a fleeting moment, before all was concealed again behind his smile. He held her hand even tighter in his and led her back home, gallantly kissing her fingertips before she fled back to the safety of her own chamber.

It had been many days since that last encounter, and Bianca had only glimpsed him for quick instants. It was truly Carnival now, and he was occupied with his own social obligations. Ceremonies and festivals, banquets, balls—lounging in velvet-cushioned gondolas with beautiful blonde courtesans. Bianca had seen him thus with the notorious Rosina Micelli, his head tipped back against the gold-embroidered cushions, eyes closed in decadent pleasure as Rosina whispered in his ear, her jewelled hand stroking his hair.

He and his father had not been back to Bianca's home until today. Rumour had it that Ermano was courting the perfumer Julietta Bassano, and Balthazar was occupied at the brothels and gambling halls. Bianca peered down at him now from her window, unsure what to think or do.

Even though she had not spoken with him in days, she had thought of him at nearly every moment. Turned his cryptic words about decay and truth over and over in her mind until she was dizzy with it. She longed to ask him what he meant, craved one more privileged glimpse into his hidden heart. Wanted to show him her own.

Yet at the same time she wanted nothing more than to run from him! From those dangerous truths he offered like emeralds.

Bianca let the curtain fall back into place, turning to the small, precious looking glass on the wall. She was too thin, with curling dark brown hair that refused to lighten no matter how much lemon juice she applied. Her cheeks were hollowed, her eyes too large for her face, her shoulders bony, and she had no bosom to speak of. But now, as she thought of Balthazar Grattiano standing so close outside, her pale skin glowed pink, her brown eyes were bright.

Yes, he *was* a strange and frightening person, unpredictable, unreadable. Not like anyone else she had ever known. If she were wise, she would stay far away from him, from all the dangerous Grattianos. Yet Balthazar made her feel alive and excited; he was like the heat of the sun on a grey, drab day. And she was powerless to turn away from that wondrous light.

Soon enough, he would be gone completely from her workaday orbit. No matter what he said about freedom and truth, about the wide new world, he would have to marry a fine patrician lady and take on his own responsibilities. Take his fearsome father's place of great power and influence. There was no escaping one's true place in life, for either Balthazar or her.

She had to seize the few moments left, when she could see him, talk to him. Maybe even touch his hand again. Such beautiful, fleeting seconds would have to last her for a long time, once she was married to a respectable tradesman with no dark depths to his soul. No mossy green eyes that burned her very heart with their intensity.

Bianca smoothed her brown curls back, securing them as best she could with combs and pins. She discarded her apron, wishing she had time to change into something finer than her blue-striped work dress. But there was not a moment to lose, if she wanted to speak with Balthazar before his father finished hearing the message of the cards.

She spun around and dashed out of her room, hurrying down the back staircase. The house was quiet today, as their tenants were off to watch a play in the Piazza San Marco and the servants were at market. From her mother's small room at the end of the corridor, Bianca could hear the hum of voices. Her mother's tone was low and soothing, as it always was. Ermano Grattiano's was strained, argumentative, angry. So foolish of him. Didn't he know by now one could never quarrel with the cards?

Bianca snatched a blue wool cloak from its peg by

the door and slipped outside, not bothering to change from her thin house slippers. Balthazar was still there, leaning against the wall. He did not read today, just watched the quiet walkway, his handsome face unreadable, his arms folded over his chest, as if he was deep in thought.

But perhaps his air of indifferent mystery was merely a product of too much Carnival, Bianca thought wryly. Of too much dancing and wine and debauchery. Their dressmaker tenant had told her all about a grand masked ball at the Piazza San Marco that had gone on until dawn. No doubt Balthazar had been there, too, with Rosina Micelli.

She longed to ask him about it all, to ask if the distant revelry she listened to from her window was as glorious fun as it seemed. Ask if he loved Rosina, or one of the other blonde courtesans. But she could not. She just leaned next to the wall beside him, and eventually he silently held out his hand to her. She slid her fingers into his cool, ungloved clasp, feeling the weight of his jewelled rings against her skin, the tenuous silken thread that was their connection.

"Do you not want your cards read, as your father does?" she asked.

Balthazar laughed harshly. "My father is a great fool, always thinking his future will change simply because he wills it so."

"You don't think we can change our future?"

"Nothing ever really changes, does it, Bianca? We

all go on in the same way, day after day, trapped. I don't need the cards to tell me what my life holds."

Bianca gazed up at him in silence, at the smooth, perfect beauty of his face that concealed so much pain. Perhaps he was right not to see what the cards revealed about him, just as her mother was right not to tell Bianca's fortune no matter how much she begged. Hope in the unknown future was sometimes all poor mortals had.

"What of the world in your books?" she asked.

"What of it?"

"Surely the future is anything but predictable *there*. Especially in those Spanish lands over the sea. It's a new world, is it not, where a person could be or do anything. Discover a life that is wondrous strange, and old ways have no place. We—you—could be whatever you wanted. Not even the cards could say what."

He smiled at her. "No more Balthazar Grattiano?"

"No more Venice, even."

"It sounds a dream-world indeed."

"Of course. But is it not there, in your books? Others have seen it, written about it. Why couldn't we?" Bianca felt her excitement growing, expanding like a silken banner in the wind as she thought of it all. Of new, unknown shores. Her old fear burned away at the thought of no more Venetian society, no more strictures, even as she knew it was impossible.

Balthazar laid a gentle hand on her cheek, his smile rueful as he gazed down at her. "You *are* a dreamer, then, my practical Bianca."

"Are you not as well?" she said, leaning into the warmth of his touch. The revelry of the sound of her name in his voice— "my Bianca." "If you don't wish to dream, to dare, why do you read all those books? Why do you study ships and the sea? If you truly think there is no other life than this, no chance to make a change, why bother? Why not just follow your father's ways of thinking and being?"

His smile darkened at the edges, his touch falling away from her. "I am not like my father."

Bianca knew that. Balthazar did not have his father's air of easy contempt towards his inferiors, of assured, comfortable confidence. She saw Balthazar's great struggle against all the feared Grattiano name meant, even if he did not speak his anger aloud. But before she could open her mouth to tell him so, to assure him she understood, the door to her house opened with a resounding crash.

She and Balthazar sprang apart as Ermano stormed out. Bianca eased back into the shadows for fear he would notice her, and turn that icy glare of his pale green eyes on to her. If Balthazar's touch held the warmth of the summer sun, his father carried naught but the freeze of deepest winter. A killing chill.

She raised the hood of her cloak over her hair, watching Ermano warily. His bearded face was white with fury, as it always was after a reading of the cards. The gods of fortune had failed him yet again. His gaze scanned the walkway, and he gestured to Balthazar, not even looking directly at his son.

"Come, Balthazar," he said tonelessly. "Let us leave the stench of this hovel behind us. I have had enough of its foulness."

As he turned to stride towards the canal and his waiting gondola, his ermine-lined cloak swung back to reveal his white brocade doublet. Bianca let out an involuntary gasp, pressing her fingers hard to her lips to hold back the sound.

One of the fine sleeves was stained with crimson blood.

Balthazar's face, too, turned pale. As white and still as an indifferent marble statue.

"Balthazar!" his father called imperiously. "Come, I do not have all day for you to dally with the maid-servants. I have an errand at Signora Bassano's shop."

The words seemed to galvanise Balthazar to action. He wrenched one of the rings from his fingers, a large ruby surrounded by pearls. He pressed it, along with a bag of coins, into Bianca's frozen hand.

"Just in case you need it," he whispered in her ear. "Remember the new world, Bianca."

Then he, too, was gone, and she was alone in the shadows of her house. She stared down at the ring, at the stone as dark red as the telltale blood on Ermano's sleeve. The silence around her was heavy, deafening, a living, palpable thing. It was as if she was the only breathing thing left on the street. In the whole decaying city.

Surely that blood could not mean what her horrified imagination conjured. Surely it was just some bizarre ritual involving chicken hearts or goat livers, as she read about secretly in her mother's forbidden books.

But she could not dismiss the whispered tales she heard of Ermano Grattiano, of his cold ruthlessness. Of the danger to anyone who became involved with him.

Bianca felt a haze of dreamlike unreality settle around her, like a drugging fog. She slipped the ring on to her finger and crept into the house, even as all her instincts screamed at her to run away. Whatever waited for her, she could not hide from it for ever.

The soft soles of her slippers made only a whisper of sound on the tiled floors as she tiptoed down the narrow, darkened corridor. Her mother's work room, where she met with those seeking her counsel, was at the end, the doorway concealed by a heavy velvet curtain.

Before she even stepped through that portal, Bianca could smell it. The sticky, coppery tang of blood. The miasma of vanished life.

She eased back the curtain, peering into the little chamber. Silvery incense smoke still hung in the air, its sweetness blending sickeningly with the blood, the remnants of Ermano's bergamot cologne, the tang of spilled wine. Atop the round table was a jumble of cards, goblets tipped on their sides. The stools were knocked askew on the floor.

And Bianca could see her mother's foot behind the purple tablecloth, the torn hem of her white gown.

Still caught in that stick web of dreams, the piercing numbness of ice, Bianca stumbled around the table and the broken stools. Her mother lay in a crumpled heap on the tiles, her eyes wide and staring, glasslike, into nothingness. Her long, dark brown hair spread around her, matted by the blood from the gaping wound at her breast.

The wound caused by the dagger still poised there in her body, its emerald-set hilt glinting in the gloom and smoke. The dagger Bianca had seen often enough in the sheath at Ermano's waist.

She knelt slowly next to her mother, reaching out to lightly touch the cold hand. Bianca could see it all in her mind, as horrifyingly sharp as if she had witnessed it herself rather than mooning over Balthazar Grattiano outside, listening to his faradiddle about truth and new lives. She saw Ermano in a rage when the cards would not tell him what he wanted, saw him destroy the instrument of his frustration—her mother. Then he just walked away.

Bianca remembered the rumours. Ermano Grattiano destroyed who and what he chose, anyone who thwarted or angered him. It was even said that, years ago, he had murdered his own mistress, the beautiful Veronica Rinaldi. He never paid for his crimes, of course, and anyone who tried to hold him accountable, who even witnessed his evil deeds, soon vanished themselves.

Bianca stared in horrible fascination at that dagger.

Ermano would surely be back for it, if nothing else. It was too valuable, too distinctive. He would be back to clean up his deed. Or he would send Balthazar to do it for him.

Had Balthazar just been using her, then? Using their ruse of friendship to help his father in this evil scheme? Betraying her feelings for him?

A sudden spasm of bone-deep grief and fear seized Bianca, banishing that distant, numb dream, those last hopes. Her hand tightened on her mother's, and a ragged sob escaped her lips. Her mother was *dead*, at the hands of a terrible, and terribly powerful, villain. And she, Bianca, was trapped. If she stayed, if she confronted the Grattianos and took the revenge her heart cried out for, then surely she would also end up dead. A dagger in the heart, and then tossed into the canal to rot alone in the swirling waters.

Who would avenge her mother then? Who would see that justice came to the Grattianos, if she was dead?

As Bianca knelt there beside her mother's body, it was as if the sheltered girl she had been fell away like a warm cocoon, a concealing shawl that held her apart from the cruel world. A wall of new ice encased her heart, hardening her, steeling her resolve. Ermano might have killed her mother, while she was distracted by the all-too-handsome Balthazar. But they would *not* destroy her. Instead she would be the instrument of their destruction.

This was one crime of theirs that would not go unpunished. She was just a girl now, but that would not always be so. She knew what she had to do, come what may.

Bianca dragged the purple cloth from the table, scattering cards and goblets, and used it to cover Maria's body. Then she hurried to a small carved chest in the corner, rummaging through the linens and boxes of incense until she found the bag of coins her mother always secreted there. Those, along with that the treacherous Balthazar gave her, would see her away from Venice, to a place of safety where she could study and plan. No doubt Balthazar had pressed the ring and money on her as some sort of salve for his guilt, or perhaps as a silencing bribe.

But she would use it to keep herself away from the Grattianos—and to help with their downfall one day.

For she would be back, somehow, and when she was it would be Grattiano blood that would flow at last.

Chapter One

Santo Domingo on the island of Hispaniola—1532

It was a quiet evening in Santa Domingo. But Bianca knew very well that would not last long.

She stood behind the high counter along the back wall of her tavern, rinsing pottery goblets and keeping a close eye on her customers. It was mostly the usual crowd, sailors and merchants biding their time as they bought supplies, loaded their cargoes, and waited for the convoys that would bear them back to Spain. A few of the men were headed in the opposite direction, from Maracaibo or Cartagena towards the mines of Peru.

They were all focused on the riches they hoped awaited them, the gold and pearls and emeralds, and drank their ale and rum with a tense, watchful air.

Bianca had been hearing disquieting whispers, though, and she was sure they had something to do with the ship that had limped into port today. Its battered sails and broken mainmast were like an omen in a town that was far too superstitious already.

But the more frightened the men were, the more they drank, and thus the more coin they spent in her establishment. Bianca was all in favour of *that*, as long as things didn't turn nasty. It had taken her a sennight to clean up after the last fight, and those were days she could ill afford to lose. She had to pay her servants, her suppliers—and she didn't intend to end up on the streets. Not again.

She narrowed her gaze as she studied the room. It wasn't vast or grand, nothing like the gilded palazzos of Venice still so vivid in her memory. It was just a long, low chamber, the walls freshly whitewashed after the last repairs. The wooden beams overhead were dark with smoke, hung with bunches of dried herbs in a vain attempt to drive away the stench of rum and wool-clad bodies in the island heat. The uneven planks of the floor were warped and sticky, covered by close-packed tables and benches.

Si, humble it might be, but it was hers. A small accomplishment, perhaps, compared to the great feats of fortune hunting she heard every day here in Santo Domingo. But it was something.

Bianca stored the last of the goblets behind the counter, checking to make sure her pistol was tucked there still. Quiet as it was, she still didn't trust that strange, heavy tension in the air. It was almost like the atmosphere that hung over the island just before a storm broke, taut and still. Something was afoot. Santo Domingo had been peaceful enough as they waited for the arrival of the next Seville-bound *flota*, but perhaps there was a raid coming.

She frowned as she remembered the last battle here with French pirates, Jean Florin and his men hanging at the mouth of the harbour as she and her late husband Juan had arrived. But that was years ago. The French had seen the folly of their actions, and ceased to harry the mighty Spanish fleets and their fortified ports. It couldn't be that. Then what was it?

Bianca glanced towards Delores, who was stirring the stew pot over the fire and humming to herself. The maid wouldn't know; she was a good worker, but cared mostly for flirting with the sailors. But Bianca knew who *would* have all the gossip, who knew everything that happened from Puerto Rico to Peru. And he was sitting right over by the wall.

She poured out a generous portion of her most expensive beverage, a punch made of rum, sugar and nutmeg, and carried it over to Señor de Alameda, aide to Governor de Feuonmayor.

Alameda was a quiet, watchful man of around thirty years old, not one to cause a fuss, yet still a regular visitor at the tavern. She suspected he was a spy of sorts, and heard more of his news at the docks than he did in the governor's fortress. Also, he was diddling Delores. Not that Bianca cared. His escudos were good, he caused her no trouble, and he sometimes passed on titbits of valuable information.

She placed the goblet before him and sat down across the small table, wiping her hands on her apron. "I hope all is well with the governor, Señor de Alameda," she said.

He glanced at her from his inscrutable black eyes, giving her a polite smile. "Ah, Señora Montero. Your company is indeed a rare pleasure. And, yes, the governor is quite well. Much occupied with the expansion of the cathedral."

"Hmm. Then that cannot be what is amiss."

Alameda took a slow sip of his drink. How very Spanish he was! Nothing ever given away. So polite, so careful, so dangerous. "Amiss?"

"I have lived in this town long enough to know when trouble is in the air," she said. "And I have an interest in what happens. Business is better when all is peaceful and prosperous."

He laughed ruefully. "That is undeniable, *señora*. A peaceful island where we can all go about our business is better for everyone. Our churches and storehouses unmolested, our shipping free of pirates…"

Bianca turned suddenly cold, despite the warm breeze from the windows, carrying the smell of the lush green island from the mountains out to the sea. She remembered those rotting bodies twisting in the wind, the smoldering shells of houses and the desecrated icons. Reports of torture, rape, murder. "Pirates? Is that the trouble?"

Alameda glanced away. "Señora Montero, pirates are always a menace in this part of the world, are they not? Desperate villains who seek to steal from the King and the Church. Surely you know that as well as anyone, for was your late husband not a sailor? But they are not an immediate threat to Santo Domingo. Quite the opposite."

The tavern door blew open, admitting a rowdy group amid shouts and coarse laughter. Delores could see to them for now, but Bianca knew she would soon have to go back to work. The time for conversation was short; she had to find out what was happening. In Santo Domingo, knowledge was power. "What do you mean, Señor Alameda?" she said impatiently.

He nodded. Like any primero player, he knew when it was time to show his hand. "I have heard reports that the *Calypso* has made its way into our port."

Whatever Bianca expected to hear, it was not that. She gave a startled laugh. "The *Calypso*? Have your spies started seeing fantasy vessels, then?"

The *Calypso*, captained by a man of near-supernatural navigational skills, was whispered about in the tavern when the rum was freely flowing: undefeatable in battle, so fleet it could outrun any storm, said to have sailed to the very edge of the earth and returned bearing unimaginable riches. Even Juan, her salty old navigator of a husband, had been awed by the tales. They had the aura of ancient, golden myths.

But Bianca had long ago given up on myths and heroes.

"The *Calypso* is real enough," Alameda said.

"And her captain? The man they say could navigate his way out of hell itself? And steal the devil's treasure while he's at it."

Alameda laughed. "He is real, too, though I doubt he has seen the underworld."

"There is hell enough on earth, especially for a man who sails the seas for his living."

"True, Señora Montero. Just don't let Father Yanez hear you speak so. None of us have chosen an easy path so far from home, not even someone as wealthy as the captain of the *Calypso*."

Bianca glanced towards the counter, where Delores was pouring rum and dishing out stew. "If the *Calypso* is so very grand, why have I never seen it? I have been in Santo Domingo for a fair number of years. I thought I knew every vessel that plies its way between Peru and Seville."

Alameda shrugged. "I've heard tell Havana is his port of choice, and too that he has his own hidden island somewhere between here and Jamaica. He is servant to no one; he certainly does not answer to Governor de Fuenmayor. Perhaps not even to the king."

A man who was servant to no one. Now Bianca *knew* he was a myth. And a most intriguing one. "Then who does he answer to?"

"That, Señora Montero, is something I would very

much like to know. I'd pay a great deal to anyone with more information on the captain of the *Calypso*."

"You know so much already."

"Me? I am merely a functionary. I seek only to mind my own business, make my fortune so I can quietly retire in Andalucia. Away from this cursed place."

And amen to that, Bianca thought, swatting at a mosquito. But much as she, too, sometimes longed to escape, dreamed of Venice and a long-lost home, she knew this was her place now. A place always fraught with dangers. "I would vow you are more than that, *señor*. Does the governor not rely on you?"

"You are too kind."

"In fact, I would vow you know everything that happens on Hispaniola. Even to the furthest *estancia* up-island." The noise of the tavern grew, spiralling louder and louder as more new arrivals poured in. "Such as why the *Calypso* would suddenly be calling at Santo Domingo."

"That is simple enough. I hear there was a great battle off the coast of Puerto Rico."

"A battle?"

"Between the *Calypso* and a pirate vessel. The villains were driven away, but the *Calypso*'s mainmast was damaged. It was made worse when she was caught in that storm in the Mona Passage a few days ago." His gaze swept over the room. "The storm that has made Santo Domingo so very crowded of late. So many newcomers to our fair city, many of them seeking shelter at the governor's fortress."

"So, the *Calypso* has come into port for repairs?" Bianca laughed. "Not so mythical after all. I would have thought anyone who could steal the devil's treasure could magically repair his own mainmast, even in the midst of a storm."

"Oh, *señora*, I would not dismiss him so quickly." Alameda laid a few coins on the table and rose to his feet. "Now I must be on my way. I have a conundrum of my own waiting at the fortress, though one I am rather looking forward to returning to. I thank you for the drink, and for the conversation. As always, it has been most enlightening."

Bianca pocketed the coins as she watched him leave, his fine clothes quickly obscured by the crowd of rougher, rowdier patrons. *He* might be enlightened, yet she was more puzzled than ever. What was it about this one ship and her mysterious captain that seemed to have all of Santo Domingo balanced on a knife's edge?

She made her way back to the counter, searching each face to see if one could belong to the unknown captain. Most of them were people she knew, sailors who usually called at her tavern when they were in port. They came to celebrate, to spend their new-found treasure, or to mourn losses at sea, bury their sorrows in her rum. The coin seemed plentiful enough tonight, but she also saw apprehension on their sunburned faces.

She glanced beneath the counter to make sure the pistol was still there. She didn't usually care for firearms; they were too unpredictable, too apt to fire off at the wrong moment. Just like the inhabitants of this town. But when havoc threatened, there was nothing like a great deal of smoke and noise to disperse it.

Bianca took over pouring out the drink, sending Delores to wait on the tables. The room was crowded indeed now, every chair filled, men lined up along the walls. The windows were all open to let in the warm tropical breeze, but it wasn't quite enough to banish the heat. The smell of rum and wool and Delores's stew.

Bianca lifted the loose curls off the nape of her neck, the wild tendrils that always escaped their pins and clung damply to her skin. For some reason— perhaps Alameda's words of "home"—she couldn't be rid of the images of Venice in her mind. Cool, white rooms, their tall doors open to terraces over the canals. The sound of music in the air, masked faces around every corner. There had been danger aplenty there, too. No one knew that better than Bianca. But there was also great beauty.

She closed her eyes for a moment, and for that one instant she stood again outside her mother's house. A girl full of foolish hopes and dreams, gazing up at the face of—

No! She slammed a goblet down on the counter, opening her eyes to the hot, noisy reality of the tavern. She would not think of that again, of Venice and Balthazar Grattiano. They were gone. This was all that mattered now. His betrayal had led to so much grief and hardship. To her life on her own.

She had work to do.

As she sent Delores off with another tray of drinks, a man appeared at the counter. Bianca stared at him curiously. He was not one of those regular customers. Indeed, she was certain she had never seen him before. He was tall, with the lean, muscled frame of someone accustomed to climbing rigging, but he was also thin, almost—hollow.

Despite the heat, he wore a hooded cloak, his face cast half in shadow. But Bianca could see enough to tell he was quite handsome, or would be if he shaved off his tangled black beard. His sun-darkened face, all gaunt angles, and his brown eyes were almost elegant, in a haunted way. Drawn with taut lines of some deep-seated sorrow. He gazed at her wearily.

For a moment, she wondered if he was a wraith, summoned by her own unhappy memories. A spirit, perhaps flown from the decks of that half-myth the *Calypso*. But then he gave her a whisper of a smile, and her strange fancies vanished. He was just a man, though certainly a very odd one. Even for Santo Domingo.

"Rum, *por favour*, *señora*," he said, his voice deep and rusty.

Bianca poured out a generous measure of the thick brown liquid into a pottery goblet, sliding it to him over the scarred wood of the counter. "You are new to Santo Domingo, yes?"

"It has been some time since I last visited," he answered, after he neatly drained the liquor. She poured out more. "This place was owned by Señor Valdez then."

"It *has* been a time. I bought it from Valdez more than a year ago, before he went back to Spain."

"A year ago," he muttered, as if that was an unfathomable length of time. Perhaps it was. Lives did change in only a moment, after all.

She found herself unaccountably curious about this wraith. People came and went on this island, all of them intent on their own business, most of them running from something. Just like Bianca herself.

"Was your ship damaged in the storm?" she asked. Perhaps he was even a crew member of the *Calypso*. That would explain why she had never seen him before. A mysterious wraith from a mythical ship.

He nodded shortly, holding out his goblet for yet more rum. "I will not be here for long, *señora*."

Here in Santo Domingo? In her tavern? In the mortal world? It was obvious he wasn't in a talking mood, so she just poured.

"Oh, *señora*!" Delores cried, hurrying behind the counter to refill her tray. The noise was almost deafening now. "They say the *Calypso* is in port! And that her captain defeated a vast fleet of pirates *and* repaired the mainmast in a storm with his own hands…"

When Bianca turned back to the counter, the cloaked man was gone. She saw only a glimpse of his back, as he headed towards a small table in the shadowed corner.

As the night went on, some of the men passed out on the floor and were dragged out by their comrades, only to be replaced by new, thirstier patrons. More men from ships seeking repairs after the storm. But Bianca did not glimpse the wraith-man again, busy as she was pouring the rum and ale and mixing more punch.

Matters seemed to have reached a crescendo of laughter and incoherent, drunken shouts when the door opened once more. Not with a great bang, as with more desperate men in search of liquid oblivion, but slowly. Quietly. Yet still everyone turned to look.

Bianca straightened from wiping spilled ale on the counter, pushing her hair back from her brow. She tensed at the sudden watchful air in the room, the way the great noise fell to a murmur—like the waves of the sea just before a storm hit.

This, then, was surely the trouble that had been coming all night.

She turned to the door. A man stood there, framed in the night-darkness. Not alone—there were six or seven others arrayed behind him. But he was all she could see.

He was tall, probably taller than any other man in the tavern as he had to duck his head through the doorway. Like the strange cloaked man, he had the lean frame of a man who had spent his life balanced on a pitching deck and climbing swaying rigging. His chest and legs were supple beneath his black leather jerkin and hose, a tall pair of worn black leather boots. She glimpsed powerful, bronzed forearms revealed by the turned-back sleeves of his white shirt. A man of action, then, of the sea and all its dangers.

His hair, a long, straight curtain of sun-streaked light brown, fell to his shoulders, bound back from his face with a black silk scarf.

And that face...

She knew it well. *Too* well. Bianca clutched at the edge of the counter, certain now that she had to be dreaming. For that face, despite the fact that it was a bit older, the skin browned by the tropical sun and the sea's salt spray, belonged to Balthazar Grattiano.

The one man she had vowed to kill if she ever saw him again.

Chapter Two

Bianca held on to the counter, watching in wary silence as Balthazar and his men made their way through the room. The crowd seemed to part for them, like Moses and the Red Sea; the roar of sound faded to whispers, crackling like summer lightning. She shivered as she watched them take their seats at a suddenly empty table near the window.

For an instant the humid taverna faded, and she was a girl again, standing on the walkway outside her house as she listened with rapt fascination to Balthazar Grattiano talking of ships and navigation, of the wide, wondrous world to be found outside Venice. Talking of glorious freedom.

He had gained his freedom, it seemed, for here he was, in the New World, thousands of miles from his privileged Venetian realm. But she was still locked in her prison. It went with her wherever she turned.

"Is it really him, *señora*?" she heard Delores say. The awed whisper dragged her back from Venice to the rough wooden floor of her taverna.

"Him, Delores?" Him—the devil?

"The captain of the *Calypso*! I had heard tell he was here, in Santo Domingo, but I did not believe it." Delores sighed. "He is certainly most handsome."

"Whatever he might be, he is a customer," Bianca said, with a brisk calm she was far from feeling. She thrust a tray into Delores's trembling hands and proceeded to fill it with goblets of punch. "And hopefully a thirsty one. Go on now."

She leaned against the counter, watching as the maid sashayed across the room to Balthazar's table. As she laid out the drinks, Balthazar glanced up at her with a sensual half-smile.

If Bianca had harboured any doubts at all that this was not Balthazar Grattiano, that smile banished them. It was the same charming smile she remembered, alluring, beautiful, carving deep dimples in his cheek that made a woman long to touch them with her fingertip. To kiss them, to feel the rough silk of his sunbronzed skin under her tongue.

A lovely, sex-laden smile—with a strange, empty sadness behind it.

He was older, yes, just as she was. Hardened by the sea and the harsh sun. Yet still Balthazar Grattiano, the love of every woman in Venice.

And still just as irresistible to women, Bianca

thought wryly as she watched Delores giggling. Most of the men who came to the tavern Delores turned away with a saucy word. She was faithful in her way to Alameda. But she seemed in no hurry to leave Balthazar's side.

Bianca didn't have much time to worry about Balthazar and his charm, though. A fresh crowd of customers came in, wanting their rum, and she was kept busy again. Slowly, inexorably, the noise level grew once more as a game of dice commenced. The throng closed around Balthazar, blocking him from her view.

From her view, perhaps, but not from her thoughts. She was all too aware of his presence, of the sparkling tension within her. He was near her again, after all this time! The man she had once been so infatuated with; the man whose father killed her mother.

And what was she, Bianca, going to do about it now?

As she rinsed more goblets, she thought of the *Calypso*, that "legendary" ship said to be able to cross the Atlantic in three weeks. To be impervious to attack and storms. And Balthazar was her captain? How had he gone from his life of luxury in glittering, sophisticated Venice to being such a great seaman, the captain of his own vessel and the scourge of the seas?

She laughed with disbelief. Perhaps his father had bought him the ship, and hired a mage to ring it round with spells. Ermano Grattiano had always seemed enthralled with the occult.

As she set the clean goblets out on the counter, she

caught a blur of movement from the corner of her eye. Somehow that flash, out of the kaleidoscope of the room, caught her attention. She turned just in time to see the mysterious cloaked stranger from earlier. The hood was still drawn up, concealing his face, but he moved with a stealthy, swift purpose. As Bianca watched, bemused, he drew a thin, lethally sharp dagger from beneath his sleeve.

Her stomach lurched. Violence was a constant threat in Santo Domingo, quarrels threatening to break out at any second, over any tiny slight, and spill out like a river of blood into the cobbled streets. A place so far from the civilities and comforts of home, a place so full of treasure and rum and rivalry—yes, danger was a constant. Hot tempers flared under the hotter sun. But not in *her* taverna. She had seen enough violence to last her a lifetime.

The cloaked man vanished into the milling crowd. Every nerve in her body tense, Bianca reached for her pistol. As she hurried around the counter, Delores let out a high-pitched shriek.

And the dreaded pandemonium broke out.

Men's shouts, the crash of crockery and splinter of wood added to the cacophony of Delores's screams. Bianca shoved her way through the thick crowd, sensing their readiness to join in any fight, even one not of their own making. One man drew a blade from his boot, but Bianca kicked it away, pushing him out of her path.

"Get out of my way, you poxy whoresons!" she shouted. "I'll not have this in my tavern."

Some of the men around her fell away, yet she still heard curses and crashes from the central knot of the trouble. At last she shoved through to see Balthazar's table overturned amidst shattered pottery and spilled rum. Delores was still shrieking, and Balthazar's men dashed around shouting, swords drawn as if to menace any who stood in their way. One of the men held the wraith's ripped cloak, though the man himself had utterly vanished.

And Balthazar—he lay on the floor, his left shoulder bleeding from a dagger wound as his men closed ranks around him.

It would almost be comical, if it wasn't so very dangerous. And threatening to become even more so, as Delores's screams and the men's bellowed threats and clashes of steel grew ever louder, like a match tossed on to dry timbers.

Bianca knew words would do no good. She had no hope of even making herself heard. So she pointed the gun at the ceiling, braced herself and released the matchlock.

The exploding recoil nearly knocked her from her feet. Whitewash from the blasted hole rained down on them as the explosion reverberated deafeningly. Thick clouds of acrid smoke billowed in the suddenly silent air.

"I told you I'll not have riots in my place of business," she said calmly. "Now, everyone get out.

Unless you mean to make yourselves useful and clean up this mess."

She swung the pistol in a wide arc, and most of the would-be brawlers fled, leaving the door swinging in the breeze. Soon only Delores and the men from the *Calypso* were left.

Bianca shoved the gun at one of them and knelt down beside Balthazar, ripping off her apron to press it against the wound. It was not terribly deep, but she could tell from a cursory glance that it would need cleaning and stitching. A mere few inches lower and the blade would have found his heart.

She was not the only one who hated Balthazar, then.

One of the men leaned over her, his bearded face peering down intently at the captain. "Is he dead, *señora*?"

Before Bianca could answer, Balthazar opened his eyes and growled, "Of course I am not dead, Mendoza. My hide is tough enough to resist such a puny blade and bad aim."

"Not so *puny* as all that," Bianca said, lifting her wadded apron to peer at the wound. "It's caused enough bleeding. You are fortunate the man's aim was off, Captain Grattiano, or I'd have to deal with a corpse in my tavern."

He stared up at her with his moss-green eyes, his gaze sharp and steady, as if he sought to peer into her very soul. "How do you know my name?"

Bianca had no answer for him. She tore her gaze

from his, shifting him so his head rested on the lap of her grey wool gown. The apron was becoming soaked, and Delores's sobbing was so loud Bianca could scarcely think.

"Oh, shut up, Delores!" she cried. "Go fetch me some water and some clean rags for bandages. Now! And you—Mendoza, is it?"

The bearded man nodded. "I'm quartermaster of the *Calypso*."

"Mendoza, what happened? My tavern is usually a peaceful enough place. The governor doesn't appreciate those who come here to deliberately cause trouble."

It was Balthazar who answered, his voice rough and taut with suppressed pain. "It was Diego Escobar," he said. "He vowed he would find me, and so he did. I was a fool to let my guard down even for an instant."

"I said we should have stayed aboard ship, captain," Mendoza said gruffly.

"We've been aboard that poxy ship for weeks," Balthazar said. "And, as the *señora* says, her tavern is usually peaceful."

"Until *you* arrived," Bianca answered.

"We will pay for the damages."

"Yes, you will. Along with all the drink you consumed," Bianca said. Delores came back with the cloths and a basin of water, and Bianca peeled back the sodden apron. The bleeding seemed to have slowed, and the edges of his torn shirt were dark brown and crusted.

Balthazar turned his penetrating stare to the men who hovered around. "And why, may I ask, didn't you go after the knave?"

"We thought you were dead, captain," one of them answered.

"Oh, so there was no need to hurry after my murderer, then," Balthazar said. Bianca thought she heard a note of wry humour in his voice, beneath that pain, "if I'm not here to see him brought to justice."

Another man tossed aside the would-be assassin's cloak. "He just vanished, captain! Like a puff of smoke. Just like last time…"

"Mayhap the man is a wizard after all," Balthazar muttered. Bianca swiped a wet cloth at the edges of his wound, and he arched up with a hiss. "Damn it, woman! Are you trying to kill me, too?"

"I am trying to help you," Bianca said, pressing him back down. As his head rested again in her lap, a long strand of his hair fell over her hand, silken and binding. "Despite the trouble you have caused me. Infection takes hold fast in this climate; the wound must be covered."

She glanced down at the floor beneath them, sticky with rum and sand. The toxic mixture would be sure to kill him as fast as any dagger-wielding madman. And, for some unfathomable reason, Bianca wasn't quite ready to let him go.

Not until he gave her some answers.

"Help me carry him upstairs," she told the men. "I can clean the wound better there."

They hesitated, looking towards the captain for any orders. And Balthazar, in turn, gazed steadily at Bianca, as if he, too, sought answers. Finally, he nodded. "Do as she says," he ordered. "And then get back to the ship to make sure the villain causes no trouble there."

"But, captain," Mendoza protested, "should we not stay watch here?"

A wry smile touched the corner of Balthazar's lips. "Oh, I would vow I am protected enough by the *señora* and her harquebus. I'm sure that's not her only weapon."

"Indeed not," Bianca murmured. She led the way up the narrow staircase to her living quarters, Delores following with the water and bandages. Balthazar let out one deep groan as his men lifted him, but was silent when they carried him to Bianca's bed.

After the men reluctantly departed, and Delores was sent to bed, the silence grew thick and hot around them. Bianca's bedchamber was small, a whitewashed chamber tucked beneath the eaves with room only for a bed, a small table and chair, and her husband's old sea chest. Balthazar Grattiano, despite the fact that he lay flat on his back, seemed to fill the whole space with his overwhelmingly masculine presence.

Bianca felt more tense, more frightened, than she had in the midst of a threatened riot.

She drew in a deep breath, and was surrounded by the smell of the tropical night wind from the open window, the wax of the candles—and of Balthazar. He smelled of clean linen, leather, salt air, sweat, blood, and that dark, mysterious scent that was his alone. She remembered that scent all too well from years ago.

But she was not that infatuated girl, hanging about hoping for one glimpse of him as he passed by, for one whiff of his cologne. And he was obviously not that young man, either. So beautiful. So angry.

She carefully removed his boots and his leather jerkin and cut away his torn shirt, conscious at every moment of his steady gaze levelled on her. Oh, the beauty was still there, undeniably. As she smoothed the damp cloth over his wound, she couldn't help but notice the lean, sculpted muscles of his torso, the smooth, gleaming skin a light golden colour, as if he worked on deck without his shirt. There were scars, too, pale, thin old ones, and one long, jagged pink cut along his ribs.

So, presumably, the anger was still there, too. That darkness that gave an edge to his angelic beauty, and once made her flee in fear.

But he was in *her* home now, in her very bed. At her mercy.

She traced the cloth from the wound along his collarbone, lightly over one brown, flat nipple, and down his chest over the light sprinkling of pale brown hair. He drew in a sharp breath, his rippled stomach muscles tightening, but he did not pull away. Did not even say anything. His skin seemed gilded in the candlelight, a taut line arcing down to the band of his hose.

Yes, he *was* still handsome, the most handsome man she had ever seen. Even after all her travels, she had never found a man to compare. But there was a hard edge to his beauty, a barely leashed violence. She would be a fool to give in again to his fatal allure.

Her gaze trailed the length of his black-clad legs, sprawled across her white sheets, the bulge of his codpiece, his lean hips. Yes, he was handsome, and she knew he was good in bed. All the whores in Venice had sung his praises, and that was long ago. He had now had years to hone his carnal skills to absolute perfection. And she was a widow, who had gone many months without a man in her bed. It was only natural she would be drawn to him now.

But only a fool would give in to lust for a villain. And she hoped she was no longer a fool.

Bianca snatched her hand away from his chest, from the warm rise and fall of his breath, the steady beat of his heart, and went back to the wound. Still he watched her in silence, always watching, as if he divined all her thoughts. Surely *he* was the wizard, and not the knife-wielding stranger!

She soaked a fresh cloth in rum and pressed it to Balthazar's shoulder. His breath hissed, but he gave no other reaction to the sting.

"I will have to sew this up," she muttered. "But you needn't fear. I've done such things many times. You'll have only the tiniest scar to add to your collection."

As she turned to reach for her sewing box, he

startled her by suddenly grabbing her wrist. She tried to yank away, but he held fast, his roughened fingers like a vise. He drew her closer, until she hovered over his bare body, unable to move or even look away. Her heart pounded in her breast, until she was sure it echoed like a drum in the silent room.

"I know you," he said, his voice soft and low in contrast to the steel of his touch. "But from where?"

Bianca shook her head. "I don't think so."

"Yes. I have seen you before—and you knew my name."

"Of course I know your name. Santo Domingo has been buzzing with talk of the arrival of the *Calypso* and her oh-so-daring captain."

"That's not it," he insisted. But he let her go, falling back to the pillows as if exhausted. A fierce frown creased his brow. "Where have we met before? Who are you?"

"I am Señora Montero," she answered. She opened her box and tried to thread a needle, despite her trembling hands. "And I am certain I would remember *you* if we had ever met before, captain. A tavern owner cannot afford to forget a face, especially if it belongs to a troublemaker!"

He gave a harsh laugh. "I would vow you know much about troublemakers, *señora*."

"And I would vow you know much about women," she said, knotting the end of her thread. "No doubt you have me confused with a female of your acquaintance in some other port. Perhaps you are growing feverish and delusional."

"Perhaps I am. Everything seems very—confused. But I will remember soon enough, *señora*. A ship's captain also cannot afford to forget a face."

Bianca held a goblet of rum laced with an herbal sleeping potion to his lips. "Remember later, then, but drink this now. It will dull the pain."

He drank readily enough, his lean body growing so relaxed and pliant he did not even move as she sank the needle into his flesh. She just wished she could be so steady, could remove herself from the acute awareness of his body heat, his every breath. At last she finished, tying off her thread before she dared glance at his face.

He seemed to be asleep, the harsh lines of his face relaxed so he seemed young again. She was free at last from those all-seeing green eyes, even if only for a moment.

Bianca threw herself into the chair, burying her face in her hands. She longed to cry, to shout out the confusion of this strange night that had borne Balthazar Grattiano back into her life! Yet she was bound in silence, in the tangle of the past come suddenly into the present.

She went to the window, pushing the casement further open to catch more of the night breeze. The sky was a heavy purple-black, dark clouds obscuring the moon and stars, blown in by that storm that damaged

Balthazar's ship. Santo Domingo was quiet enough now, in the hours before dawn. Only a few houses near the banks of the Rio Ozama were lit from within. The governor's fortress, high on its hill overlooking the town, was a blank, silent behemoth.

Soon, the streets would come to life. She would have to face cooking, and cleaning up the mess downstairs. She would have to face the man in her bed. But for now it was as if she was alone in the world. Alone with Balthazar Grattiano.

Bianca rubbed wearily at her aching neck, turning to the small looking glass hanging on the wall. She almost laughed aloud at the sight that greeted her in its silvery reflection. How could Balthazar possibly recognise her, when she hardly recognised herself? Her curling brown hair stuck every way from its pins, tangled and wild. Her cheeks were a hectic red, her eyes lined with purplish shadows. Her grey wool dress, never fashionable in the first place, was stained with Balthazar's blood.

She unlaced the simple bodice and tossed it with her skirt over the chair, standing before the glass in only her chemise and stays. As she brushed out her hair, yanking at the stubborn tangles, she knew that Balthazar would not long think he had her confused with some past dalliance. He had always preferred blondes with lush bosoms and full, pink lips. And she—well, she was a thin, dark tavern owner. Any meagre attractions she had as a girl in Venice were surely coarsened by a life of hard work on a tropical island.

Not that it mattered, of course. Balthazar and she would have their reckoning soon enough. And then it wouldn't matter a bit what he thought of her bosom, or she his codpiece. For now, she was almost too weary to think of anything at all.

Bianca loosened her front-laced stays and slipped into bed, as far from Balthazar as she could get on the very edge of the mattress. She wrapped a blanket tightly around herself, but even as she fell into slumber she could feel his heat, reaching out to wrap seductively around all her senses…

Chapter Three

It was the old dream again, the one that Balthazar always thought long-buried until it rose up to haunt him. Like a monster of the deep—*Here Be Serpents*. Here lay the past.

A vast storm raged, silver lightning flashing overhead from the bowels of black, roiling clouds. Cold, jagged whitecapped waves broke across the bow; the screaming wind drove past the bare masts, flying the caravel through the air as if it was naught but a child's toy. Rain beat on the deck's planks, hard enough to bruise. The ceaseless pitching of the sea, the driving rain, the howling dread of his men who feared to be swallowed by the sea—Balthazar saw it all again. Like a painting of the judgements of hell come to life before his very eyes.

Yet still he dragged on the rudder, trying desperately to steer the ship away from her certain death, even as he knew in his heart that all his efforts were in vain. All he had worked for, all the men who trusted and followed him, were doomed.

It seemed a fitting end. For had he not spent all his life fighting against the dark inevitable? Against his own tainted blood, his sins. And all for naught.

His muscles ached as he strained against the rudder. He would not let it win! Not the sea, that pitiless mistress. Not the black emptiness that always threatened to swallow him. Salvation lay ahead, if he could just fight hard enough. But as he felt at last the blessed yielding of the rudder under his slippery grasp, a terrible sound split the sulphurous air. The crack and splinter of wood.

Balthazar shook the wet strands of hair from his eyes, staring up at the damaged mainmast of his ship. It listed, wavering in the gale. Soon, all too soon, it would crash to the deck, driving a hole through the wounded ship that would take them all to the bottom.

And atop the mast perched his father. Ermano Grattiano, dead these seven years by Balthazar's own hand, clung to the splintered wood like a demented bat from hell, his black cloak and white mane of hair flying wildly in the wind. Even from that distance, his green eyes glowed, and he held out his bejewelled hand beckoningly.

"I told you that one day you would be mine, Balthazar," he shouted, his voice clear and ringing over the howl of the storm. "We are one flesh and blood; you cannot escape me. You have killed my body, but I will always be with you!"

Balthazar shouted out his own fury. In his burning anger, he climbed the slippery, tumbling mast, not feeling the cold or pain. He was intent only on destroying the evil within himself, once and for all.

But Ermano only flew higher, ever distant, ever beyond reach. At last the mast fell entirely, sending Balthazar plummeting towards the battered deck—and certain death.

But he did not land in the cold sea. The waves did not rise up to claim him at last. He fell back on to a soft bed, amid a tangle of sheets and blankets.

He opened his eyes, staring wildly up at the dark wooden beams bisecting a whitewashed ceiling. The stench of lightning was banished by a warm, soft breeze from an open window.

This was not his cabin aboard the *Calypso*. There was no constant pitch and sway of waves, no watch bells or shouts from the deck. For a moment, he could not remember what had happened, he was still caught in the nightmare. In the storm, which had been all too real. And his father, who lived now only in his mind.

He tried to roll to his side, and the sudden stabbing pain in his shoulder reminded him. They had come ashore in Santo Domingo, seeking comfort after their travails in the Mona Passage. The battle with Diego Escobar and his pirate lot, the storm that damaged the mast and crippled them. They sought warm, dry beds, drink, food free of rot and weevils. Perhaps a pretty woman. What he had found was Diego, and his dagger.

"Damn the man's eyes!" Balthazar cursed, as hot needles of pain shot down his arm. Diego had fought them on the seas, where Balthazar was greater and Diego knew he had no chance of victory. So, he had crept to Hispaniola and waited like a spider for his moment.

Ermano Grattiano might indeed be dead, but there was never any shortage of villains waiting to take his place. Diego was proving to be one of the more determined. Revenge was a potent motivation for anyone; it could even drive a man to piracy and murder. Balthazar knew all too well about revenge.

As he lay back on the bed, the rest of the night came flooding back to him in waves of vivid colour and noise. The flashing dagger, the shouts and commotion of running feet and utter confusion. The explosion. And the woman who peered down at him, her brown eyes filled with sparkling anger, concern and…

And what? He, who had spent years at sea and in rough ports learning to read men as if they were nautical charts because his fortune, his very life, depended on knowing their nefarious plans and deepest desires, could not read *her* face at all. Her eyes were a beautiful veil, opaque as fine Seville lace. Perhaps her life, too, balanced on knowing the thoughts of others while always hiding her own.

What had she read of him, as she stared down at him

in that cacophonous tavern? As she tended his wound so carefully? And where, by all the gods *where*, had he seen her before?

Suddenly, there was a soft rustle of sheets, and that face was above him as she leaned over him. She must have been sleeping beside him in the bed, for her hair was loose, a river of wild curls over her shoulders, and she wore only a thin white chemise. The candles had burned out, and she was lit by the faint, chalky moonlight streaming from the open window.

He frowned as he stared up at her, studying her in the shadows. That sense of recognition was still there, but it was like a dream that faded with the dawn. The more he grasped for it, the more elusive it was. Yet it was still there, as tantalising as a Venetian perfume.

She was not beautiful, not like the courtesans of his youth, or like Marguerite, Nicolai Ostrovsky's French wife. Golden, charming creatures of light and air. This woman, his physician tonight, had a thin face with high, sharp cheekbones, a long nose, full lips, and brows like silken raven's wings. She obviously did not hide from the tropical sun, for her cheeks and nose were scattered with freckles. Her slim hands, slightly rough from work, had been calm and quick as they tended to him.

Not a pampered lady, then, but not a dockside whore either. He had surely never tupped her, or danced with her at some Venetian ball. But still that feeling persisted. She was not a stranger.

She reached out and gently touched his brow with

one of those hands, her fingers cool and steady. The sleeve of the chemise fell back to reveal a thin wrist unadorned by any jewelled bracelets or rings. She smelled of clean water and soap, of ale and some rich tropical flower. Sweet and exotic, strange and familiar, all at once, like the islands themselves.

She smoothed back his tangled hair, her touch resting lightly on his cheek. His rough beard, the product of long days at sea, surely abraded her skin, yet she did not draw away. Her dark eyes watched him, gleaming like obsidian in the night.

And Balthazar felt the most unaccountable, irresistible urge to turn his face into her touch, to kiss the soft inside of her wrist, just where her lifeblood beat so strongly. To taste the palm of her hand with his tongue, until she gasped and that veil was torn away. Until she showed him her true self.

But he merely watched her, warily waiting to see what she would do.

"Do you feel feverish?" she said softly. "You are a bit warm. I should change your bandage."

He felt the ripple of tension in her arm, as if she would pull away, and he reached up to gently grasp her wrist. To hold her touch to him, just for a moment more. It seemed so very long since he had touched a woman, inhaled her essence, felt her softness. It was a refuge, one he knew could not last.

A refuge in a mystery, for he *still* could read nothing of this woman!

"What is your name?" he said urgently, his hand tightening on her wrist. Here, wrapped in the velvet of an island night, alone with her, it seemed vital he know her name.

"I told you. I am Señora Montero." Despite the Spanish name, the impeccable cadence of her Spanish words, he could hear a different accent lurking just beneath. A slight, unguarded music that was not there before, emerging only because she was tired.

It was almost like his own accent. Venetian, even after years of sailing the Spanish Main.

"What is your given name?" he asked.

She smoothed her touch along his cheek, her finger-tips lightly skimming the line of his jaw. Feathering over his lips.

He captured the tip of her finger between his teeth, tasting her at last. She tasted of salt and flowers, like something deep and needful.

Her breath hissed, and he felt her shiver. In that moment, there was only the two of them wrapped in the secrecy of darkness. No past, no future. It mattered not at all who she really was.

The ache in his shoulder, too, was distant as he wrapped his good arm around her waist and drew her atop him. She also seemed caught in the dream-moment as she slid her body against his. Their lips met in a kiss, soft at first as they explored each other, the tastes and textures and feelings. Then she sighed against him, and the murmur of it, the whisper of her breath mingling with his, awakened something within him.

He touched her tongue with his, and a wave of heat enveloped them, a blue-white flash like the lightning of the storm. Their kiss was fast, artless with a primitive need, a blurry clash of mouths and bodies and sighs.

Through the humid rise of passion, Balthazar felt himself harden, felt her caress on his naked chest. He reached down and grasped the hem of her chemise, dragging the thin cloth over her legs, her hips. She was slender but strong, her thighs parting to straddle his hips and hold him her willing prisoner beneath her.

She moaned as his avid touch skimmed over the soft skin of her inner thigh, the arc of her hip. She cried out, her mouth torn from his as she arched up, her back supple as a bow. Balthazar, too, lurched up from the bed, his hands on her hips as his mouth slid from hers, along the line of her throat.

His tongue touched the frantic pulse at the base of her neck, and he felt her very life flowing into him. After facing death, the raging sea, the dagger, her warmth and lust were intoxicating. He kissed her collarbone, the slope of her shoulder, as he pushed her chemise back to bare one breast.

Her bosom was small but soft, the nipple a dusky disk that lengthened and hardened as he blew a gentle breath over its pouting flesh. He drew it deep into his mouth, suckling it hard as she gasped.

Her fingers drove deep into his hair, holding his

mouth to her breast, her legs tight on his hips. Through the thin fabric of his hose he felt the damp heat of her womanhood.

"Balthazar!" she cried hoarsely. "I…"

Suddenly, like a cold wave, she pushed him away. As he fell back to the pillows, she scrambled off his body, her feet landing with a thud on the wooden floor. The ache of his wound came flooding back upon him as she spun around, as he lost her taste and warmth, the passion that came upon him so suddenly, so irresistibly.

He pushed himself up on his elbows, panting as he watched her draw the chemise back over her shoulders, hiding her beautiful breasts. She, too, was breathing hard, her shoulders trembling. She wrapped her arms around herself, until finally she gave one last shuddering breath and peered back at him over her shoulder. Her profile was as pale and pure as an ancient relief in the moonlight.

"You know my name," he said. "And you speak with a Venetian accent."

A bitter smile touched the corner of her mouth, still swollen with his kisses. "Of course I know who you are, Balthazar Grattiano. You are famous from Seville to Peru. The captain of the *Calypso*, the master of the seas—and of ladies' bedchambers."

He watched in tense silence as she wrapped a shawl over her shoulders and walked towards the door. There was no haste to her movements, only the taut line of her back, the soft sound of her rushing breath.

Or maybe it was *his* breath. He felt as if he had been climbing the rigging in a stiff wind for hours.

"My name is Bianca," she said quietly. Then she vanished, closing the door behind her.

Balthazar groaned, collapsing back to the tumbled bed amid the smell of her soap, the salty essence of their lust. His body was still hot and hard, aching with the need to drive itself into her welcoming womanhood. His blood pounded in his ears, his shoulder throbbed.

And yet—Bianca? Who the hell was *Bianca*? He knew no one called...

Then, as if in a flash of fire, he remembered all too well. Bianca.

"Bianca Simonetti," he muttered, pounding his fists into the yielding mattress. Of course. Yet another avenging spirit from the past.

Chapter Four

Bianca leaned back against the closed door, her hand pressed hard to her aching stomach. She had just kissed Balthazar Grattiano! Had let him put her breast in his mouth, straddled his near-naked body like a dockside whore. And, what was even worse, she had *liked* it.

Nay, more than liked it! The pleasure had been so deep, so hotly overwhelming, that she had forgotten who she was, who he was, where they were, even the terrible past. She had forgotten everything but the sensation of his lips on her skin, the hard steel of his penis under her hips. The raw need that had bound them together, tighter and tighter, until she vowed she would explode like her gun.

Bianca moaned, covering her flushed face with trembling hands. A man she had not seen for years, a man who had betrayed her friendship in the worst way, appeared again in her life, and what did she do? Kill him, take her long-delayed revenge? Nay, she nearly had sex with him in her very own bed!

Behind the closed door, she heard the squeak of floorboards, a muttered curse, as if Balthazar tried to get out of bed. Bianca ran down the narrow staircase, heedless of her bare feet, not even sure where she was going. The tavern was deserted in the pre-dawn gloom; the hot air still smelled of spilled ale and rum, greasy leftover stew and the acrid tang of gunpowder. The broken furniture from the fight, good now for nothing but kindling, was pushed back against the wall.

Bianca turned towards the kitchen at the back of the building. It was hotter in there, the fireplace banked and smoldering for the day's cooking, but Delores still slept in her pallet by the hearth. Bianca slipped past her and out the door into the night.

It was nearly morning. A greyish-pink light tinged the edge of the thick blackness, and soon flickering lights would appear in the windows of the shops and houses. The bells would ring out for Mass from the half-finished cathedral on the plaza. The governor's palace fortress, high on its hill above the rest of the town, slumbered behind its impenetrable stone walls, its vigilant cannons. It was silent now, yet soon enough would come to life and tend to its business, the business of every inhabitant of Santo Domingo— tending to the flotas, the treasure fleets that wended their way to Spain a few times a year.

Bianca gazed out over the town, so deceptively

peaceful in the dawn. Santo Domingo had been her home for a long while now, longer than most of the European inhabitants. They could not bear the heat, the strange food, the insects and storms. Could not bear to be so far from the culture and comforts of Spain. They came only to make their fortunes, to serve the king and thus win a place at court. Then they made a dash back to Seville and Madrid, putting the strange witchcraft of the islands behind them.

But Bianca had come to love it. Oh, indeed there were times when she longed for Venice, but after so many years of wandering, of hardship and struggle, she had found a home of sorts in this rough port town on the Rio Ozama. She had built a business, one that prospered and required of her only honest hard work, and not the degradation of her body. The loss of her soul.

She gave a wry laugh. It was not always grand to haul unconscious drunkards out her door at three in the morning, to scrub sticky floors and negotiate with hard-bitten merchants for her rum and sugar and ale. There were certainly times, many of them, when she wanted to bash an obnoxious customer over the head with a cauldron and be done with it! To run screaming into the jungle, never to be seen again.

But there were also times when she could leave the jostling tavern behind and walk along the banks of the river. Could smell the salt breeze from the not-so-distant sea, tinged with the sweetness of greenery and exotic flowers. Could see the sky overhead, the purest, clearest blue, lit by a blinding yellow-white sun. Could absorb the natural beauty and peace into herself and hold it close to her heart.

Santo Domingo was rough, true, especially compared to Venice. Despite the fortress, the cathedral on the plaza, the substantial houses where only thirty years before there were just grass huts, it had the air of a temporary holding place. Of a land where the bonds of civility were thin indeed, and the threat of violent raids and rebellion hung heavy. Yet Bianca had lived in worse places, and she had found a refuge of sorts here.

But now that refuge was torn asunder. Balthazar Grattiano was here, in her very home. Bianca frowned. What was he doing here, so far from Venice? From his jewels and silks, his expensively beautiful courtesans. He did seem to be a ship's captain now, one spoken of with awe, even in a hard place like this. One obviously respected by his men. Something shattering must have happened to him to bring him across the ocean, just as it had with her.

But what could it possibly have been? Balthazar Grattiano was a veritable prince in Venice, the sole heir to a wealthy and powerful, and ruthlessly cruel, father. He had no need for the riches of the New World, unless it was solely Grattiano greed. One kingdom was not enough.

If he could appear so suddenly in her life, would Ermano be next?

Bianca shivered, remembering her mother's glazed, staring eyes. The blood, the dagger. The terrible fear that drove her to flee, to never see Venice again. Was it all beginning again?

She shook her head fiercely. "Nay! I will not let it," she muttered. This was *her* home. She would not flee the Grattianos twice.

And she would discover what Balthazar did here. Then she would know how to act.

The pale pink light of dawn was spreading over the sky, banishing the dark of night and with it her cold flash of fear. She was not the frightened girl she had been then, alone without her mother and heartbroken at the betrayal of a handsome young man. She was a woman grown, and she would not allow the Grattianos to steal one more thing from her. Not her home, her pride *or* her due revenge.

Bianca sighed. Well—perhaps Balthazar *could* steal one more kiss from her. She *was* a woman, after all, and he was still the most handsome man she had ever seen. But that was all, and it would only be on *her* terms.

She whirled around and hurried back into the kitchen, where Delores was yawning as she stirred the fire. The morning brought a new day's hard work, and it couldn't be disrupted by a beautiful ship's captain lying wounded in her bed.

Unless he had managed to vanish from her life as quickly as he appeared. She could hear no stirrings abovestairs, but she went about gathering water, bandages and a bowl of the reheated stew anyway.

"Is he still here?" Delores asked.

"Of course," Bianca answered. "He's not in much of a condition to just be wandering off." Though, wounded or not, he had been in fine *condition* when he kissed her, and caressed her naked hip.

Delores sighed. "How very beautiful he is, *señora*! It would have been terrible to see him killed last night."

Aye, terrible for him to die before she could get answers—or kill him herself! "Beautiful or not, Delores, we don't have time to be mooning over him," Bianca said, suddenly deeply impatient with Balthazar, Delores, the world and especially herself. "We have too much work to do."

Delores nodded, turning away from the now-blazing fire to start peeling and chopping cassava. Despite the fact that she did rather like to giggle over handsome sailors, Bianca had to admit Delores was a good worker who actually seemed to enjoy the workings of a tavern.

"Especially with all the people seeking refuge from the storm in town. I heard there was even a Spanish contessa at the fortress! But I think we need more meat, *señora*, if we're to feed everyone," Delores said. "I used the last in the stew."

"I will go to market myself this morning, then," Bianca answered. She suddenly felt a deep urge to run away. And if she could not go to the jungle, to the tangled interior of the island, she could at least go to the market on the plaza. The warm morning breeze would help clear her confused mind, and she would be away from Balthazar. "You keep an eye on our wounded customer."

Delores brightened. "Oh, yes, *señora*!"

"Not too close an eye," Bianca warned. She left Delores to her tasks, carrying the tray of water and bandages upstairs with her. She lingered outside the door, listening closely for any signs of movement. After what had happened last night, she wasn't at all sure she could trust herself with Balthazar, even in the clear light of day.

Bianca scowled at the memory of the humid darkness, the feel of his sea-roughened hand on her naked skin. It seemed the armour she had built so carefully around herself, link by impenetrable link, over the long years was more vulnerable than she thought. But she couldn't allow that to be. She couldn't *be* vulnerable.

All appeared silent behind the door, the heavy quiet of early morning. She slipped into the room, finding Balthazar sound asleep in her bed. It had not been a quiet sleep; the bedclothes were tossed and tangled, his arms thrown wide as if he fought a battle in his dreams.

She remembered his shouts and murmurs in the night, the monsters in his nightmares. She set the tray down on the table and tiptoed to the bed, gazing down at him in search of any sign of dangerous fever.

A fierce frown creased his brow, but he seemed to sleep deeply. The wound had seeped through the bandage, a reddish-brown colour untainted by yellow infection.

She carefully smoothed the tangled hair back from his sun-browned face, watching the glint of light on the small gold hoop in his ear. She remembered the pearls and diamonds he had worn in Venice, the riches that set off his fine looks to such perfection.

Bianca glanced at the clothes tossed over her chair, the leather jerkin, the torn shirt and scuffed high boots. The fine silks, too, had been cast away with the jewels.

"What have you been doing all these years, Balthazar Grattiano?" she whispered. "And what in St Iago's name are you doing *here*?"

He groaned in his sleep, rolling away from her on to his side. Bianca drew the sheet up around him, careful not to wake him. Much as she wanted, needed, answers to her questions, she couldn't face him again quite yet. Not until she had repaired that chink in her heart's armour.

She quickly washed her face and brushed out her hair, confining the unruly curls in a knitted caul. She dressed in a plain brown bodice and skirt of light wool, and a pair of sturdy boots. She was certainly no fine lady of Venice, she thought as she studied herself in the looking glass, tying on a wide-brimmed straw hat. Balthazar would surely never have kissed her if he saw her now, as she truly was! But she would do for the market.

And when she returned, hopefully she could also know what to do about that man sleeping in her bed.

Chapter Five

Bianca hurried out of the tavern, her basket over her arm, and turned towards the town's central plaza. The street of her establishment, and indeed most of the streets of Santa Domingo, were narrow, closely packed with houses and shops, but they were cobbled like those of any European city. In the morning light, the yellow stones and red brick of the buildings gleamed, and the air was cool and clear with the tang of salt. Only later, when the sun rose overhead, would the thick heat set in and the shutters of the houses be drawn closed.

She descended the sloping streets, answering the greetings of her neighbours as they opened their shops for business. Later she would have to stop at the bakery, and look in at the office of her sugar supplier, who brought in goods from the inner-island plantations. But for now she was intent on her errand.

The cathedral bells had rung out long ago, and soon the plaza would be crowded and the best meat and vegetables gone.

At last she emerged from the maze of streets into the open, central part of town. Santo Domingo was built atop a hill, to give a natural defensive position against any who would try to attack. The governor's fortress, the storehouse of treasure and seat of the *cabildo*, sat at the highest point, locked behind thick walls and guarded walkways. There was no sign of any Spanish contessa there this morning, though, as Delores claimed. As Bianca gained the ramparts, she could see the ragged, green-black mountains that hid the island's jungle interior, which she had never visited. A soft breeze swept down from the lush mountains, carrying her on her way.

She hurried past the gallows, blessedly empty of swinging bodies today, and found herself gazing down at the harbour. The mouth of the Rio Ozama formed a natural port, with anchorage for dozens of ships. Usually, unless the flota was in on its way to Spain, there were not so many vessels as that. But the storm had driven many to seek shelter. The sapphire-blue waters were crowded with a forest of masts, the ships' decks crawling with the rush of activity. From her place on the ramparts, Bianca could hear an indistinct chorus of shouts and sea ditties.

She paused to stare down at the crowd of vessels, wondering which one was the famous *Calypso*. They had said the mainmast was damaged, but many of the ships were undergoing such repairs. Surely such a one would stand out, like the flagship of a mighty fleet. It would bear the mark of magic.

Yet she saw no such thing, only the usual caravels and carracks, tiny pinnaces, weary after the storm. As she watched men climbing the riggings, swabbing down the decks, she remembered her voyages with Juan Montero. The endless creaks of a vessel at sea, the wide open vistas of the shimmering water. It had not been an easy life, but the freedom of it all, the vast mystery—oh, it had been glorious!

"Señora Montero?" she heard someone say, the words jolting her from her daydream of the high seas. She turned to see Mendoza, Balthazar's quartermaster, hurrying towards her.

"Ah—Señor Mendoza, yes?" she said.

"Yes, indeed. I was just on my way to your tavern. How fares the captain?"

"Well enough. He was sleeping when I left, and has no sign of fever. My maidservant is watching over him."

A smile actually broke across Mendoza's glum, rough countenance, glowing through his thick beard. "That is excellent news, *señora*! The men will be relieved to hear it. They have been praying for the captain through the night."

"Have they?" Bianca said. "No doubt they fear to lose their wages and their posts, if the captain were to die."

Mendoza looked startled. "Not at all, *señora*. The

men will be paid no matter what, and there is always a berth for an honest sailor in the Velazquez fleet. But there's no other captain we'd be as proud to serve under as Balthazar Grattiano."

Bianca gazed down at the bustling port, remembering the near-mythic tales she heard whispered of the *Calypso* and her captain. "He cannot have been a captain for long," she murmured.

"Nay, he first went to sea near seven years ago, apprentice to the navigator on the *Elena Maria*," Mendoza said. "He bought the *Calypso* two years ago, and his crew has followed him ever since. With a fair wind, he can see us to Spain in three weeks."

"Three weeks?" Bianca said, startled. "He *must* be a magician."

Mendoza laughed. "So some people say. But it's only if charts and astrolabes be magic. He can steer a ship through any storm, too. He's one hell of a sailor, *señora*. The crew would follow him anywhere."

"Not everyone, so it would seem. What of that man who tried to kill him in my tavern?"

A dark scowl obliterated Mendoza's grin. "Diego Escobar."

"Was that his name, then? Who is he? Why did he want to kill your captain?" Bianca thought of the cloaked man, of the dead darkness in his eyes. Had he, too, lost something precious to the Grattianos? She could well believe that an entire crew of men would follow Balthazar; his charisma had been such in

Venice, too. But she could also believe that someone sought revenge for some insult or crime.

"He was a navigating officer, come aboard a year or so ago from Vera Cruz," Mendoza said, his tone reluctant, as if she forced the tale from him. "He and the captain were friends, until…"

"Until what?" Bianca urged impatiently, taut with suspense.

"'Twas a woman."

"Oh." Of course. A woman. Somehow, Bianca was rather disappointed it should be something so sordid, so ordinary. "No doubt some doxy this Diego thought was his, until she transferred her affections to the captain."

"No, no, *señora*! It was not like that."

It was *always* like that. Bianca saw it in her tavern every week, and cleaned up after it, too. But she gave Mendoza an encouraging smile, hoping he would continue with his tale. "Then how was it, pray tell?"

"Diego had a wife, a native woman he met before he joined the *Calypso*. Esperanza. We all knew about her, but we didn't think anything of it. Lots of the men…" His voice trailed away, as if he was embarrassed to speak of such things with a European woman.

"Lots of the men have sex with native women, with their wives back in Spain all unknowing," Bianca said.

"Yes," Mendoza answered, still obviously uncomfortable to be gossiping about such things with her. Yet she found she could not let him squirm free. She had to know what happened.

"But Diego married the woman, in the church in Havana," he went on. "She had been baptised and everything. Afterwards, we put out to sea, heading to Peru for a shipment of silver. That was when it happened, a few days out of Cuba."

"What happened?" Bianca whispered.

"The captain found that Diego had his wife aboard, in the hold. She was pregnant, and ill."

Bianca could imagine. The ceaseless pitch and roll of the waves, the dank stink of the hold. It was surely no place for a pregnant woman. "What was he thinking of?" she muttered.

"It was like he'd gone moon-mad, *señora*," Mendoza said. "The captain insisted on setting the woman ashore, but Diego argued. Threatened, even. But Captain Grattiano wouldn't hear him. He made to turn back to Cuba, even as we lost precious time, and he left her there with a nurse, in a house of her own."

For once, Bianca thought Balthazar was quite right. "What else could he have done?"

"Naught, of course. But she died anyway, poor soul, and her baby, too. Diego vowed to kill the captain, to have revenge for what he had done."

"And he happened to catch up with him in *my* tavern." Bianca shook her head at the madness of it all. The whole blood-soaked scene had not been for money or position, then, but for love. The greatest insanity of all.

"Captain Grattiano will pay for any damage,

señora," Mendoza hastened to say. "We're all very grateful for what you've done."

"You shouldn't thank me yet," she said. "Go, see to your captain. I must finish my marketing."

"Of course, *señora*."

As they parted, Mendoza on his way to the tavern and Bianca turning towards the steps that led down to the plaza, she suddenly called back, "Señor Mendoza!"

"Yes, *señora*?"

"Which ship is the *Calypso*?"

He pointed towards a vessel in a small, sheltered cove, somewhat apart from the other vessels. "'Tis that one. The repairs are nearly finished, you see. As soon as the captain can travel, we'll be setting off."

"Setting off for where?"

Mendoza smiled again. "For home, at last! It's been an age since we saw Vista Linda."

Vista Linda. Home. Where would that be? But before she could ask him, the quartermaster set off, whistling a sea chanty into the breeze. Bianca turned again towards the plaza, more puzzled than ever.

Her mother had always dealt in the uncertainties of life, the mysteries. Love, death, changes in fortune— she could glimpse it all. Bianca preferred the realities. Work, companionship, a cosy fire, a goblet of good wine. Things she could see, quantify. Despite all the allure of the vast, wide sea, of adventure and freedom, she knew that such things did not last.

Balthazar Grattiano was like the sea. Changeable,

stormy, ever beautiful and intriguing. And, like the sea, he could swallow up all she had, all she was, in a moment. A person had to be tough, cruel even, to survive in this New World, and the Grattianos had never been noted for their gentle benevolence. Why, then, had Balthazar bothered to turn back to Havana for the safety of a woman? And what had he done to make his crew so devoted they would follow him there so willingly?

Well, most of them followed. Bianca shivered as she remembered that man, Diego, and his dead eyes.

Those thoughts all swirled around in her head, indecipherable as a dream and twice as confusing, as she entered the main plaza of Santo Domingo. At one end of the cobbled square rose the cathedral, Santa Maria La Menor. Unfinished, it was still grand and imposing, gleaming a pure white in the harsh morning light. The doors stood open, beckoning the faithful into the cool, shadowy gloom, where they could lay their sins before the gilded altar.

Bianca turned away from the solitary splendour of the church to the bustle and noise of the market. At the centre of the plaza was a raised stone cross, and around this were arrayed the tables and booths of farmers and merchants. Every week they took the long journey from their inner-island estancias and smallholds to ply their wares to town dwellers.

Bianca surveyed the fruits and vegetables: brilliant oranges, lemons and guava, mounds of starchy cassava. There were barrels of sugar, left from what had not been exported from the island's thirty-four mills, jars of molasses for rum, and small buckets of precious spices. But these were not what she wanted. She examined the beef from the cattle stations, the pork from the wild pigs who ran free all through the mountains. Her patrons liked familiar, Spanish sorts of food, and these would make the hearty stews and roasts she sold so well.

As she paid for her purchases, she remembered Venice, and the tales her mother told of banquets in the grand palazzos. The long, damask-draped tables covered with platters of chicken amarosa, trout and leeks with lemon sauce, capon, plump strawberries, bright Majolica bowls overflowing with sweetmeats, goblets of fine wines. The hundreds of wax candles casting a warm glow over the silver and gold plate, the satins and jewels of the patrician diners. It all sounded like a fairy story to her, as far from their simple home on a back alleyway as the gods on Olympus!

And how much further it was from *here*, an entire world away. There was no capon for her simple table, just pork haunch and roasted cassava. Rum and ale in place of wine.

"Did you hear, Señora Montero?" one of the merchants asked, as she examined his vegetables. "One of the storehouses was robbed last night! I hope there are no pirates abroad again."

"Especially with a contessa at the fortress," his

wife added. "They say she is Señor de Alameda's special guest…"

Bianca made appropriate noises about how shocking it was, but she walked away still distracted by her own thoughts. She had not remembered home in a very long time. It did her no good to remember, as this place was her life, her reality, now. The bittersweet, jewel-like beauty of Venice was lost to her, just as her mother was. Just as the coins from the storehouse were lost to "pirates".

It was surely Balthazar who made her think of it now. Who made her so very confused and uncertain. Who made her…

Who made her wish she had baked peacock to offer him instead of stew. She should not care one whit what the man ate, where he went, or what he did. What he had done these last seven years.

She should dump the stew over his handsome head and push him out her door.

Bianca had to laugh at the vision of Balthazar with dark, greasy broth dripping down his face. No matter what happened to him in these last long years, surely it had never been anything so undignified as that.

As she turned back towards the tavern, the heavy basket balanced on her hip, she remembered what Mendoza had said. It had been nearly seven years since Balthazar went to sea. Thus he must have left Venice soon after she herself fled. Why was that?

Ah, yet another mystery. Surely enough of them surrounded Balthazar to fill that now-empty storehouse. She was a patient woman; she would discover all in time, and then she would know how to act. But for now she had work to do. The sun was high in the cloudless sky, and the hours were getting away from her.

She couldn't allow even Balthazar Grattiano to interfere with her business.

Yet as she hurried along the ramparts, now crowded with people out to gossip about the thefts, she couldn't help but glance towards the cove where the *Calypso* sheltered. It was not a large ship, she noticed. A mid-size caravel, perhaps seventy feet long and twenty-five feet wide. Once her mainmast was repaired, it would have the square-rigged mainmast and foremast, and a lateen-rigged countermizzen just aft the mizzen.

It was not a conspicuously rich or impressive vessel, especially marked with storm damage as she was, but, after her years with Juan, Bianca could see the true worth of any ship. "The best ships that sail the seas," Juan used to call caravels, and this one was a beauty. Lightly built, versatile, it could go anywhere, even sail in crosswinds with a skilled captain at her rudder. With a stern rudder, and those lateen sails, it would be very responsive—especially at the hands of someone like Balthazar.

Bianca had no doubt that Balthazar was a skilled captain indeed, as capable of charming a ship as he was of charming a woman.

But Bianca was determined *not* to be charmed. Not this time. Not ever again.

Chapter Six

Balthazar eased the clean shirt over his head, gritting his teeth against the ache in his shoulder. It was surely a mere scratch to other wounds he had received; it didn't even bleed now, after Bianca's careful ministrations.

Ah, yes. Bianca Simonetti. Bianca Montero now, it seemed. Balthazar laced up the shirt, remembering the girl he had known in Venice. She had been pretty enough then, if too thin and simply dressed. She had smiled at him shyly, hardly daring to look at him directly when he would come to her mother's house with his father. But he had liked her. Her intelligent conversation, her questions about his books on navigation and geography, made those irksome visits enjoyable. He even came to look forward to the times his father would insist he accompany him to those silly tarot readings, for it meant he could talk to Bianca.

He knew women aplenty in Venice, women of great

beauty and practised charm. Bianca Simonetti had neither, but her dark eyes were fascinating, her mind full of curiosity and longing that matched his own. She listened to what he said, truly listened, unlike anyone else ever had. And she made him think in turn, with questions and observations he had never considered.

But then she had vanished—she and her mother dead, they had said. And his own life had exploded in one fiery night. He had been forced to make a new existence on the high seas. Over the years of exploring new lands, Bianca Simonetti had become a memory. A regret—one among so many.

Once she told him her name, he could see the girl in the woman's face, in those brown eyes, now so hard and wary. She, too, had made her own existence. And now their lives had intersected again, and she had saved him.

Balthazar glanced around the bedchamber. It was larger than his cabin aboard the *Calypso*, but not by much. There was room only for the bed, a table and chair, and a scarred old sea chest. The walls were whitewashed, and there was one shuttered window, half-open to let in the morning breeze, but no rugs or paintings. No velvet cushions or ivory boxes.

The tavern downstairs was also simple and serviceable, though cleaner than most he had seen in the islands. Whatever had happened to her in these last years, she obviously worked hard for her livelihood. The eager, curious girl he remembered was gone, the light in her extraordinary eyes dimmed by a cautious, simmering anger.

Until they had been alone in the dark of the night.

Balthazar went to peer out the window. The town of Santo Domingo spread out before him under the sun, a sea of yellow, white and red that arced down to the harbour and up the hillsides. It could almost have been any seaside settlement in Spain, with its dark red roofs, the bell tower of the new cathedral, and the forest of masts crowding the sheltered port. But just at the edge of town, at the very boundary of a tenuous civilisation, the dark jungle waited.

Santo Domingo had not been Balthazar's first choice of a haven. It was *too* settled now. His years of sailing the seas, of being his own master, had made him too fond of solitude. Of the rougher, wilder ways of the smaller, further-flung islands, like his own Vista Linda. There no one cared about his past, his family name. Almost everyone else had secrets to hide, secrets even darker than his own. He earned any respect on his own terms, as Captain Grattiano.

Even though he had a licence to trade in Santo Domingo, the administrative capital of the Spanish Antilles, Balthazar preferred other ports for his trade. Only the damage to the *Calypso* forced him here, but now he was glad they had come. For here he had found Bianca.

Most of his youth he had tried to forget, to drown under the salt waves of his new life, but there had been brighter flashes of light in Venice. Bianca Simonetti was one of them. Utterly unlike any other woman he knew, she was not one of the silent, haughty patrician ladies his father urged him to marry. Or like the beautiful, artificial courtesans he spent so much time with. He liked her intelligence, true, but he had also wanted to kiss her on those long afternoons outside her mother's house. To sense the awakening of her hot sensuality and know it was his alone.

She had wanted him, too. He saw the flush of her cheeks, the quickening of the pulse that beat at the base of her slender throat. But she *was* young, and innocent. For all his careless debauchery, something in him could not bear to dim that glow inside of her, those idealistic dreams that he himself had never known.

He had been old and damaged. Bright innocence could never survive in his father's house. Only by striving to equal Ermano in cunning and cruelty had Balthazar lived at all, but it had made his heart twisted. Bianca was not like that. She was a small, shimmering pearl, its perfection tucked away in a dark casket where only he could see it.

Balthazar thought of the woman who kissed him last night. She had Bianca's dark eyes, her lush lips, but the bright hope had vanished. Was the girl he once knew hidden there, somewhere deep beneath the hard, cool surface?

As he watched out the window, he saw her coming up the street, a heavy basket over her arm. A wide-brimmed hat shielded her face, but he was familiar with her body now, with the shift and warmth of it against his, and he recognised it in the way she moved. She wore a plain brown gown, the square neckline revealing the edge of a white chemise and a modest expanse of sun-browned skin. She wore no jewels, and he wondered what she would look like in loops of pearls, chains of emeralds.

And nothing else. *Aye*, he thought with a smile, chains of jewels framing her bare breasts. Looping down past her navel, her flat belly, just touching her womanhood.

Bianca stretched backwards, her hand at the small of her back as she wiped her boots at the doorstep. Even the prosaic movement had an unconscious grace to it, but also weariness. He wondered again what had brought her here, to this life in a Santo Domingo tavern.

She pulled off her hat and wiped her wrist over her brow. As she tucked a loose curl back into her knitted caul, she glanced up and her gaze met Balthazar's. For a mere instant, her expression was unguarded, her eyes wide and startled as a doe. She seemed younger in that moment, unsure and vulnerable.

Then her armoured visor dropped back into place, an unreadable mask. She gave him a brusque nod and hurried through the door.

Balthazar turned from the window, finishing the lacings of his shirt. Mendoza had brought the clean clothes and toiletries from his cabin, and promised to bring more men back the next day to fetch him to the *Calypso*. For once, his crew dared to override his orders and refused to let him walk Santo Domingo alone. Diego Escobar had not been apprehended, nor had he come near the ship. He was still out there, filled with that seething, murderous fury.

Nor was he the only one, Balthazar thought as he heard Bianca's light footsteps on the creaking stairs. The innocent desire from years ago might be vanished from her eyes, but he had seen there something he knew all too well.

Anger. Simmering anger directed right at him.

She opened the door with just a soft click, no ferocious slams or bangs. She did not look at him, just hung her hat up on a peg and turned to the small looking glass. Her cheeks were flushed a pale shell-pink over her high cheekbones, the only sign of emotion.

She tucked her loose curls back into the net, and he remembered how her hair had looked last night. Long and tumbled over her shoulders, a mass of wild dark curls.

"You are awake," she said. "And dressed, too. You must be feeling better."

"Mendoza brought provisions from my ship," he answered, as cautious as she. "I won't trespass on your hospitality much longer, Señora Montero."

Her gaze shifted towards him in the glass, her lashes shielding her eyes and thoughts. "You should let me examine your wound. If you move too soon, it will reopen, and all my hard work will be for naught."

Balthazar laughed. "You are the physician, of course. I would never want to go against your instructions."

"Your men rely on you, do they not? They need you to be healthy." She motioned to him to sit on the edge of the bed, coming to stand between his legs.

He shrugged. "Any of my officers could guide the *Calypso* as well as me."

"That is not what I hear."

"Oh? What do you hear?"

Bianca turned to him, her slender fingers nimbly unlacing his shirt. Her movements were quick and efficient, as if she was indeed a physician, but he saw a tiny smile just at the corner of her mouth.

What would it take, he mused, to make her truly smile? To laugh? To make her come to hot life, as she had been all too briefly last night, in his arms.

"I have heard you possess magical powers," she said, her touch gentle as she eased back his shirt and loosened the bandage. "That you can steer a ship through any storm. Can set any course and cross the widest of seas in mere days."

Balthazar snorted in disbelief, though he was secretly rather pleased. Any rumours of supposed strength and invincibility, magical or not, made pirates and enemies think twice before they attacked his ship. They made the best men sign on to his crews, and even the greediest officials did not harry him for his cargoes.

But he had the distinct sense Bianca was not impressed.

"I have some skill with the astrolabe and the compass," he said. "I can read a chart. And my ship is well built, fast and stable. Any sailor worth his rum learns to understand the waters, the clouds, which way the wind blows."

"Some better than others." She nodded towards the small sea chest Mendoza had brought from the *Calypso* with Balthazar's supplies. "Your men seem loyal to you. I met Señor Mendoza in town; he was very concerned about you."

"Mendoza has sailed with me for a long time. He is an excellent quartermaster."

"And he says *you* are a fine captain."

"Mutiny and dissent are a great danger at sea, Señora Montero. You must see its bloody results here in Santo Domingo often."

She nodded shortly, probing at her neat stitches in his shoulder. Balthazar winced, but did not pull away. She leaned close to him, and he could smell her scent of soap and clean water, wool and flowers, the salt breeze caught in her hair. The gentle swell of her breast, plump and alluring, rose above the edge of her brown bodice with every breath.

He felt his manhood stir in his hose, and he shifted uncomfortably on the bed. He *had* been too long without a woman.

"I have seen the bodies of mutineers hanging on the

gallows," she said, turning to reach for a jar of salve on the table. "Their hands cut off, their entrails dangling…"

Not even the gruesome image could settle his erection. What a fool he was, Balthazar thought wryly. And a pervert, too, if the description of tortured mutineers only made him want to tumble Bianca to the bed and kiss those lush lips, caress her naked breasts, until she moaned with need.

"My men have no need to mutiny," he said hoarsely. She smoothed some of the greasy salve over his wound, and he hardened even further, like implacable iron. "They know I am stern, but fair. If they do their work, if they are loyal, they have nothing to fear from me."

"Did this Diego do his work?"

Balthazar frowned. "For a time."

"Until he fell in love?"

"I see Mendoza was chatty."

"I found it a very interesting tale."

Was she disapproving? He could not tell, her face was so perfectly serene, her eyes opaque. No matter. Her condemnation of his actions could hardly sting his conscience any more than his own did. He had done what he could for Diego's wife, the *only* thing he could. A ship at sea, rough, crowded, stinking, was no place to bear a baby. Diego should have known that, if he had not been driven insane by his passion. Balthazar had to be the rational one, the captain. Had to set the woman ashore.

Passion, love, had no place in such a life. Yet the memory of Esperanza Escobar's sobs, her pale, ill face, haunted him.

"A ship's captain who dares these dangerous waters makes many enemies," she observed coolly.

"Are you one of them, Bianca? An enemy?"

Her hands went still in the midst of wrapping a new bandage. Her gaze skimmed up to meet his. There, at last, was a flicker deep in her dark eyes, a spark of some unfathomable emotion.

"I hardly know," she murmured.

He reached up to clasp her wrist. The bones felt delicate under his fingers, her pulse beating like a frantic wild bird. Her breath caught, but she did not draw away.

"I thought you dead," he said softly. He had thought her one of the terrible casualties in those bloody days during the Carnival of 1525. Days when his life had changed so completely.

"Did your father tell you that?"

He shook his head. "It was your maidservant in Venice. She said you and your mother were both dead."

"I *felt* dead, for a long time. I felt I was deep in a dark hole in the ground, and could see and feel nothing at all."

Balthazar stared up at her, amazed. He, too, knew that feeling of black, numb blindness. It never quite left him. "What brought you back to life?"

She smiled then, her lips parting on a breath. "What

is life, Balthazar? Can anyone really say? But when I felt the hot sun of this place on my skin, I could see again."

She drew away from his grasp, reaching up to frame his face with her hands. Her palms, slightly roughened from the hard work of a tavern, were gentle against his skin. Her thumbs traced his brows, his temples, the line of his cheekbones.

"I never thought to see *you* again, Balthazar Grattiano," she whispered.

"Nor I you," he answered.

She kissed him, her lips soft, tentative, tasting of fruit and sunshine. It wasn't desperate, as their gropings in the darkness had been, born of sheer lust, the drive to erase nightmares. This was more of a greeting, an explanation. A discovery.

Balthazar's touch alighted on her shoulders, feeling the tension beneath the lean muscle and bone, the smooth cloth of her gown and heat of her skin. She felt like a wild animal, set to dash away at any fright. Gently, slowly, he slid his hands along the arc of her back, rubbing in soothing circles until she sighed against his lips and relaxed into him.

Their kiss deepened, lips parting to taste, feel. Balthazar touched the tip of his tongue to hers, clasping her waist to pull her even closer. She tumbled into his lap, her arms twined about his neck as their kiss caught fire.

Oh, yes, he *had* been too long without a woman. Usually he wanted to savour his lovers, to take time to study every inch of their bare skin, every curve and angle. To make them cry out, even as he himself stayed somewhat distant from the erotic scene, the heady emotions.

Now, he wanted only to see Bianca's nakedness on the bed, hear her moans, her voice calling out his name. He *needed* to push up her skirts and bury himself inside of her, like a callow boy driven to clumsy haste by his first woman.

His lips slid from hers along her jaw, catching her earlobe in his teeth. She gasped, arching back over his arm, the line of her throat vulnerable to him. He kissed her there, biting at the curve of her shoulder and licking it to soothe the sting. He blew a cool breath over her skin, watching in fascination as she shivered, as her pulse skipped just beneath her skin.

Had he thought her cold? Nay, she was as full of life as that island sun, as full of heat and light. And as likely to burn him if he got too close.

She had not answered him when he asked if she was his enemy.

He rested his head against the soft swell of her breast, listening to her heart beating. It seemed to echo inside of him, the very rhythm of life itself. *Her* life. His, too.

He closed his eyes, inhaling deeply, as if he truly could draw her into him. Find the essence of her again, the spark buried so deeply beneath the violent past, the uncertain present.

She stroked his hair as she held him against her, smoothing the strands along his back, gently caressing.

"Are you real?" she whispered.

"I don't know," he said. "But if this is a dream…"

"Can we not awake?" she said, kissing the pulse at his temple. "Or will all turn to a nightmare?"

Balthazar closed his eyes, remembering the visions that tormented him when he dared to sleep. His ship breaking apart, his father flying out of hell to remind him who, what, he was. Whose blood flowed in his veins.

He felt Bianca shift herself from his lap. He didn't open his eyes, but he could hear her straightening her hair and clothes. Hear the uneven rush of her breath.

"I fear you're bleeding again," she said quietly.

He opened his eyes to find that her mask was back in place, along with her skirts. One glimpse, that was all he was allowed.

She turned away, reaching for the door latch. "I will fetch more bandages," she said. "You should rest."

Then she was gone, the door shut softly behind her. *She* could almost be the dream, if her delicate, elusive scent did not linger around him.

Balthazar fell back to the bed, hardly aware of the sticky blood trickling through his bandage. Soon, he would be gone from here, turned towards home, or what passed for home in his life. And she would be here, in Santo Domingo. His enemy.

He had left her once. Could he bear to do it again?

But he knew he had no choice in the matter. Despite

the burning lust between them, he knew she hid secrets from him, as he did from her. She would not go with him even if he asked. The past was still too strong. Sex couldn't erase it. All the waters of the sea couldn't wash it away.

Yet still, that scent lingered all around him…

Chapter Seven

Bianca leaned back against the rough planks of the door, hand pressed to her pounding heart. A wild urge rushed through her, the need to run and run until she reached the edge of the sea itself. To run until her lungs burst and her legs burned—until she couldn't see Balthazar's face in her mind any more. Until she could escape from him, and from herself.

She shook her head, closing her eyes against the spinning world around her. She had fled once from the Grattianos, when she was young and terrified, and had no idea what the world really held. She had come all the way across the ocean. She could not flee again.

She had to face Balthazar, and herself.

Bianca hurried down the stairs. Face him, aye, she would do that. Just not quite yet. Not with the taste of him still on her lips, the lingering heat of his hands on her body. She would wait, until her blood ran cooler and she remembered all that happened in Venice.

Someone had taken away the broken furniture, and Delores was sweeping the floor free of splinters and broken pottery. The window shutters were open, the hot afternoon wind carrying in the clangs and shouts of noisy commerce.

"We should have another busy evening, Delores," Bianca said, reaching for a bucket of water set near the door. She scrubbed fiercely at a scarred, sticky tabletop, imagining it was Balthazar's handsome visage under her rag. She would erase his maddeningly charming smile, and—and those *infuriating* dimples!

"Do we have enough ale, *señora*?" Delores asked.

"I spoke to Señor Garcia at the market, and he promised to deliver a barrel before dusk." They went on to speak of commonplace matters, business affairs Bianca could understand and solve. Unlike the matter of men, of course. She could not understand *them* at all.

If only Balthazar was a ledger book or a barrel of ale…

Soon, the room was set somewhat to rights, the floor clean and benches and tables shifted to cover the gaps. As Bianca inspected the space, Delores dumped the dirty water out the window.

"What of the captain?" she asked.

Bianca frowned, sure she heard a distinctly sly tone in the girl's voice. "What of him, Delores?"

"Will he be staying with us a bit longer? He seems quite—comfortable here."

"I am sure he'll be gone by tomorrow at the latest," Bianca said, shrugging indifferently. An indifference, of course, she was very far from feeling. "His quartermaster said they're eager to be gone, as soon as the repairs are made and the winds are favourable."

"And where will they go?"

"Home, he said." Wherever that was.

"It is a pity, *señora*." Delores sighed. "I don't think there's ever been such a handsome man in Santo Domingo! Señora Valdez's maid said—"

"Enough, Delores," Bianca cried. She had heard enough gossip about Balthazar Grattiano, about his fine looks and magical skills at the rudder. What she needed now were facts. Where had he been, where was he going, and how had he really come to be in Santo Domingo? And she probably would not hear such things from besotted maidservants.

She feared she herself was becoming *besotted*, and that would never do.

"Well, he is sure to pay us well for his board, anyway," Delores went on. "They say his hold is filled with pearls and gold."

"I doubt that's true," Bianca said. "The ship was riding too high in the water."

"So you have seen the *Calypso*, *señora*? Is it truly black, with black sails?"

"It was a ship like any other," Bianca said impatiently. "And the sails were struck, though black would be terribly impractical in this heat."

"Oh, *señora*! Have you no romance at all?"

Bianca laughed, remembering how very "romantic" she had been as a girl. Waiting for hours, just hoping for one glimpse of Balthazar Grattiano. And look where "romance" had got her. "This is not a poem. Captain Grattiano is not El Cid."

Delores pouted. "He could be. He certainly looks the part."

Before Bianca could answer, the front door opened, admitting Señor de Alameda. Despite the bright day, unlike the *Calypso*'s sails he wore his usual black. Rich fabrics, simply cut, and a wide black hat. Delores blushed and giggled as he gave her a smile.

"Señora Montero, Delores, good day to you both," he said. "Already hard at work, I see."

"There was much to be seen to this morning, *señor*," Bianca answered.

"Ah, yes. I did hear that after my departure last night there was some drama."

"A bit of a drunken fuss," Bianca answered. It was not like Alameda to leave his business in the governor's fortress in the middle of the day. She thought it prudent to discover what his errand was before they went chattering on too freely. "Nothing we haven't cleaned up after before."

"The perils of running a business in Santo Domingo."

"Quite so," Bianca said. "Can I offer you some ale, Señor de Alameda?"

"Perhaps later. It is actually this drunken fuss that brings me here."

"How so?" Bianca asked, tensing under his cool gaze. She wanted no trouble with the governor or his henchmen. As a Venetian woman running a tavern in a Spanish land, she had to be very careful.

"There has been some trouble at one of our store-houses," Alameda said. "A small theft last night. I would like to speak with your lodger, if he is well enough." He paused. "He is not dead, is he?"

"Not at all," Bianca said. "The wound was not deep."

"But enough to keep him from returning to his ship."

"Yes, though I am told he will return there shortly," Bianca said.

"Eager to depart, eh? It seems I have arrived just in time."

Bianca could think of no excuse to keep Alameda away. She nodded, and said, "Delores will show you up, *señor*. Captain Grattiano was awake and dressed an hour or so ago."

Or almost dressed, until she arrived and tore his clothes off again. To her shame, Bianca felt her cheeks burn at the thought, at the vivid memory of Balthazar's lean, scarred, naked chest.

She turned away as Delores led him up the stairs, the two of them whispering together as they no doubt set up an assignation. For an instant, she was tempted to follow and listen at the door as Alameda talked to Balthazar. But whatever information she gleaned would surely be not worth the effort. Whatever trouble Balthazar might be in with the cabildo, it was surely no more than he could deal with. The Grattianos always wriggled out of any tight spot quite handily.

The difficulty was, should she let him wriggle away from *her*? Escape the reckoning that had been coming for them for so long?

Bianca whirled around and hurried out to the street, before she could change her mind. She retraced her path from that morning, but rather than turning towards the plaza she went down the steps that led to the port.

It was the hottest part of the day now, and the jostling crowds of the morning had thinned, as many people sought a shady place to rest. Most of the anchored ships were quiet, bobbing serenely up and down on the green-blue waves.

Not the *Calypso*, though. There, men swarmed like ants over the decks, the mainmast once again in place. She could not tell from this distance, but surely they were busily storing provisions, readying the sails and rigging. Preparing for a new voyage, as they were obviously eager to slip down the Ozama and out to the open sea.

She could envision Balthazar at the rudder, his hair

tossed in the wind, grinning as he steered his vessel out to freedom again.

And, as she stood there watching the ship, a wild plan slowly took form in her mind.

Chapter Eight

Diego Escobar braced his palms against the railing, staring out at the night-dark sea, at the endless gloom of the sky overhead. He did not see the stars, the gleam of moonlight on the waves, did not even see the distant breakers that signalled land. All he saw were the visions in his mind, looping over and over like a trapped rat. A life in permanent stasis.

He saw again Balthazar Grattiano's face, the flash of surprise as Diego raised his dagger to him. The chaos of the tavern, the panic that had allowed Diego to make his escape, had frozen, narrowing down to that one moment. That one point. His enemy. The cold-hearted, all-powerful captain who had shown no pity for Diego's wife, for the poor baby. Who had ruined Diego's life without a pang.

Well, Grattiano had paid for it. He was surely dead now, bleeding out his life on that tavern floor just as

Esperanza had bled when she had struggled to birth their child. Diego had taken his revenge, the revenge that had been his only reason for being of late.

Why, then, did he feel no satisfaction? No completion. He felt only—empty. The same cold emptiness that had filled him as he had cradled Esperanza's lifeless body in his arms. All the warmth and joy she had brought him, the laughter and shining innocence, were utterly vanished, gone for ever.

Was this, then, how the rest of his life was to proceed? In hollowness and blood? The one glimpse of happiness he had with Esperanza had been the illusion. This existence of piracy, life as an outcast, was the reality.

His hatred of Grattiano had once burned as hot as his love for Esperanza, but even that was now vanished. There were only cold ashes, and the sure knowledge that all goodness was gone from the world.

Diego clenched his fists on the railing, remembering again the way it felt when his dagger had sank into Grattiano's flesh, when his blood had spilled at last. How long he had planned for that moment, how he had savoured it in his thoughts! But the reality was not the same. It gave no satisfaction. It did not restore his wife to him. It did not even restore his honour, lost when he turned to piracy.

He remembered, too, the woman at the tavern. Her brown eyes were wary, yet kind, as she gazed at him over the counter. He could see in their depths that she, too, had known hardship and loss. She could obviously sense there was something not right about him; anyone who ran a tavern in a place like Santo Domingo had to be cautious. But she hadn't turned him away. Her small kindness had been the first he had seen in a very long time, and he was sorry for starting a riot in her establishment.

It could not have been helped. Grattiano was invulnerable aboard his ship, his little kingdom. There was no hope of defeating him at sea, despite Diego's best efforts. Santo Domingo was Diego's only chance and he took it, despite the woman's kind eyes.

Now Grattiano was in hell. And Diego would surely join him soon enough.

He heard a rustle behind him, a footstep on the deck, and turned to find Mauro, the first mate of his new command, the *Firebrand*. The *Firebrand* was not the *Calypso*, not the tightly run, swift vessel of Captain Grattiano. It was an older ship, crewed by men whose best recommendation was their willingness to do anything for gold. They wanted riches, plunder, and they followed Diego because he was even more ruthless than they.

It was not what he had looked for when he had left Spain all those years ago, seeking fortune, adventure and honour. But piracy was all he had now.

"Shall we make land at Tortuga, cap'n?" Mauro asked.

Ah, so that was the dark mass Diego saw ahead. Tortuga, the lawless land where even the King of Spain dared not reach. A haven for murderers and brigands. For him and the *Firebrand*.

"Aye," Diego answered. "No doubt the men are eager to spend their coin."

Mauro grinned, his gap teeth yellowed in the moonlight. "That they are," he said, with grim satisfaction. While Diego took his revenge on Balthazar Grattiano, some of the crew stole from the more unprotected, smaller storehouses of Santo Domingo, making off swiftly with their ill-gotten gains. The raids were small and relatively quiet, but useful for keeping them occupied and distracted. For now.

Diego looked again towards Tortuga, looming closer over the waves. He could see the twinkle of lights now, the flickering welcome of brothels and taverns. His home now, such as it was.

And a fitting one, at that, for a man who had lost his soul.

Chapter Nine

It was deep into the night by the time Bianca barred the tavern door and turned towards the stairs, leaving a yawning Delores to finish putting out the candles. There were still shouts echoing from the streets, drunken howls of laughter, but all was silent inside.

Bianca slipped off her shoes at the foot of the stairs, tiptoeing carefully so the warped wood wouldn't creak. She paused outside her bedchamber door, listening closely for any sound. Balthazar still slept there, despite the way his men had argued to carry him back to his ship. He was there for one more night, before he departed.

One night, then he sailed out of her life yet again. She had to move swiftly.

She could hear only the sounds from the street as she pressed her ear to the door, the pounding of her own heartbeat in her ears. She shivered with uncertainty, yet when she closed her eyes she saw her mother again. Lying lifeless in her own blood, stained tarot cards and shattered glass all around her. She saw Ermano and Balthazar Grattiano in their rich satin and jewels, their smug certainty that the world was only constructed for their benefit. Their pleasure.

She opened her eyes, staring blindly at the rough planks of the door. She frowned, thinking of Balthazar not as he had been then, the reckless, beautiful debaucher, but as the man whose wound she had stitched. He was scarred, both in his body and his soul. She could see that when she looked in his moss-green eyes, so flat and dark, but only because she, too, was scarred. Knocked about by life, by the fear and shame she fought so hard to keep down.

He sailed the seas now, held his own in untamed lands that held no pity for any man, that were ruled only by ruthlessness and warfare. He was respected by his men. And still loved by women, if Delores's sighs were any indication.

Or Bianca's own reaction to his nearness. She felt her cheeks burn again as she remembered their kisses, his rough, hot touch on her naked skin. Oh, yes—he *did* still have a way with women. And after winning the hearts of women in Europe, from Venice to London, he had turned his attentions to the New World.

Even when she was an innocent girl, Bianca had not been immune to his attractions, to his handsome looks, his fierce intelligence and dark intensity. The air of sadness that clung to him like a fine, alluring perfume. She was not immune to it now, even after all that had happened. But she could not forget, either.

Couldn't forget all the Grattianos had stolen from her.

She could not leave her mother unavenged. Yet neither could she kill an innocent man. That was the Grattiano way, not hers.

Bianca clenched her fist, feeling the bite of her nails into her skin. Why had he come here at all? Now, after all these years! When she had finally gained a small measure of peace.

Yet he *had* come, and she had to face the past again. Face it, and put it to rest once and for all.

She slowly opened the door, careful to make no sound. One candle was still lit on the table, burned low and sputtering in the breeze from the half-open window. It cast its small, pink-gold glow over the tumbled bedclothes, over the man who slept in her bed.

His arms were thrown wide, as if he still fought fierce battles in his dreams. His bare torso was tawny against the sheets, the bandage on his shoulder stark white. He lay perfectly still, the slight rise and fall of his breath the only movement.

Bianca hurriedly unlaced her bodice and skirt, slipping out of them until she wore only her chemise and stockings. Hardly daring to even breathe, she took her small, lethally slim dagger from its hiding place in her trunk.

Clutching its plain, worn hilt, she climbed on to the

bed, straddling Balthazar's lean hips. The instant the cold steel of her blade touched his throat, his eyes opened. He stared up at her in the flickering light, not moving, not afraid. Completely expressionless.

Bianca, though, still trembled with uncertainty. She forced herself to breathe slowly, carefully, keeping her hand steady on the blade.

"Where is your father?" she asked. "Does he follow you here? Does he own the *Calypso*?"

Between her thighs, she felt him shift, as if he would toss her away. She pressed the dagger closer to his pulse, and he stilled. "What makes you ask that?" he muttered.

"I well remember his greed," she said. "The Grattiano greed, which destroyed all before it. Surely he has seen the great wealth Spain extracts from the New World. I can't imagine he would be happy with only a Venetian kingdom, when all the gold and emeralds and pearls of this place could be his."

"I'm sure he would not be," Balthazar answered, still so expressionless, so unmoving. Yet his stare never left her, that green gaze that held them bound together in a terrible spell only the two of them could enter. "He always had an eye for treasure, whether it belonged to him or not."

"And peoples' lives," Bianca whispered, almost to herself. Ermano had always thought the lives of others belonged to him, as well.

"Quite right," Balthazar said. "Souls were his possessions, too."

"Were?"

"Indeed. He is dead, you see, and has been for over seven years."

Bianca stared at him in cold shock. She should not be so surprised, of course. Years had passed, and Ermano had not been a young man even back then. Yet still, he had seemed a veritable demon, a spirit who made a bargain with the underworld and would thus live for ever, enjoying his ill-gotten wealth.

"Dead?" she murmured.

"I know. Hard to believe he *could* die. And yet I saw it happen myself."

"And now you are the great lord Grattiano. The master of all Venice," she said. Was he indeed the new Ermano? He hardly looked it, this lean, hard, sea-scarred man in her bed. Yet she had learned too well that appearances deceived. Nothing was ever as it seemed. "Why do you come here, then? Why are you not eating off gold plate in your marble palazzo, sipping wine with some expensive courtesan?"

He smiled humourlessly. "I think, Señora Montero, that I could converse much better without a knife at my throat."

Bianca eased the blade away just a bit, turning it from his skin as he stretched his neck. She kept him pinned beneath her, every muscle in her body held taut.

"That is better," he said. "You could have merely asked, you know, *cara*. No need to employ weapons."

"I thought you might need a little persuasion. The

Grattianos have never been known to share their secrets freely."

"Of course not. Information is power, here more than anywhere. We know better than to spend our power indiscriminately."

Bianca remembered the jewels and furs of Venice. The grand palace, the beautiful blonde whores. "Unlike your coin."

"Ah, now, there is always more coin to be had. But information—not always."

"Exactly why you should share your 'information' with me," Bianca said, letting the candlelight dance along the edge of her blade. "Now."

"For you, beautiful Bianca, anything." He shifted again between her legs, and she felt the powerful muscles of his thighs, the hot skin, the rough abrasion of his hair.

"I am here because I choose to make my own way in the world," he continued. He stretched his arms behind his head, resting there as he watched her with cat-like laziness. "I no longer have an interest in my father's Venetian holdings. Most of his property there has been sold, anyway, to benefit my brother's shipping concerns."

"Your *brother*?" Bianca gasped. Her mind whirled with revelations, with all she had missed while she made her own way in this parallel world. She did not know what shocked her more, that Venetian property *could* be sold, or that Balthazar had a relative. "But you are an only child. Your father…"

"Was determined to breed more heirs on the body of Julietta Bassano. Yes, I know."

"It was why he wanted his cards told by my mother so often."

"He wanted assurances of more sons, strong warriors who would not be a disappointment like me."

Bianca stared down at him, at his powerful, beautiful body sprawled beneath her. She didn't see how anyone could be disappointed with such a one as he. But then, she had never understood the Grattianos. It was what drove her here in the first place.

"So, where did this other son come from?" she said.

"Oh, he was a bastard," Balthazar said lightly. "Got off a courtesan years ago, before I was born. My father thought both mother and child disposed of, until he reappeared. Much to my father's detriment."

"His detriment? Did this long-lost son kill him?"

"Oh, no, *cara.*" Suddenly, in a movement quicker than lightning, Balthazar grabbed her wrist. Bianca cried out in surprise—she had been so caught up in his bizarre tale that she forgot he was her captive. He squeezed until her hand opened, the blade clattering to the floor as he rose up above her.

He spun her to the bed, pressing her deep into the mattress. His eyes burned as he stared down at her, holding her arms pinned to her sides.

"Marc did not kill our father," he said, his voice as calm as if he discussed the weather. "I did."

Bianca stared up at him, aghast. Had he just said…?

But she had not time for thought, for coherence. His mouth came down on hers, hard, desperate, his kiss blotting out all else. There was no past, no future, just this man at this one moment.

She parted her lips eagerly, touching his tongue with hers. He tasted of ale, of that dark sweetness that was only him. He groaned, deepening the kiss until there was only the blurry, humid heat of wild need.

She felt him pull the hem of her chemise up to her hips, and she wrapped her legs tightly around his back, holding him to her. His penis was hot and hard as iron against her inner thigh, and that ache of desperate desire grew deep in her belly, deep in the wet core of her being. She had never felt anything like this terrible, desperate need, this sense that the world would shatter if she could not kiss him. Touch him.

Feel him inside her, at last.

She arched her body up into his, her head falling back to the pillows as his mouth trailed to her throat, the curve of her shoulder, easing away her chemise until she was bare to him.

He nipped at the soft skin along her collarbone, soothing the little sting with the tip of his tongue. That wonderful, talented tongue, which slid along the swell of her breast, circling her aching, pouting nipple until she cried out with longing. Still, he teased her, moving closer, then further away, his breath warm on her flesh. At last, at last, he took her into his mouth, suckling at her aching nipple as she lost herself in him completely.

As he kissed her breast, the arch of her ribs, she felt his hand slide between her legs, one finger easing inside of her. Pressing ever deeper until he found that one perfect spot.

"Balthazar!" she cried, and he quieted her with another kiss.

"Do you want me?" he muttered roughly against her mouth.

"Of course I do," she whispered. And she always had, even when she was too young to understand what "wanting" truly meant. To understand this hot, desperate *need*.

Now her desire was a flame beyond all imagining.

"Only me?" he said.

Bianca didn't know what he meant. But she *did* want only him. No other had ever been able to replace him, not even her husband. No other ever could, despite the secrets and lies that still lay between them like a burning sword.

"Only you," she said.

In one swift movement, he drew the chemise over her head, leaving her completely naked beneath him. He stared down at her hungrily in the flickering light, just before he plunged deep inside of her, to her very core, and they were joined at last.

Bianca closed her eyes tightly, shutting out everything but the feel of him, the burning, abrasive delight of him inside her, his body heavy atop her as he paused. She clutched at him tightly, her nails dug into his shoulders to keep him with her.

Then she felt him move, the slow friction of it, as he drew out almost to his very tip, then plunged in again, deeper and deeper, faster. Bianca caught his mouth with hers, their gasps and moans mingled. The sensation built and built, burning like the brightest tropical sun, heat dancing along her skin until at last she shattered into a hundred bright stars.

As she floated above herself, her head arched back, she heard his own cry echo out. "Bianca!" he shouted, his body taut as a bowstring over hers. "Bianca." In that one moment, he was hers, and hers alone.

He collapsed beside her, their limbs still entwined, the world still spinning. Bianca stroked his damp hair, spreading its silken length over her breasts and stomach as everything slowly stilled. As her breath drew out, and her burning flesh cooled.

He lay next to her, unmoving, his face turned from her on the sheet. His breath was rough, his heartbeat erratic as it flowed into hers. They were surely as close as two people could be, yet still an ocean apart.

Balthazar Grattiano had always been unknowable to her, an irresistible enigma. He was unknowable to her even now, more than ever.

She would just have to find a way to change that. If it was even possible.

Chapter Ten

Bianca lay on her side, half-drowsing as she watched the stars outside her window. The sky was still a dusty black, but she knew that all too soon those stars would twinkle off, one by one, and the sun would edge up over the horizon. A new day, with new decisions and choices.

For now, though, the night seemed endless, a dark cave of blissful silence.

Balthazar lay wrapped around her, his arm heavy over her stomach, his breath soft against her bare shoulder. She felt his lazy kiss on her shoulder blade, the play of his fingers through her hair. She stretched against him, curling into the warm safety of his body.

Here, in the quiet heat of night, the lazy ache of the aftermath of their lovemaking, she could almost imagine she dreamed. That she had tumbled down that dark hole of hers into another realm, another life. One where she was not Bianca Simonetti, and he was not

Balthazar Grattiano. They were no one at all, just a man and woman entwined under that magical island moon.

Bianca ran her fingertips over the back of his hand, feeling the small scars and burns that marred his elegant patrician's fingers. They were not the soft hands of a nobleman now, decorated with jewels. They were the hands of a sailor.

But who was he, really?

Bianca closed her eyes, sighing as his lips found the curve of her neck and left a delicate, burning ribbon of kisses along her skin. Why could he not just be her dream-man, just for this one night? Why *could* they not be a man and a woman?

Yet even as she tried so desperately to hold on to that fantasy, she found it slipping away.

"How did your father die?" she murmured.

Balthazar's hand stilled. He rolled away from her, on to his back, and Bianca felt suddenly chilly. She reached for the sheet, drawing it up over her nakedness.

"He was shot," Balthazar answered tonelessly. "With an arrow."

"An arrow?" she said, not sure she heard him aright.

He laughed, a harsh sound completely devoid of humour. "Not a weapon for a gentleman, eh? My father thought the same when I would practise with targets in the courtyard. He would laugh, call me a damned peasant and none of his getting."

"I would wager he was not laughing in the end," Bianca muttered.

"No, indeed. But if the arrow hadn't done it, the poison would have." He paused. "Poison. Now *there* is a weapon for a gentleman."

She felt the mattress tip as he rolled from the bed, and she glanced back to find him picking up his clothes from the chair. He pulled the shirt over his head, not even wincing as the rumpled cloth slid along his wounded shoulder.

It was obvious he signalled an end to the conversation, yet Bianca burned with curiosity. Questions swirled around madly in her mind, questions she needed answers to! For years she had blamed Balthazar for being a Grattiano, for pretending to be her friend while he allowed his father to ruin her life.

Or perhaps she blamed him for her own girlish fantasies, for the ruin of foolish dreams.

Whatever Balthazar had been—spoiled aristocrat, full of anger and dark depths, ladies' man—she wouldn't have thought him a cold-blooded killer. Oh, surely he *was* capable of coldly dispatching an enemy in battle, but to shoot an arrow into his father…

It must have been terrible. Something truly horrifying surely led him to that moment. And Bianca could not say she was at all sorry Ermano was dead, no matter how it came about.

Yet she didn't know what to say to Balthazar. The gulf of years and hard experience lay deep and wide between them, and surely neither of them had ever been people to easily share their deepest emotions.

She had no idea how to bridge that gulf, yet she found she wanted to. Desperately.

Bianca sat up, wrapping the sheet around her bare breasts as she watched him dress. His movements were quick, gracefully brisk and cold as he fastened his hose and reached for his boots. He, too, seemed to feel the chasm, the wide ocean that flowed between them despite the smallness of the room. Despite the salty smell of sweat and sex that still hung thick in the air.

"Where do you go now?" she asked. "Back to Venice?"

He shook his head, running his fingers through the tangles of his hair. "I haven't been to Venice in many years."

Not since his father died? Since his kingdom was dispersed? Perhaps he, too, had been driven away by violence and blood.

"Not at all?" she said. Tucking the sheet around her, Bianca got up and reached for the comb on her table. She gently pushed away his hands, which were making an even greater mess of his hair, and started to work the tortoiseshell teeth through the long strands. He went very still, but did not push her away.

"Venice is my brother's problem now," he said shortly. "Not mine."

Ah, yes, the mysterious brother. One more thing to unravel in the life of Balthazar Grattiano. Bianca moved the comb gently, her touch soft on his hair. The tense line of his shoulders. "So, all you have is the *Calypso*."

He laughed. "Are you after my wealth, Bianca?"

"If I was, I would be a fool indeed," she answered lightly. "You can't be worth half as much as the Spanish grandees who pass through Santo Domingo."

"I hope not. Wealth is a trap."

"Only for those who have it," she muttered. "The rest of us can only hope for such a wondrous snare."

"I have my ship, and my house, my own island here in the New World where I can live my own life. It is enough." He suddenly spun around, catching her hand in his as the comb fell to the floor. "Bianca, can I see you when I come back to Santo Domingo?"

She stared up at him in the starlit darkness, at the angles of his face spangled in moonlight. How beautiful he was, her lonely, distant angel. But there was something new in his eyes, a glow deep inside like a distant fire on a cold night.

She raised her free hand, lightly tracing his jaw, the taut skin whisker-rough, the soft curve of his lips. He caught her fingertip between his teeth, nipping at it until she shivered, and he caressed it with his tongue.

"We will surely both be old and grey before you find your way back here," she whispered. "If we are alive at all."

"We've survived this long," he said, holding her hand against his cheek. "Survived storms at sea, the tropical heat and fevers. There must be a reason for such a thing."

"A reason for us to meet again? You may be right,

Balthazar Grattiano. Very well, you may see me again. If you can find me."

He drew her to him, his mouth meeting hers in a kiss that seemed to taste not of farewell, but of a most uncertain future.

Little did he know, Bianca thought as she wrapped her arms around him, feeling his body harden against hers. Finding her would be all too easy, once her plan was carried out. She would turn her back on what she had built here, knowing how precarious life was, knowing she might never come back. She would risk it, just to know at last.

Chapter Eleven

Balthazar stood at the prow of his ship, his spyglass trained on the rapidly vanishing hills of Hispaniola. The white-hot island sun beat down on the red roofs of the town, glinting off the gun trained on the port. It grew further away by the second, a mirage of civilisation fringed by the dark mountains. He watched it until the *Calypso* turned a bend in the Rio Ozama and slipped out into the harbour of Azua that led at last to the open sea.

He slowly lowered the glass, only half-aware of the rush of activity around him. Sailors scurried up the riggings and over the deck. It seemed a frantic dance, but Balthazar knew well how carefully choreographed it all was. Every movement perfectly calibrated to turn the ship towards open water, headed home at last.

Home. It had always seemed a foreign word to Balthazar, a concept he could not quite grasp. Surely a home should be a warm and welcoming place, like his brother Marc and Julietta's villa. Their corridors and high-ceilinged rooms rang with the laughter of their children, with the bustle of business and lively conversation.

Balthazar loved to visit them, yet he also left with no regrets when it was time for another voyage. As much as he loved his nephews and little baby Beatrice, as much as it meant for him to have a brother, that was *their* place. Their world, built by the two of them to be their sanctuary, their little universe of love and light after so much darkness. He could warm himself in its glow for a moment. But he did not belong there.

No more than he had ever belonged in his father's cold marble palazzo.

Balthazar turned away from Santo Domingo, facing out to sea again. Mendoza was at the rudder, and a fine wind filled the sails, carrying them out with the tide. This ship had been the most home he ever knew. The very wood of her decks and canvas of her sails were part of him; the salt water of the ocean flowed in his veins. When he bought Vista Linda from the Spanish merchant and built his house on its highest hill, he thought *that* could be his place. And it was beautiful, peaceful.

But the sea, the wide world—that was still his home. A place of freedom, and no rest.

Usually when he left land he felt a soaring exhilaration in his soul. The rush of adventure, the unknown. Today, as they steered the wounded *Calypso* towards Vista Linda, he thought only of Bianca Simonetti.

He leaned his palms against the rail, staring down at the emerald-green waters and seeing Bianca's face there. Her wide, wary brown eyes, the slender curve of her body beneath that thin sheet.

She slept when he had left at dawn, curled up on the bed they had shared, her brow wrinkled as if she worried even in her dreams. She did not even stir as he had kissed her gently, staring at her as if he could memorise every curve of her face, every freckle, every soft breath. She said he could see her again, but only God knew when that would be. They lived here in the most dangerous of worlds, and one chance meeting was surely all the miracle they could expect.

"Maledetto!" he growled, pounding his fist against the rail. He had found her again, Bianca! Found her against all the odds in the world. And the newfound passion in her arms was so very—amazing.

Yet he had left her. Had ran from all the anger and difficult questions he saw in her eyes, back to the cold safety of the sea.

Balthazar glanced back to find the coast of Hispaniola slipping ever further away. The waters turned from a warm green-blue to white-tipped indigo. Soon Bianca would be beyond his reach altogether.

He spun around, his mouth open to shout out orders to come about. Yet even as he called out, he heard a scuffle below decks, echoing from the open hatch.

It was not the normal noise of a voyage just begun, the clank of pulleys and crack of sails, bellowed course directions from the watch, the splash of waves against the hull as a constant counterpoint. The hatch should not even be open now, with all the new supplies and cargo safely stowed.

Yet Luis, the boatswain and pilot, appeared out of the hatch, dragging a parcel behind him and cursing all the while. The sailors nearby even stopped to stare, agog at any unexpected events on Captain Grattiano's tightly run ship.

Balthazar himself stared, scowling. Luis pulled the last of that parcel, a bundle of brown cloth, behind him and dumped it on to the deck, kicking out at it.

The parcel cried out. "Poxy whoreson!" it shouted roughly.

And Balthazar saw it was not a bundle of cloth at all, but a lad. A stowaway. He walked slowly down the steps to the main deck, his arms crossed as he examined the thin figure clad in brown woollen hose and doublet, a black knitted cap pulled low over his head. They often had seamen begging for a place on the crew, but never one desperate enough to hide aboard before.

Yet Balthazar had not time to deal with such annoyances. Not now, when his thoughts were full of Bianca.

"Mendoza!" he shouted. "Turn back to Santo Domingo. We have a knave to set ashore."

He reached down to grasp the lad by the collar of his doublet, knocking his cap askew. One long, dark brown curl escaped, falling along a startlingly graceful neck.

The stowaway shoved Balthazar's hand away, standing up straight as it pulled off its cap. Bianca glared up at him, shaking her hair free over her shoulders.

"You cannot turn back, Captain Grattiano," she said. "The wind is against you."

As Balthazar stared at her in utter astonishment, he heard Mendoza roar with laughter. "Looks like we have a new crew member, captain."

"I can swab a deck or mend a rigging rope with the best of them," Bianca declared. Her words were bold, but her eyes—her eyes still held that deep caution. That distance.

A distance that had suddenly grown much narrower.

Balthazar caught her against him, his lips coming down hungrily on hers as his crew broke into raucous cheers.

Bianca sat on the edge of Balthazar's high-set berth, swinging her booted feet above the planked floor. She gazed around at the small cabin, the space crowded with a table covered with nautical charts and books, a washstand, a sailor's chest. There was a worn blue carpet on the floor by the table, and on the wall was a single portrait, incongruously framed in shining gilt. A painted image of a pale, brown-haired lady in green brocade and dark furs. Bianca recognised it from the one time she had been in the Grattiano palazzo—it was Balthazar's mother. Ermano Grattiano's last wife, the tail end of a most unfortunate parade of spouses.

Bianca stared into the painted hazel eyes, into their quiet, troubled depths. Anything to *not* look at Balthazar, who paced the tight confines of the cabin like a tiger in a menagerie.

When she had conceived this wild plan, this crazy idea to stow away on the *Calypso*, it had seemed to make a sort of senseless sense. She and Balthazar had so much unfinished business, and she could not just let him leave again. He had said he would come back, but she had lived long enough with men of the sea to know how unlikely that was. Sailors were always distracted by the next discovery, the next prize, by new lands and uncharted waters. One port could seldom hold them.

And, even if he did remember, there were storms and pirates and disease. Despite appearances to the contrary, surely even Balthazar was not immune to such things.

So, if she wanted to close the book on her own past, to make peace with her strange relationship with Balthazar Grattiano, she had to follow him into his world. To confront him.

It had made perfect sense in the middle of the night. But now, sitting here in his cabin, with all the creakings and shouts of a vessel at sea just outside the door, she felt a cold, sick sensation in the pit of her stomach.

As she had packed Juan's old trunk and instructed Delores on running the tavern in her absence, her blood ran too hot to allow doubts. Then, crouched in the *Calypso*'s hold, amid barrels, piles of sails, the smells of fish and stagnant bilge water, the reality crashed over her.

She was being a fool. A foolish, infatuated girl, when she was old enough to know better. She was running off to sea after a man who—well, she hardly knew what he was. What he thought.

Yet she could not show such doubts to him. Foolish she might have been, but the die was cast. There was no going back, not for either of them. She had left Santo Domingo behind, maybe never to see it again. She had to play the game now.

She tilted up her chin, sitting straight and still on the edge of the berth. If she *had* to be a fool, she would be a brave one at least.

Balthazar finally ceased his pacing, coming to stand behind the table with his hands braced on a pile of charts. His stillness, the tension of his powerful shoulders beneath his linen shirt, spoke louder than words of barely leashed anger.

Anger at her? At what she did today? Any sensible woman would surely hide beneath the berth now, but Bianca felt strangely distant from it all. As if she watched a *commedia dell'arte* scene played out for her amusement.

Only she wasn't at all amused.

"Why, Bianca?" he asked at last, his voice rough and low.

"I do not know," she answered truthfully. "It seemed a rather good plan back in Santo Domingo."

"Oh? And does it seem a good plan now?"

She watched his long, elegant fingers curl into tight fists. "Not especially."

He gave a bark of laughter. "Nay. Women aboard ship lead to trouble."

"Like Diego's wife, you mean?"

"Exactly so. She thought it a fine idea to hide down in the hold, too."

"Well, *I* am not pregnant." Not that she knew, anyway. "And I am not a complete stranger to the sea. My late husband was a navigator, and I travelled with him before we settled in Santo Domingo. I know my way around a ship well enough."

"How to swab a deck?"

"Yes. I can cook, too."

He stared at her intently, his green eyes dark as a primeval forest in the gloomy light. "And warm the captain's bed?"

Bianca's throat went suddenly dry and tight. She swallowed hard, and said, "That remains to be negotiated."

"No matter what your admirable skills, *cara*, they don't explain why you are here. Why you would leave your home to stow away on my ship."

"I hardly know," she answered. "I just knew that something is left undone between us."

"Do you still think us enemies?" he said. He stalked out from behind the table, coming to stand beside her perch on the berth. He did not touch her, just leaned his forearm on the wall above her enclosure, staring down at her. But his warmth, the clean scent and sheer power of his body, reached out to wrap all around her like caressing fingers. Like ribbons of intoxicating smoke.

Bianca braced her palms on the mattress behind her, unable to look away from him, unable to hide any longer.

"I no longer know *what* we are," she said. "But your family once did mine a terrible wrong, and I cannot be at rest until justice is done."

"Are you going to kill me, then? Pull your dagger out in the dark of night again?" he said, his tone light and conversational, as if he asked about the weather. "Will that satisfy your *justice*?"

Bianca shrugged, suddenly deeply wary. This had all been a very bad idea indeed. But now it was too late to reverse her actions. Too late for many things.

"My father hurt many people," Balthazar went on. "I was young, and angry. I did not know how to stop him. And for that I will always repent." He leaned over her, easing her back on to the berth as he planted his palms on either side of her. She stared up into the harsh light of his eyes, mesmerised.

"But," he said softly, "I do not really think you came here to kill me."

"Why did I come here, then?" Bianca whispered.

"For this." And he kissed her. She knew his kiss now, knew the shape of his lips, the taste of him, the way they fit together. They came together as if they had always been just so, as if this deep hunger for each other was a part of themselves they could not deny.

And yet the sensations were completely new, completely surprising. She would have thought that their coupling in Santo Domingo would slake the old desire, the old dreams. But it was not like that. Her need for him only flamed higher, ever more out of control.

Bianca clutched at his shoulders, her hands sliding around his muscled back to the supple groove of his spine, pulling him closer. The world shifted beneath her—the rock of a ship at sea? Or the cracking and remaking of everything she knew?

She wrapped her legs about his hips, arching into his body. This, despite everything, despite all the pain and hatred, the prison of silence, this felt right. The two of them entwined on a narrow berth, the smell of salt water and tar around them, the groanings of the ship blending with their own muffled cries. This was real and right, in a way palatial Venice could never be.

Was this, then, the real Balthazar she held in her arms? She hardly even knew herself now. She knew only this kiss.

A bell clanged on the poop deck just above their heads, announcing the change of the watch. Startled, Bianca pulled away from Balthazar, staring towards the single porthole to the outside world. The light had mellowed to a soft amber, tinged with that strange sparkle only the open sea could impart. Had so many minutes passed, then? It felt only an instant.

Balthazar slowly straightened to his full height, his head mere inches from the wooden ceiling. He stared down at her, his breath harsh, as if he was as surprised as she.

"I have to go," he said. "But when I come back, Bianca, you will tell me why you are really here."

Bianca lay back on the berth, watching in silent bemusement as he ran his fingers through the tangled length of his hair. He stalked to the door, pausing without turning back to say, "And don't leave this cabin."

"My trunk," she managed to say. "It's in the hold."

"Someone will bring it to you."

"You just don't want your men teasing you about your female stowaway. About how your great manhood lured her aboard, she couldn't bear to be without it—"

"Bianca!" he interrupted harshly. Yet she could vow she heard laughter in his voice, lurking beneath. "I would think *you* would not want that, either."

She shrugged. "It makes no difference to me. It wasn't your codpiece that drew me here, Balthazar Grattiano."

He glanced back at her over his shoulder, one brow raised. "Was it not?"

"Nay!"

"Ah. Well, then, pray remember that when I get back I expect an explanation of what *did* draw you here."

Then he was gone, shutting the door behind him. Bianca listened closely, but she heard no click of the key turning in the lock. He expected his words alone to hold her in place.

And they would, for now. He was the captain of this ship, after all, and she knew well the importance of hierarchy in this tiny wooden world. Besides, she was too tired, too confused, to fend off bawdy jokes.

Bianca reached for the pillows, sliding them beneath her head as she stared up at the wide wooden slats. The *Calypso* was well constructed; there were no gaps there. Yet still she could hear booted steps from the deck above, the indistinct hum of voices. Far beneath her, she felt the swell and roll of the waves, a soothing, timeless rhythm she missed in all her time on land.

Her gaze slid down the scrubbed walls, finding the portrait hanging in the shadows. Signora Grattiano. How strange it was to find her here in this New World, that fine lady of patrician Venice. She stared back, her painted hazel eyes so very sad.

Bianca rolled on to her side, unable to face that lady any longer. Sad resignation had never really been Bianca's way. It availed a person nothing. Yet she could feel that lady's lassitude seeping slowly into her.

Or maybe it was the realisation of what she had done. Running away, hiding here for—what? She hardly knew. It was like when she had run away from Venice all those years ago, an impulsive bolt into the unknown. Yet then she ran *from* danger.

Today, she ran right into it. Into its very arms.

Balthazar demanded to know why she was here. She did not know. She had nothing to tell him that would make any sense.

She only had that feeling, deep inside, that one way or another the two of them had a reckoning coming. A final battle to send the past to its silent grave once and for all.

Chapter Twelve

Bianca must have dozed off, for she was startled awake by the sound of the door opening. She blinked, half-afraid it was Balthazar, catching her unprepared as usual. But it was one of the ship's boys, carrying in her small trunk. Another followed, with a tray he placed on the table amid the charts and books.

She closed her eyes again, lying still until she heard them leave. "She's thin, isn't she?" she heard one of them mutter as the door shut behind them. "No bubbies at all! Cap'n won't like that."

Bianca pressed her hand to her mouth, holding back a crack of laughter. No bubbies, indeed! That had been the curse of her youth, being so thin and scrawny while she watched Balthazar cavort around Venice with buxom courtesans. Now—well, it was the least of her worries.

She stretched on the berth, opening her eyes to see

that the light outside was darkening at the edges. The end of their first day at sea. When would this voyage end?

She climbed down, going to study the tray. There was a ewer of wine, a bowl of water for washing, and a plate of fruit, cheese and dried meat. No stale biscuits so early on. Nibbling at a bit of papaya, she opened her trunk, the scarred old seaman's chest that had once belonged to her husband.

If she never made it back to Santo Domingo, it was all she owned now, too. A grey woollen skirt and bodice, clean chemises and stockings, a straw hat, a couple of books. A bulging purse of coins. And, hidden in that purse, a ruby-and-pearl ring that Balthazar himself had once pressed into her hand.

She took off her boots and hose, her boy's doublet and shirt. Beneath it she wore a flat strip of linen, bound tightly around her chest. As she unwrapped it, she muttered, "See, I do have bubbies." Nothing spectacular, of course, but Balthazar had not complained.

The small looking glass over the washstand reflected her back to herself as she dipped a cloth in the water, running it over the red grooves beneath her breasts. The glass was wavy, distorted, showing a wild-haired, brown-skinned woman. A woman who would do insane things like hide aboard a ship departing for lands unknown.

That was surely not her. Not really. But the sudden rush of freedom, the feeling of being untethered from the world, was intoxicating.

She unlatched the porthole, swinging it open to let in the damp, salty wind. It washed over her naked skin, a benediction of sorts for a new life. Beyond, she could see only water, tinged golden-pink by the sunset. The open horizon.

The door opened again behind her, and she tensed at the thought it could be one of the crew. But the sea breeze carried a new scent to her, that clean, dark smell that was only Balthazar's, and she relaxed.

"I do like the new garb," he said teasingly. "It suits you far better than that doublet."

Bianca laughed, shutting the porthole against the encroaching night. She turned to face him, feeling suddenly bold. Who knew that nakedness could be a finer armour than wool and steel?

"I just thought you might," she said. "Though I did hear tell that my lack of bubbies might be a detriment."

He crossed the cabin in two strides, his eyes hooded and dark with intent. He pulled her close to him, one palm reaching out to weigh her breast. He massaged and squeezed gently, as if he evaluated that estimation. One rough fingertip circled her nipple, closer and closer until at last it caressed her aching, pebbled skin. Bianca moaned, her head arching back as she thrust her breast closer into his touch.

"I would say they are exactly right," he muttered, lowering his head to take that swollen nipple into his mouth.

Bianca buried her fingers in his hair, holding him

to her as the tension inside her grew more and more taut, until she feared she would snap.

"And I think," she gasped, "that you are entirely overdressed, captain."

She reached for the hem of his shirt, dragging it up and over his head. The cool air washed over her damp breast, making her shiver, yet she did not waver from her task. She unfastened his hose, pushing the fabric down until his manhood was freed, rigid as iron.

"Bianca..." he said tightly.

"Be quiet," she answered, and for once he obliged. She slid down his body until her knees rested on the carpet-covered floor, her palms trailing along his smooth, lean-muscled chest, his hips. The thin arrow of hair leading to her goal.

Lightly, teasingly, she traced the length of his erect penis with her fingertips. It was heavy under her touch, pulsing with desire. Something deep inside her, something damp and secret, responded to that primitive need. Everything around her grew blurry and hot, the night narrowed to just the two of them, bound together in the passion that could not be explained or denied.

She eased the tip of her tongue along him, tasting the warm saltiness of his skin, of his very essence. He groaned, the deep sound shimmering through her. She felt all his muscles go tense as she took him fully into her mouth, her tongue twined around him.

His hips jerked, his clasp closing over her hair as

he pressed her closer. But then he pushed her away, just as she tasted him.

"Bianca, I cannot bear it," he gasped.

"Neither can I," she answered. This hot desire, it was all she knew when she was near him. Enemies or not, they were bound together in ways she could never understand.

He fell to his knees beside her, folding her into his arms as their mouths met in a rushed, needful kiss. There was nothing of art or practice about it, just a frantic meeting of heat and light. Of all she was.

She felt him draw her down, until their kiss broke and she lay on her elbows and knees, the carpet deliciously abrasive under her skin. She sensed his dark presence behind her, the spiralling passion that matched hers as his hands traced her breasts, the arch of her back, her buttocks.

He drew her back and up, and she felt him slide inside her, deep and fast. Deeper than he had ever been before, as if he could touch her very soul. He held her still, his grasp tight on her waist as his hips pumped into her.

Bianca moaned, the pressure too much, too wondrous. She arched back into him, feeling his chest along her spine, the tight joining of their bodies. His sweat mingled with hers, their breath and heartbeats as one.

At last, that taut pressure broke, a shower of hot, unbearable pleasure. She felt the warmth of him inside her, the trickle of it on her inner thigh as he called out her name.

She collapsed to the floor, weak and sated. He fell beside her, his legs tangled with hers, his face turned to the wall.

She traced his damp shoulder, his trembling back, the length of his hair. She could not think, not reason. All she could do was *feel*, floating above herself on a cloud of delight and exhaustion.

She closed her eyes, feeling her heartbeat slow, her hot blood cool in her veins. The rush of it seemed to echo the splash of the waves against the ship, the rhythm of Balthazar's breath under her touch.

She had no idea how much time passed as they lay there—minutes, hours? But at last she felt him stir, felt him sit up beside her. She could not open her eyes, even as he wrapped his arms around her, lifting her with him as he stood. She wanted nothing to burst this shimmering dream. Not yet.

He laid her gently on the berth, tucking the blankets around her. But rather than join her, she felt him move away. She heard him pull off his boots and loosened hose, heard his bare footsteps cross the cabin and the splash of water.

She finally opened her eyes to see him rinsing out a cloth in the basin. Now that the great storm of their passion was passed, like the still lull after a storm, there was the old quiet between them. The questions she did not even know how to ask.

She propped her head on her palm, watching him as he wrung out the cloth, his face so solemn, etched in shadows as the day died outside the porthole. He came back to her side, sitting on the edge of the berth as he reached for her bare foot, still in silence. Slowly, gently, he bathed her skin until every sign of their love-making was washed away.

There was nothing to be done to erase the memory of it from her mind, though. That hot, sharp need of his kiss, his touch, lingered there, haunting her.

Perhaps she had hoped to erase Balthazar and all that was between them, to banish him from her life once and for all. But all that happened imprinted him on her spirit more indelibly than ever. He was part of her, and she of him, and there was no blade sharp enough to sever that.

Bianca lay back on the pillows, closing her eyes as his touch, the cool water and rough cloth, eased over her body. How long had she been taking care of herself? Months, years—for ever, it seemed. Struggling to feed herself, to keep a sheltering roof over her head. Struggling just to survive, all alone. How delicious it felt to have someone else care for her, even if only for a moment!

And even if it was only an illusion.

When every inch of her skin was clean and bare, she felt Balthazar draw away. She reached out and caught his wrist, taking the cloth from his grasp. She sat up, gently urging him down to the bed in her place.

He stretched out beside her willingly enough, but

Bianca could feel the tension in his lean body, the wariness that was so much a part of him now. A part of them both.

She eased the cloth over his arm, the sharp angle of his muscled shoulder. Fascinated, she traced light patterns over his golden skin, over each scar and mark. Over the new knife wound, healing now to a bright pink. Every flaw only seemed to increase his beauty. The boy she had been so infatuated with in her youth was a hardened warrior now.

And she—she found she had just become a cautious old woman, weighted down with the past. Only in his arms, with their bodies joined, could she feel like the dreamer she once was. The silly girl who dared to think romance and adventure were real, that they were something worth striving for.

She knew better now, of course. Romance and adventure were a great deal of trouble, an illusion constructed to lure the unwary over the edge of a cliff.

But with him…

Bianca shook her head. With him, all was confusion. They only had this one quiet moment.

On the deck above, the bell clanged for another change of watch, and she heard the crack of the sails in the evening wind. They were far from land now, adrift in the vast unknown.

She lay down next to Balthazar, her body curled around his in the narrow confines of the berth. His hand reached for hers, their fingers entwined.

"You said you came to look for me in Venice," she said quietly.

"What?" he said. His voice was rough, as if he had started to drift into sleep.

"You said our maidservant told you I was dead. When you came to look for me."

His head turned on the pillow, his green-gold gaze searching hers in the gathering gloom. "Have you been thinking of that all this time?"

"Nay," she said. In truth, she had not remembered until this moment. She had been too busy planning how to sneak aboard this ship. But it suddenly seemed very important. "I just—wondered."

His thumb traced over her palm, a looping pattern that made her shiver. She tightened her fingers over his, resting her cheek on his shoulder. They were, had been, as close as two people could be. Was that yawning chasm easing closed? Could it even start to?

"After the last time I saw you in Venice," he said, "so much happened so quickly."

Bianca nodded. She remembered all too well—her mother's dead body; the mad, fearful flight. She was so sure Ermano would come for her next, all she could think of was running for her life. Of how much she hated the Grattianos.

"After my father died," Balthazar continued, "after I knew that I had to leave Venice, find a place on a ship, I wanted to tell you goodbye. To tell you…"

"Tell me what?"

"I hardly remember now. It seemed so important then, that you know I would seek the New World."

"But I was gone."

"Your maid would not even let me into the house. She had obviously been weeping, and she told me both you and your mother were dead." He squeezed her hand. "After so much loss and upheaval, it felt like a punishment."

Bianca frowned in puzzlement. "A punishment?"

"I had sinned horribly when I loosed that arrow on my father. God took you, my friend, in retribution."

"Were we friends, Balthazar?" she murmured.

"Perhaps I was not *yours*. But I had always been so isolated. Cut off from others my own age. When you were kind to me, interested in my books…"

It was so very close to her own old thoughts of him, of her girlish joy at their meetings, that she felt her throat tighten with tears. She swallowed hard against them, and said, "Have I changed so much since then?"

"Changed?"

"You did not know me at first in Santo Domingo."

"I did not expect to find a dead woman, a ghost, there. I thought you must be a fever-dream. But you have changed, just as I have."

"It has been many years."

Balthazar rolled on to his side, staring down at her as if he could read her thoughts. Banish the blinding mist of all that time. "What happened to *you*, Bianca Simonetti? How did you come all this way?"

"Oh, Balthazar," she said sadly. She raised her hand to touch his cheek, the whiskers rough under her hand. A muscle tightened in his jaw. "Too much has happened to speak of tonight. To speak of ever, mayhap. Just for now, for this night, I want to be Bianca Simonetti again."

He studied her intently, his head tilted into her touch as the silence between them lengthened. Finally, he gave her a brusque nod. "For tonight, we will be as we were then. As we should have been."

He lay back down against the pillows, holding her in his arms as he tucked the blankets around them. Bianca snuggled into his embrace, lulled by the rhythm of his breath, the creak of the ship's timbers and the splash of the waves. Outside the porthole, the moon cast its chalky white glow over their entwined bodies, limning everything in its dream-sparkle.

She did not know what would happen tomorrow, or the next day. The world was all upended yet again, everything thrown into chaos. But for that moment, she was safe with Balthazar.

Chapter Thirteen

Balthazar lay very still in the darkness, his arm around Bianca's hips as she slept next to him. Her breath was soft and steady, her body warm under his touch. For all that she had left her life behind, run off to hide on his ship and set out for ports unknown, her sleep was peaceful.

But he could not sleep at all. She would surely rue her choice soon enough, yet he could not regret that she slept beside him now. That they were together, no matter how long it lasted. He had lived all his life alone; the years ahead seemed destined to be just as solitary. Bianca was an unlooked-for gift.

She sighed in her dreams, cuddling deeper into his embrace. The night, so deep and dark outside the porthole, had turned chilly, but the sea was steady enough. No storms on the horizon. Not yet.

Balthazar drew the blankets closer about Bianca's

bare shoulders, pressing a kiss to her brow. His old sins were dark indeed. The tainted blood of his father that ran in his own veins.

Bianca had plenty of reason to hate him, hate the Grattiano name, after what had happened in Venice. Yet he was selfish enough to take what she gave him now, the softness that lurked in her heart and which he craved so deeply. Take it, and relish it.

He kissed her again, and carefully slid from the berth. She murmured wordlessly, her forehead wrinkling, but then she rolled into his warm, abandoned space and fell quiet again. Balthazar put on his robe and opened the porthole, letting in the magic starlight. The silvery glow fell over his table, the old rug on the floor—the spot where he and Bianca had coupled so feverishly. He forgot himself in her body, in the overwhelming heat of their passion, but now his blood ran cooler.

His gaze moved to Bianca's trunk, its lid closed. The pale light illuminated the carved initials "JRM". Surely the monogram of her husband the navigator. Whoever *he* had been.

Balthazar frowned as he thought of the unknown man. Where had Bianca met him? It had to be after she had left Venice; Montero was a Spanish name. What was her life like then, in all the years he had lost her? That life that led her to Señor Montero. Had she been as fierce, as giving, in *his* bed as she was in Balthazar's?

He felt the strongest, most overwhelming surge of

raw jealousy. Violent jealousy, towards a dead man! A man who surely had more claim to Bianca's body and affections than Balthazar ever could.

His hands curled into fists as he resisted the urge to bash in the bloody trunk. To wake Bianca and demand to know all her secrets, to break her puzzling silence and beg for all of her.

She wouldn't give it to him, no matter what. She was the most stubborn, most self-possessed woman he had ever seen. And it only made him desire her more.

She murmured in her sleep, unaware of the storm inside him. The bell had rung for the watch change at the helm long ago, the course called out. Most of the crew would be sleeping now, the officers in their wooden bunks under the quarterdeck, the sailors wherever they could find a space. Perhaps there, under the black sky, he could find a moment of peace.

Balthazar left the cabin, hurrying up the steep flight of stairs onto the deck. The sailor who kept watch by the *ampoletta* gave him a nod. He made his way to the prow, staring out over the open sea as he filled his lungs with the salty, cold air. The darkness was broken only by the glowing white foam of the waves.

It was only here, so far from Venice and all he knew in his life before, that Balthazar had found his only peace, his purpose. The sea could be mastered by no man, yet they understood each other. Understood the wild, angry freedom that couldn't be constrained. The sea was his real home, as much as he had ever found a home.

Did Bianca feel the same? Had she, too, found a place to belong in this dangerous new world? For he sensed that she, like the ocean, could understand him.

If he could just let her. If *they* could just be free of all that came before.

But for all the wondrous gifts the sea could bestow, she could not make a man new-born, not wash away sins.

He heard a laugh behind him, and turned to see Mendoza and Luis cooking in the *fogon*. The three-sided metal box was lashed to the deck, a cooking pot hung on its rod over the flames. The smell of smoke and roasting pork clung to the cold breeze.

As he walked towards them, the men glanced up, giving him a pair of wide grins.

"Hard work tonight, eh, captain?" Mendoza said. "Here, have some meat, some ale."

"'Twill fortify you for more hot work later," Luis said. He passed Balthazar a tankard of ale.

He took it gratefully, sitting down close to the warm fire. The two men laughed, but did not question him about Bianca. They knew better than to pry, after being on his crew for so long. And Balthazar had no answers, anyway. Not for them; not for himself.

"Your wound is healed, captain?" Mendoza asked, turning the skewers of meat over the flames.

"A scratch, that's all it was," Balthazar answered.

"And Señora Montero is a good nurse, eh?"

Balthazar winced, remembering her needle jabbing into his skin. "That she is."

"The saints must have been watching over you," Luis said. "Diego was fiercely determined."

"He'll be back, no doubt about it," Mendoza said darkly. "Once he hears you still live."

Balthazar took a long drink of the ale, wiping his mouth with the back of his wrist as he remembered the fiery glare of Diego's eyes as he had brought down the dagger. He remembered Esperanza's cries as she was carried from the ship, Diego's curses.

"I would expect no less, from a man so set on revenge," he said.

"He won't find us on Vista Linda," Mendoza said stoutly. "No one knows the island."

"Even if he did, he would have to get through all of us," Luis said. "He'll not escape again."

Balthazar nodded, but he knew that no threats, not even steel or shot, could deter someone as angry as Diego Escobar. Someone who had lost his very soul to grief and inescapable fury. Only death—his own or Balthazar's—could stop him.

Balthazar knew this well, for he had lived his own life in just such a blindly violent state. He had *been* Diego.

Perhaps he still was. And, if Diego's wife made him feel as Bianca did…

Then he understood the grief and fury. He and Diego would surely meet again, very soon. One of them would not survive the encounter, not this time.

What would become of Bianca then?

Chapter Fourteen

A crash of breaking glass, of shouts and shrill laughter, woke Diego from his restless sleep. His eyes flew open, his dazed stare meeting the soot-stained rafters above his head. The door and window were still barred, but were too thin to keep out the riot that was Tortuga at midnight.

The whore next to him muttered in her sleep, rolling closer to him. In the faint light of one smoking lamp, her pale skin was streaked with dirt, her rouged nipples smeared to the same coppery colour as her hennaed hair. She smelled of cheap rum, and even cheaper sex.

For an instant, he remembered Esperanza, her honey-coloured skin, the way her long black hair smelled of flowers. Her sweet, sweet smile.

Suddenly disgusted with the whore, with himself, with everything, he pushed himself away from the woman, sitting up on the edge of the bed. A flickering torch passed by outside the window, borne by yet more drunken people revelling in the tawdry night and ill-gotten coin. Coin from blood and death, which would be gone by morning, thrown away on drink and women.

The glow of that torch was cast over the sparse rented room, the packed dirt floor, the mouldy straw mattress, the tangle of clothes tossed over a rickety stool. How very far it all was from what he had hoped for when he left Spain! When he had said farewell to his home and sailed off so blithely into hell. He had found no riches here. He lost his one treasure, Esperanza, to the greed and callousness of life here.

To the greed of one man. Balthazar Grattiano.

Strange, Diego mused as he reached for his hose and boots. He had imagined that once Grattiano was dead, he would feel some satisfaction, some peace at last. But there was only that cold hollowness. Perhaps he would feel like that for ever, until he met his own end at the point of someone else's sword.

There was no use in regrets now. He had made his choice, the only one he *could* make. Esperanza was dead. He soon would be, too. He just had to carry on in this life he chose until that day.

Diego finished dressing, and checked the bottle he found on the floor. Empty, of course. He remembered drinking it with the red-haired doxy, gulping down its fiery oblivion before they fell to their rough coupling. He should go out for more, but he found what he truly wanted was not the haze of drunkenness, but to be alone. To be alone in silence for one single moment.

Yet that was the one thing that was impossible in a hellish place like Tortuga. The one thing that could not be bought with any amount of escudos.

As if to confirm that thought, there was a fierce knock at the door, a pounding that shook the room to its very rafters. The woman didn't wake, though; she merely rolled over and started snoring. Diego rushed for his sword, clutching the hilt as he threw open the door. Maybe *this* was his fate come for him at last.

It was only his first mate Mauro, swaying perilously on his feet as he stood on the threshold. A little blonde in a torn red dress stood beside him, holding him up even though she hardly looked any more sober. Diego's grip slackened on the sword, but he did not set it aside. Only a fool would go unarmed around here, even for a moment.

"Cap'n!" Mauro slurred urgently. He swayed to one side, the blonde giggling as she hauled him upright. "I heard at the tavern…"

Diego frowned as he stared at Mauro. There was always much news to be found in the taverns, if a man was alert enough. But little of it could be urgent enough to leave such pleasures in the middle of the night.

And none of it could be good.

He stepped aside, letting Mauro and the woman come in. Their presence made the already cramped space even tinier, even mustier with the smell of liquor and unwashed bodies.

The whore in his bed woke at last, scowling. "Here, it costs extra for groups," she complained.

Diego ignored her. "What did you hear at the tavern?"

Mauro's sunburned brow furrowed in thought. "I heard that Grattiano is alive!"

For a moment, Diego just stared at Mauro, certain that he had not heard right through the stale cloud of rum. "Alive?"

"Aye! Felipe saw him himself. Going back aboard the *Calypso* in Santo Domingo, as alive as you or me."

"The *Calypso*," the blonde said. "It's real, then? I thought it was just a story."

"M'sister says she tupped that Grattiano once," the redhead said, sitting up in bed with her breasts still bare. "She said he was amazing, went on for hours and hours."

Both women sighed.

"But then, my sister was always a bloody liar," she added. "But still…"

"Shut up!" Diego snapped. "Felipe is sure of what of he saw? He wasn't on the *aquadiente* and imagining things?"

Mauro shrugged. "He seemed sure enough. And no one in Santo Domingo was talking about Grattiano being dead after we left."

And surely the death of someone like Balthazar

Grattiano would be all they *would* talk about. Diego's hand curled into a fist around the sword hilt, as he fought down the urge to plunge it into Mauro's heart for bearing such tidings.

He had been a fool indeed to leave Santo Domingo so hastily, to assume his errand was complete when he saw Grattiano fall. He should have known such a foe would not die easily.

He had failed his wife yet again.

Diego shoved past the crowd, out the door. "Go and sober up," he said tightly. "Then find the rest of the crew, drag them out of whatever hellhole they're in. We leave at dawn."

"But, cap'n…" Mauro protested.

"Dawn!" Diego insisted, slamming the door shut as the whore slid back down on the bed, her eyes wide with sudden fear.

He had to find Grattiano again. And this time he would not fail.

This time, Balthazar Grattiano would die.

Chapter Fifteen

Bianca slowly came to consciousness, like swimming up through warm, clear water to the shimmering light above. Whatever her dreams were, they did not want to release her from their clutches. She burrowed beneath the blankets, seeking one more moment of oblivion. Of floating free in that shining water.

But sleep was not to be. Her legs were sore, as if she had been swimming all night, and her belly rumbled with hunger. She pried her eyes open, peeking over the edge of the sheet. She hoped, feared, Balthazar would be there, watching her.

She was alone, though, the golden morning light bright on the empty cabin. A fresh ewer of wine and plate of fruit waited for her on the table, and a man's fur-trimmed robe was draped over the chair.

Bianca pushed back the bedclothes, slowly swinging her legs over the edge of the berth. She *was* sore after last night's lovemaking, but it was a delicious sort of ache. One that had her humming a silly little tune as she got out of bed and hurried over to the table.

She slipped on the dressing gown. It was much too large for her, of course, the sleeves falling over her hands and the hem trailing on the floor. But it was warm, and its rich folds still smelled of Balthazar. She snuggled into it, revelling in the satin and fur luxury that whispered of another world than the rough one of Santo Domingo. A world of glittering beauty, of ease and privilege.

Bianca had never known such a world, not really. Even in Venice, her life had been far more work than ease. But she glimpsed such things every day, silken gowns seen on latticed balconies or in passing gondolas, the flash of gold and jewels and fine Burano lace. The scent of rosewater, jasmine, and violets from Julietta Bassano's shop. Music, hushed and secret laughter, sparkling eyes behind masks. *That* was Balthazar's world, one he gave up to come here and face the perils of the sea.

For what? Perhaps that was why she had left her tavern to follow him aboard the *Calypso*. Balthazar Grattiano had always been an intriguing mystery to her dazzled, girlish eyes. As slippery as a length of finest satin, always just beyond her grasp. She wanted to discover what he truly was, once and for all, before she put a final end to whatever it was between them now.

She poured out a goblet of wine and took a long,

fortifying sip. Trying to decipher Balthazar was hot work indeed. She couldn't do it in a day, maybe not even a lifetime. Yet she had to try.

Starting with what had really happened with him and his father.

As she munched on a slice of papaya, she glanced at the papers piled on the table. They were hand-drawn charts, she noticed, maps of various island coasts with carefully calibrated measurements.

She flipped through them, marvelling at the beautiful work. Her husband had been a navigator, so she saw how accurate and well drawn these maps were. Yet truly they were also beautiful, etched in delicate shades of blue, green, lilac and earthy sepia, sketches of tiny ships and natives in their strange dress along the margins.

She turned the charts over to find more drawings hidden beneath, detailed scenes of plants and trees, of native dwellings. And on the bottom was something even more extraordinary, a charcoal portrait of a dark-haired woman and two small boys. These were not islanders. The woman wore a fashionable Italian gown with brocaded ribbon trim on the sleeves and bodice. Her oval face was gently smiling as she gazed down at the children, one infant on her lap and one standing beside her, clutching at her skirt.

It was truly beautiful. Every grey charcoal line spoke of tenderness and loveliness, of the peace a family ought to bring, but which Bianca had never known.

In the corner were the hastily scrawled initials "BG". Balthazar Grattiano.

Bianca stared again at the little boys. There was something about them, something familiar about their eyes, the crooked slant of their smiles. Were they, then, Balthazar's sons? His family?

Was he running away from domesticity, even more than he ran from his father's death and dark legacy?

The bright morning faded a bit around her as she looked at those children. Something seemed to break inside her, a brittle crack so loud she vowed she could hear it. Which was so ridiculous, really. She had no heart at all any more, not since her mother's death. And she cared naught for Balthazar, beyond making him pay for his family's crimes.

Why, then, did her throat ache as if she longed to weep?

Bianca sat down hard on the nearest chair, the sweet fruit suddenly like ashes in her mouth. She had entirely lost sight of why she was here, of who Balthazar was. Who *she* was. She was too enthralled by their hot lust for each other, by fantastical dreams that were utterly impossible.

She took another gulp of the wine, wishing she could drown in it. And drown Balthazar right along with her.

She reached for a pile of books, blindly opening the volume on top in hopes of distraction. Ptolemy's *Geography*. Of course Balthazar would not have poetry or romances. She opened it, diving into descriptions of the Spice Islands, the 360 degrees of longitude.

She was still reading of Africa and how it extended far south beyond the equator when the cabin door opened. She glanced up, startled, to find Balthazar standing there. His hair, bound back by a black scarf, was tousled by the sea winds, his shirt unlaced to reveal a vee of sun-browned skin. In that instant, he did indeed seem part of the ocean, salt waves, sun, open sky. Of delicious, intoxicating freedom.

She stroked the soft sleeve of the robe. How many Balthazars were there, really? Three? Twelve? A hundred?

For a moment, the grin he gave her made her long to run into his arms. To feel his mouth on hers, taste all that salt and sun, and forget everything in the pleasures of his beautiful body.

But even sex had its complications, a vast array of them. And she could not let her armour drop again. There were those children…

"Reading Ptolemy?" he said. The cabin door slammed behind him as he came to pour himself the last of the wine. His strong, brown throat tensed as he drank, and Bianca had to turn away.

Unfortunately, her gaze fell on the faded rug under his scuffed boots, and she remembered all too well what happened to them *there*.

"Yes," she answered tightly. "I hope you don't mind."

"Of course not." He sat down across from her,

reaching over the charts to spear a piece of fruit with his dagger. "I remember how it was in Venice, being able to talk about books with you. About navigation, new lands, exploration."

"I remember, too. You were the only person who ever spoke to me about such things. Everyone else was always so…"

"Settled? Resigned to their place in the world?"

"Yes, exactly so. Our maidservant disapproved of my reading. She said if God placed us in one spot we ought to stay there, not go sailing off into heathen lands."

Balthazar laughed. "Perhaps she was right. Look what trouble we get into in 'heathen lands'."

"Not as much trouble as we had in Venice, the blessed land of St Mark."

"Very true. But what if God put us in Venice, a place of boats and water, just so we could learn how to come here?"

"Then I wish God would not work in such mysterious ways," Bianca muttered. She wished some divine voice would come into her head now, tell her what to do. What the truth was. But then surely such a voice would be the devil, tempting her to abandon her course and forget all but the sensual power of Balthazar's kiss.

"He is silent indeed," Balthazar said. "Especially when it matters the most."

"And yet surely sometimes He works through us to create great beauty," Bianca answered. She tapped one of the charts with her finger. "Did you draw this?"

He frowned down at the map, as if he never saw it before and didn't know how it got there. "Aye," he answered finally.

"You seem reluctant to admit it. Anyone else would be boastful. It's wonderful work."

"Do you think so?"

"Certainly. The detail and accuracy are amazing. My husband was a navigator, so I do know something of nautical charts. He would have given anything to possess such fine maps."

"Ah, yes. Your husband. Tell me, Bianca, who was this Señor Montero?"

Bianca laughed. "You, Signor Grattiano, are trying to change the subject, I think! To talk of me rather than you."

"Too clever of you. I never like to talk of myself. It's a dull subject."

"But why? These *are* very fine work. The best I've seen."

"So my brother Marc says. He wants me to come back to Venice, or maybe go to Seville or Cadiz. Open a shop, where I can draw and sell my charts. There is vast demand for such things, he says."

Back to Europe—to his children? That dark-haired woman in her fine gown? Bianca felt a sharp pang deep in her belly at the thought. But she pushed it away, down into that dark chasm that held all her hurts, her old pain. "That seems a sound idea. The sea is a hard life; a man can't follow it for ever."

Balthazar shrugged. "It seems the sea is the only thing I'm truly good at."

"Oh, I would not say it was the *only* thing," Bianca said.

"Nay?" He arched his brow in question.

"No, indeed."

He leaned over the table, reaching out to toy with the fur edging of her robe. His finger grazed her skin, and she shivered. His eyes grew hooded and moss-dark as he stared at her breast, just visible beneath the brocade.

"What else am I good at, then, *señora*?" he asked hoarsely.

Bianca shook her head, catching his wandering fingers in her hand. "You are quite arrogant enough, I think! I will not add fuel to the flames of your confidence."

He laughed, and leaned closer to give her a quick kiss. "Then you should dress, *cara*, before I'm tempted to try to evoke your praise. It grows too hot in here."

It was indeed *hot* in the cabin, but Bianca was sure it wasn't from the sun climbing overhead. She snatched up her own clothes, the hose and shirt draped over her trunk, feeling suddenly rather shy. In the dark of the night, any intimacy with him seemed allowable, needful. But in the bright light…

Things were so very different then.

"May I come up on deck with you, then?" she asked, fastening her doublet. "I won't get in the way."

"Aye, you did say you knew your way around a ship."

"I came from Europe on one, did I not?"

"And around the islands with your navigator husband, no doubt."

"That, too. I can mend a sail, if needed, or swab a deck."

"Don't tell Mendoza. He'd put you to work straight away," Balthazar said.

"So, he is not one who thinks women aboard a ship bring bad fortune?"

"Only some women." He opened his trunk to pack away the robe, and Bianca glimpsed more books, clean shirts.

And a carved Irish bow, tucked along the side with a quiver of arrows.

He took out a cross-staff and slammed the lid, cutting off her glimpse of the shining weapon. Was it the same one he had used to dispatch his father?

"I would imagine someone has been telling tales," he said.

"Tales?" Bianca said, still bemused by the bow.

"Of women on board who bring bad luck. Or one woman in particular."

"Mendoza, of course. I wanted to know who that man was in my tavern, why he wanted you dead."

"Many men want me dead. Women, too, I would imagine," he said. "Diego Escobar is just more persistent than some."

Bianca froze. "Does that mean he will come after you again?"

"Most probably. He disappeared in Santo Domingo. But we live in a small world, and once he hears I am not dead…" He turned and caught a glimpse of her unguarded face. "Oh, Bianca. How shocked you look. I doubt he will be able to find us where we are going."

"You said he was persistent."

"But I am more so, as you well know. And I am determined to stay alive for a few more years yet." He held out his hand to her, beckoning. Tempting. "Come, the day gets away from us."

Bianca slowly slid her fingers into his clasp, feeling his strong touch close around her, so warm, so strong.

So—alive.

He led her up the narrow steps and through the door on to the deck. For a moment, she was blinded by the brilliant sunlight after the gloom of the small cabin. She shielded her eyes from the glare, studying the scene before her.

For an instant, the months and years melted away, and she was on that first ship as it made its way from shore. There was the same ceaseless flow of activity, of movement and noise. Men hurried all around, pumping water from the hold, scrubbing the decks, climbing the riggings to check for frayed ropes. Laughter, shouted conversation, and the off-tune words of sea chanties blended with the crack of the sails in the wind, the groan of the ship's timbers as they ploughed through the waters.

Even after so long ashore, she remembered it so well.

The salt spray in the air, the pitch and roll of the deck under her feet. And she remembered, too, how very alone she had felt then. Married to a man she did not yet know well and who was quite a bit older than she, setting a course away from everything that was known.

She felt alone now, too. Cast adrift on a wide, wide sea where anything could happen.

Then Balthazar turned to her, holding out his hand. His lips quirked in a questioning half-smile, his head tilted as if to say—will you jump with me? Jump forward into nothingness, into that great unknown.

Yet Bianca knew it was too late for choices. She had jumped into that abyss when she had crept aboard the *Calypso*. Now all she could do was catch Balthazar's hand and pull him down with her.

She slid her fingers into his strong clasp, following him as he made his way along the deck. The men made way for him respectfully enough, but she glimpsed their hidden grins they looked at her. *Tough but fair*, she remembered Mendoza saying of Balthazar, and it was clear they did respect him. But everything was known aboard the tiny, confined world of a ship. Even—especially—sex could not stay hidden for long.

Bianca could feel the warmth that flooded her cheeks, but she held her head high as she followed Balthazar up the steps to the bow. A tall, thin man in a straw hat kept watch there, and he gave Bianca a shy bow as she and Balthazar approached the rail.

"Bianca, this is Luis, the *Calypso*'s boatswain," Balthazar said. "Luis, may I present Señora Montero of Santo Domingo."

"*Buenos dias, señora,*" Luis said, still shy.

"Señora Montero has offered to help mend sails and cook for us," Balthazar said, his brow arched teasingly at Bianca. "What do you think? Are we in need of her assistance?"

"Mayhap when we reach land, Captain Grattiano," Luis said. "There's always plenty of work to be done then."

"So, we are close to our destination?" Bianca asked, gazing out over the horizon. All she could see was endless dark blue, frosted with edges of white.

"Not far now," Luis said. "The *Calypso* always makes good time." He was hailed by one of the other sailors and hurried away, leaving Bianca and Balthazar alone by the rail.

"A magical ship indeed," she said, leaning her elbows on the polished wood to gaze down at the breaking waves. The warm sun felt good on her skin, like a taste of bright freedom after a long, cold confinement.

"Hardly magic," Balthazar said, coming up beside her. He held a cross-staff in his hands, and as Bianca watched he raised the long edge to his eye, moving the sliding cross-piece until the bottom edge aligned with the horizon and the top edge with the rim of the sun. Bianca knew the task could not be easy on a pitching deck, yet he made it look simple.

"Merely good craftsmanship," he said. "My

brother's shipwrights are among the finest in Europe."

"A well-made ship is naught without a good captain," Bianca said. "One who knows the sea."

"And respects her whims?" Balthazar said with a laugh. He put down the cross-staff and leaned over an astronomical chart laid out on a table.

"Can you read her whims there?" Bianca said, peering over his shoulder at the numbers that meant so little to her. Even if she could decipher it, she feared she would be distracted by the flex of his shoulders beneath the thin linen shirt. The long sweep of his dark hair, brushed by the wind away from his neck. The clean scent of him.

"I can see the sun's declination," he said, pointing to a number with one brown, elegant finger. "See, Bianca? This is the sun's degree of angle overhead for today's date. By subtracting this from the cross-staff reading, I can see the *Calypso*'s latitude. So, we are truly not far from home. If our fortune holds and we are not blown off course."

"And who drew these charts?"

His palm flattened on the parchment. "I did."

Bianca rested her hand on his shoulder, staring down at those mystical numbers. "Surely these *are* a kind of magic. A map to the ocean and the sky themselves."

He glanced at her, his eyes jewel-bright and unreadable in the sun. "And I am a sorcerer for knowing how to read them?"

Bianca felt suddenly breathless. The noise of the bustling ship vanished around her. There was only Balthazar, and that wild sea that was so much a part of him.

"You have a magic in you indeed, Balthazar," she murmured.

"Is that how I lured you here, Bianca?" he said. "With magic?"

"I'm beginning to think so. Once I bought the tavern, I vowed I would never leave land again. Never venture into the unknown."

"Yet here you are."

"Here I am." She forced herself to turn away from him, from that all-seeing gaze that gave nothing away. She went back to the rail, studying the horizon that only he seemed able to read. "I forgot how very beautiful it was."

"The sea?"

"The whole wide world." She felt the shift of his movement behind her, the heat of him against her back. Surrounding her, like that sun itself. He *was* the world, all the wondrous, mysterious, frightening, alluring world in one man.

"I remember when I was young," she said, "and you would talk to me of the lands in your books. Places of new languages, new ways of being, where the *Libre d'or* had no meaning. Where a person could be anything they wanted."

"I remember," he said quietly. "You were the first person who ever understood."

"And did you?"

"Did I—what?"

"Become what you wanted."

She felt him draw closer, right next to her by the rail. Only their shoulders touched, yet it felt as if they were the only people in the world. The two of them bound as one by the waves.

"Did *you*, Bianca?" he asked. "Did you become what you wanted?"

She reached for his hand, and again had that dizzying sensation of launching herself into open air, not sure where, or even if, she would land. Where that horizon dropped away and there was nothing at all. No past, no future.

"I hardly know what I am any longer," she said. "Or what I wanted back then."

"Aye," he said. "Venice seems a hundred years ago. But one thing turned out as I hoped."

"This ship?"

"Finding you again, Bianca Simonetti."

Startled, she turned to him, her gaze scanning his face. The sunlight always turned him to gold, an ancient idol. His brow was creased as if he questioned her, but she could still not read his thoughts. They were always hidden.

"Do you hate me still?" he said.

"I…" Bianca shook her head, confused. "I hardly know." And she did not. Her feelings for Balthazar Grattiano were all tangled, like a piece of frayed rigging caught in the wind.

"One day, Bianca," he said, "one day soon, you will have to tell me what happened to you between Venice and now."

"I know," she answered. But, please God, not yet. Not yet! "As will you."

He gave a bitter laugh. "Are you sure you want to know?"

Nay, she was not *sure* at all! Yet she had come all this way.

She leaned against the railing, staring blindly down into that blue abyss. She had jumped. Would she now fall—or soar?

Chapter Sixteen

Balthazar peered through his spyglass at the horizon, searching for a hint of land, some cove they could make for before nightfall. He didn't like the look of the water, so smooth, nor the wispy clouds racing overhead. The weather was changing, and after the fierce storm they had weathered in the Mona Passage he was doubly wary.

The *Calypso* carried a fine cargo now in Bianca, and he could not put her in danger.

He heard a ripple of laughter, and it made him smile in response. The sound had an almost startled quality, as if the laugh was not used much, and thus was all the sweeter. He lowered the glass, turning to peer along the railing to the quarterdeck.

Bianca was stirring something in the large pot hung over the fogon, still wearing her boy's clothes with her hair pinned atop her head and bound with a scarf. The warm breeze stirred the loose curls, and she brushed them back impatiently from her flushed cheeks. Two of his men sat close to her, slicing onions and cassava root, gazing at her raptly as if they were suddenly her willing slaves, drawn in by the enchantment of her smile.

And they were surely not the only ones caught in that spell! He could not look away from her, and found himself longing to hear that laughter again.

She shook her head as she stirred, listening as the men told her what was no doubt some wildly exaggerated tale of their seafaring exploits. The rest of his crew still went about their tasks, yet he could see how they all glanced in her direction, how they drifted ever closer in their chores.

Women on board ship could be a curse indeed. Yet sometimes they could be a blessing. Marc's wife Julietta had sometimes gone aboard the *Elena Maria*, the flagship of the Velazquez fleet, for shorter voyages, and she always seemed to inspire everyone to work even harder. She brightened the hard world of the ship with just a smile, a flick of her satin skirts.

And Bianca had that same quality. She was dark and quiet, self-contained, just as Julietta was. Hard to read. Yet he sensed her keen interest in all that happened around her, her easy, unobtrusive manner aboard ship that proclaimed her experience with a seafaring life. She asked the men questions, nodding and smiling at their answers as she cooked a meal that would no doubt be the tastiest any of them had aboard ship.

Balthazar felt a sudden, unfamiliar emotion—peace. Calm. Despite the uncertainties of the weather, despite his own uncertainties of having Bianca so close, he felt peaceful and still, for the first time ever.

It was a dangerous feeling indeed, lulling him into that dream of smiles and laughter, of a soft, warm bed, kisses and talk. A friend who had understood what he was before he became Captain Grattiano. Understood, perhaps, because they were the same deep down inside. Seekers, craving home even as they needed freedom.

When all they had, really, was this one moment.

Bianca glanced up to find him watching her, and for an instant the wary mask she usually wore fell away. He saw his own puzzlement and yearning written there in her dark eyes. He wondered again what had brought her to this point in time, to this place where against all odds they had found each other again.

She gave him a little smile, and the mask dropped back into place. She turned her attention to the cooking, stirring in a handful of the vegetables his men so obligingly sliced for her.

Balthazar turned away, too, back to the horizon and the search for a safe port.

The sun was beginning to set, a strange orange-red amid shimmering streaks of gold and lavender. But not far off was a new bank of clouds, grey and thickening. Mendoza came up beside him, watching that same changing sky with a frown on his bearded face.

"The weather is changing," Mendoza said.

"Aye."

"Just rain, captain? Or…?"

Balthazar knew what he meant. Or was it a storm like the one that snapped their mainmast and drove them into Santo Domingo? They had made the best repairs they could, but the *Calypso* was still vulnerable. "Not like the last time, I think. The air doesn't feel as heavy. Still, we are not at full strength. We should find a port for the night."

"Any place near?"

"San Pedro should be just a few leagues off. It's not much, but it has a protected cove. Not too rocky, out of the way of wind and waves. We can make for that, ride out the rain."

Mendoza laughed. "If you can persuade the men to cease flirting with Señora Montero and do their work!"

Balthazar glanced back down at Bianca. Indeed, most of the crew *had* clustered around her, abandoning their chores altogether to tell her more tales and watch her smile. "If *she* asked them, I'm sure we could get them to do anything."

He reached out and clanged the watch bell, watching in satisfaction as their startled attention flew towards him. How dare they all flirt with Bianca! Make her smile when he, Balthazar, seemed incapable of that impossible feat.

"Scurvy knaves!" he shouted. "We're making for San Pedro before dark falls. So stop ogling a pretty face and get to your posts. *Ora!*"

Mendoza still laughed. "I don't think her pretty face is *all* they're ogling! She also has pretty—" He quickly sobered when Balthazar turned a fierce glare on to him, and he hurried away to his own tasks.

Balthazar snapped the spyglass back up to his eye, watching as a rugged coastline slowly moved into distant view. All around him, his shouts had the desired effect as his men sprang into action along the decks and into the rigging. Was that *jealousy* he felt? That bitter pang? First for the late, unknown Señor Montero, now for his own crew. His control must be slipping beyond his grasp, which was the most fatal error at sea. It had never happened before.

It could not happen now.

Even amid the clamour of sudden activity, he heard footsteps as she came up the stairs, felt her presence beside him. He lowered the glass, staring down at her. She watched him with her usual calm wariness, but he sensed something else beneath. Something deep in her eyes.

"I can keep watch, so you can take the rudder," she said.

"I thought you were cooking."

"I put the lid on the pot, and left one of the ship's boys to watch it," she said. "He has strict instructions to keep it from burning. Even if it does rain, we can have a decent meal."

Balthazar grinned as he handed her the spyglass. "Cook, lookout—you *are* useful, Señora Montero."

She smiled in return. "Did I not tell you so?" She

turned the glass on to that shore, still too distant, as he turned to the rudder. The wind was brisker now, colder, filling the sails as they crept slowly towards land.

"How red the sky is," she murmured. "I don't like the look of it."

"Nor do I. But we'll find shelter before it hits, never fear."

"I'm not afraid," she said. "Is this ship not under the command of the famous Captain Grattiano?"

"I do hate to contradict a beautiful lady, but I fear I have no command of the skies. They rain down on the *Calypso* as much as any other vessel."

"But you surely have command of the waves. The mermaids, the sirens, the naiads—they would do anything you said."

"Sadly, though, Neptune is a man, and not likely to be swayed by *me*. Perhaps you, though, he would listen to."

"Me?" Bianca laughed. "Not with those pretty naiads at his disposal."

"My crew obviously listens to you. They were gathered around you like eager subjects with their queen."

"Only because I am going to feed them something besides hard biscuits and dried beef." She scanned the horizon, slowly back and forth. "The water colour is changing. It's looking brown now."

"We are close, then. If we can make it around the shoals, there's a protected cove just to the north."

"How do you—ah, yes. Your charts. You must know every coastline between here and Lisbon."

"Not every one." Balthazar smiled ruefully. He obviously did not have a map of the human heart. It was a hazy mystery always, beyond every compass and cross-staff.

They worked together in silence until at last the *Calypso* slid into safety in the cove, beyond the worst of the ripening wind and the dangerous rocks along the shore. Balthazar ordered the anchors dropped and most of the sails struck. They would ride out whatever came here right here, through the night.

Bianca carried her stewpot below decks just as the slate-grey clouds rolled in full force and released their heavy, cold burden of rain. The men followed her through the hatches, their tasks as complete as they could be. All that was left was to wait out the storm, the ship at anchor and riding up and down with the swells.

Only Balthazar was left to pace the deck, constantly scanning the horizon as the rain misted on his face. He had seen his ship through worse storms than this many a time, had even relished the hot rush of energy that driving through a howling gale evoked. Battling the sea and winning was the greatest of victories.

But with Bianca aboard the *Calypso*, the stakes were greater than ever.

Bianca settled herself in a corner of the hold, amid stores of firewood and barrels of provisions. She stirred at the thickening stew, listening to the drumbeat of rain on the planks overhead. As the steady pattern increased, grew more erratic, and droplets dripped through the tiny gaps, she felt herself growing nervous. It seemed just some tropical rain now, a sudden storm punctuated by the angry rumble of distant thunder, yet she knew all too well how quickly such a storm could spin out of control.

But the men did not seem at all concerned as they gathered in the crowded, dark, damp hold. They found spaces atop the piles of extra sails and coils of rope, amid the masts that jutted at right angles, increasing the crowded conditions. One of them even took out a small pipe and started playing a lively tune.

If *they* were not concerned, Bianca thought, surely she had no reason to be, either. Still, as thunder clapped overhead, sudden and loud, she couldn't help but shiver.

As she slid the stew pot away from a drip of water, Raul, one of the men who had talked to her on deck, came to sit beside her.

"Can I help you, *señora?*" he asked.

"You can stir for a bit, if you like," Bianca said, handing him the long spoon. She wrapped her arms around herself against the damp chill. "I must say, Raul, the crew here is by far the most courteous I have ever encountered!"

He laughed shyly, stirring the bubbling brew far more vigorously than required. "Captain Grattiano won't stand for brawls or quarrels, *señora.*"

"Feuds can be fatal aboard a ship," Bianca said. "I see the results all too often in my tavern." She paused. "The captain is very strict, then? There are many floggings aboard the *Calypso*?"

"When needed," Raul said. "But that isn't often. Most of us have served aboard ships that…" His voice trailed away, and he did not look at her.

The captain is strict but fair, Bianca remembered Mendoza saying. His men were loyal to him. "Ships that are not as neatly run as the *Calypso*."

Raul nodded. "We're all fortunate to be here, *señora*. To work for Captain Grattiano. He's a fine captain, none like him in these waters."

"Hmm," Bianca said. But she knew that a ship's captain was only as good as his crew, and a truly gifted commander knew how to invoke loyalty and hard work. "Is that why no one is afraid to ride out a storm at anchorage in a strange harbour?"

Raul laughed. "After what we saw in the Mona Passage, *señora*, we can't fear much! Not this little rain."

Another beat of thunder rumbled overhead, making Bianca jump and Raul laugh even more. "I have been on land too long, I fear."

"It's easy to forget," he said. "I had the fever two years ago, and spent weeks in Havana. The smell of the waves, the wind—it was all new again."

"Yet even if this *was* another fearsome storm, you would have no fear, would you? Because you would follow the captain. You would trust him."

Raul nodded. "Most of us will surely meet our ends at sea, *señora*. We don't have illusions about that. But Captain Grattiano, he would never ask anything of us he would not do himself. He sees that we get our fair share of profits, that we're looked after. It's more than any of us could expect."

"Yet that's not all there is to it, is there?"

"What do you mean, *señora*?"

"I mean…" Bianca lowered her voice to a whisper. "In Santo Domingo, they say the *Calypso* is a magical ship."

Raul peered at her closely. Accusations of "magic" of any kind were dangerous; the Inquisition had ears everywhere, even in the New World. Yet whatever he saw in her eyes seemed to reassure him. He nodded, and said, "Perhaps it is, at that."

"How so?"

"During that storm, when the mainmast crashed down and we were sure death was near," he said quietly, "something happened."

Bianca leaned closer, eager to hear this tale. *She* knew all too well that Balthazar did have a strange magic in him. A spell that lured her irresistibly to his side, despite everything. What was it about him that did that, drawing not only her, but this crew, and all of jaded Venetian society, too?

"The storm in the Mona Passage was a terrible one," Raul said. "The wind howled like a demon, and we could hardly see for the rain, or stand upright the ship was pitching so badly. I thought we could go right over the rail. But the captain, he stayed at the rudder right through, even when it looked like the waves would wash him away. Then…"

"Then what?" Bianca whispered, enthralled.

"The captain, he stared up at the top of the mainmast. And we saw lightning. Or what must have been lightning, though it looked like none I ever saw before. It was like a star, come down to earth."

"A star?"

"Aye, dancing up the mast. It was all glowing, blue and silver. It flew from shroud to shroud. That was when the mast fell, and we had to heave it overboard before it could sink us."

"And the star?"

"It just danced away, like it had never been. But I would vow, *señora*, that the captain saw it before it even appeared! He summoned it, and it saved us."

Bianca swallowed hard, her throat suddenly dry. Magic, indeed, though perhaps not what Raul thought. She had heard of such rare occurrences, coronas, and she doubted Balthazar could summon them at will. But she knew that he had the power to make people *believe* he could do such things. Make even her believe it. And that was a strange sorcery indeed.

"Never fear, Raul," she murmured. "I will say nothing of this."

He nodded, and she took the spoon from his hand. "I think we can eat now," she said. "Do you think the captain will come below soon? He will catch the ague in such a rain, even if it is not a fearsome storm."

"Only when he is certain the ship is secure," Raul answered. "But the rest of us will be most grateful for a hot meal."

Bianca laughed, and happily obliged them by spooning out portions of stew and accepting a flagon of wine in return. Despite the swell of the waves, bearing the ship ever up and down, the mood below decks seemed almost merry. Even the steady drip of rain from above, splashing into the food and on top of heads, didn't seem to bother anyone. The pipe music grew faster and higher; some of the men lurched into an awkward gavotte.

Bianca found herself laughing at their leaps and twirls, at the giddy tune that drowned out even the thunder. Mendoza seized her hand, pulling her into the dance.

"Nay, nay!" she protested, shaking her head through her laughter. "I am not a fine dancer."

"And does it look like the rest of us are?" Mendoza said. "Compared with our gallopings, you shall dance like an angel!"

He seized her by the waist, spinning her around and around in an approximation of a stylish *volte*. He did not even drop her as the ship rode the crest of yet another wave, only relinquishing her when she was claimed by another partner.

She forgot the storm, forgot all the uncertain days

ahead as they danced. She spun around and around, thinking of that star that danced over the masts of the *Calypso*. Free and bright, shimmering like a signal fire in the midst of darkest despair.

She had never known a home, not really. Even in her mother's house, she had always sensed Maria's disappointment that her daughter did not share her gifts. That Bianca—brown-haired, prosaic Bianca—had no magic in her. The years of wandering, of hard work and hunger, and then of being married to a man she did not really love, they wore her down. "Home" was not something she could even aspire to, a place of warmth and secure comfort, a place where she truly belonged.

As she clapped her hands and twirled amid the music and the rain, the rough laughter, she forgot all of that. For that moment, in the world Balthazar had created here, she had a place to belong.

The hatch above them suddenly opened in a burst of wind, and Bianca spun around to see Balthazar lowering himself from the deck. His shirt, sodden with rainwater, clung to his shoulders and chest, his tied-back hair dripping. Tiny, crystalline droplets made his brown skin shimmer as if he was painted with silver. Despite whatever dangers he faced alone on deck, he glowed with vibrant, powerful *life*, a force that drew her irresistibly to him.

He grinned as he saw the festival they had created in the cramped, smelly space, the music, dancing, and wine-splashed laughter. He seized Bianca's hand, twirling her close to him.

Her own doublet was quickly soaked, but she did not care. She craved that life of his, that heat, needed to be ever closer.

He held her hand, guiding her in a graceful circle that reminded her of the old Balthazar, the elegant courtier who danced with the most beautiful women at the Carnival masked balls. Who wore the finest silks and jewels carelessly, as if born to them and thus taking all his fine things for granted.

He danced like that man, but he no longer looked like him, in his rough, sea-soaked garb, his beautiful face harshened by a growth of beard and the constant tropical sun. He did not laugh like him, either. As far as she knew, the old Balthazar never laughed at all.

Yet this one, the Balthazar that held her by the hand now, did laugh. As he adroitly guided her through half-forgotten steps, spinning her faster and faster, they laughed together. How ridiculous they were, the two of them, dancing a fashionable, courtly *passamiento* as the sea roiled around them! How absurd that they were together at all.

And yet—yet she had never been as happy as she was then. Dancing and laughing in the hold of a creaking, leaking ship in the midst of a rainstorm. Gazing up into the bright green glow of Balthazar's eyes.

She had dreamed of such moments as a girl, of moments when Balthazar would see she was more than a strangely well-read girl he could pass an idle afternoon with. Would see she was a desirable woman, would take her hand and lead her into a glittering ball at one of the palazzos along the Grand Canal. Of course, in those dreams she wore a fine velvet gown and jewels, and miraculously had straight, shining hair and fair skin.

This was the reality now, with all its old anger and resentments, its dangers and uncertainties. Rainwater dripped down on their heads, and a sailor's pipe was their orchestra.

But Bianca laughed, laughed with a burst of sheer joy as he lifted her in the air, spinning her around and around. The clapping men, the angled masts, the piles of sails, grew into a blur, a mere flash of dim colours and echoing sound.

Was this, then, the *real* Balthazar? And was she now her real self? She had been hiding for so long she did not know. Yet for this moment, she was free.

He lowered her slowly to her feet, against the warm strength of his shoulders, his chest, and she clung to him as her boots splashed into the sludgy water covering the planks. Still dizzy from the dance, from that unaccustomed fizz of giddy happiness, she held on to his hands, staring up at him.

Usually his eyes were the mysterious mossy-green colour of an impenetrable forest. Now, they glowed like rare jewels. Like the clear, sparkling light of a Venetian summer.

How very *alive* he was, she thought again. A vital force of nature, drawing everyone close to him, pulled in by a primitive craving for all that heat and light and beauty.

Suddenly, she shivered. Such heat surely burned out, flaring away and leaving the world in darkness once again. It could not last. Balthazar's life-force was as ephemeral as this moment. Gone like the lightning.

Not for the first time, Bianca wished she had her mother's gift for the cards. Could see the future, Balthazar's future, and her own. Yet Maria's gift could not save her. The Grattianos were too unpredictable even for the tarot.

Yet still, Bianca had some dark feeling of foreboding as she stood there in that dark hold, her hands in his. Something was coming, something to shatter the bright veil they drew around themselves now.

She shivered again, and Balthazar frowned. "You're cold," he said.

"Nay, I just…"

"Of course you are, standing around in this damp hole." He took her arm, drawing her back to her spot next to the now-empty stew pot. Bianca went with him, unprotesting, as he found a fairly dry blanket and draped it over her shoulders. He held her hands between his, rubbing them until she felt some warmth creeping back into her numb fingertips.

That flash of foreboding presentiment was gone, swiftly as it came, and she just felt tired and drained. She longed to curl up against Balthazar and go to sleep, sleep for hours and days until she felt warm and safe again.

"You must be colder than me," she said, trying to shrug off the blanket and give it to him instead. "You were out on deck."

"I am accustomed to it now," he answered. He tucked the woollen folds more firmly around her. He smoothed her damp curls back from her face, tracing the line of her cheekbone, her nose and brow, lightly with his fingertips. His touch was callused, but gentle, careful as he caressed each freckle over her nose one by one. "I'm a hardened old sea dog now, you know. Who would have thought it, back in Venice?"

Bianca stared up at him, mesmerised by his touch. "I would."

One brow arched in question. His hands alighted on her shoulders, but he did not move away. Even through the blanket, the wool and linen of their clothes, she could feel his heat.

"Did you, Bianca?" he asked. "Or did you just think me the spoiled, indolent son of Ermano Grattiano, good for nothing but running his father's errands and spending his coin?"

"Perhaps I thought that once," she said. "But that was before I ever talked to you, before you shared your books with me. I knew then that you would do more. That you *were* more."

"Some would say there could be no 'more' than to be wealthy and aristocratic in Venice."

"We are not those 'some', are we?"

Balthazar laughed. "Obviously not. For here we are, as far from Venice as can be."

"Do you regret it? Do you miss your life there? The grand palazzo, the fine clothes and banquets?"

"Never. In Venice, I was nothing. Nothing but my name."

"And here?"

He gave her a crooked smile, letting her go to lean back on a coil of rope. "Here, I am still nothing. No human can triumph over the sea, not really. At least it is 'nothing' on my own terms."

His own terms earned him a place of near-legend in a harsh and ruthless land, Bianca could see that. Sailors on other vessels feared him; his own men respected him, would follow him anywhere. She understood that burning desire to be free, to make one's own destiny. To go in the direction the wind filled the sails.

But how long could that last, for any of them? And what place did *she* have here, if any at all?

Before she could say anything, the *Calypso*, relatively calm for the last several minutes, gave a sudden lurch. She grabbed the empty, lidded pot before it could topple over, and the laughter and music around her faded away. The ship tilted again, her timbers creaking, and new water poured through the gaps in a steady stream.

The storm had gathered fresh strength.

"Stay here," Balthazar told her. He headed towards

the hatch, pulling himself up and through, disappearing back into the darkness and rain. Several of the men followed him, and those who were left gathered around Bianca's corner.

She drew her knees up to her chest, wrapping her arms tightly around her legs as she listened to the drumbeat of rain quicken over her head. She could surely be of some help on deck, but she knew not to argue with captain's orders.

Instead, she sat there, closing her eyes tightly as she pictured Balthazar in the midst of the storm, lightning's glow reflected in his eyes, his hair streaming like a banner behind him as he scrambled up the rigging. Impervious even to the wind and rain, clinging to the ropes as his ship pitched beneath him and the ocean swirled in black depths.

Was this, then, that flash of presentiment she had of danger? Would that waiting sea reach out and drown him at last?

She hugged her knees closer, thinking of him, picturing him striding the slippery decks. Nay, she felt no immediate doom there. Yet that dark feeling had been so brief, so quickly closed off. A flicker of magic as ephemeral as that lightning.

If he toppled into the waves now, never to be seen again, what would she do? How would she feel? Bianca hardly knew. Life had suddenly become just one moment, one second, after another.

"Never fear, *señora*," one of the ship's boys said reassuringly. Bianca opened her eyes, and he smiled up at her. "The captain will see this through. He always does. Ever since my parents sent me here to learn to sail, I have never been afraid."

She smiled at him in return, and saw that he was a handsome child of about eight or nine, with dark curls and clear blue eyes that reflected none of the fear held by most boys of the sea. Ship's boys did the hardest, dirtiest tasks, and were usually severely punished when they failed. Not this child, obviously.

Bianca remembered the sketch of the woman and the two little boys.

"I know I need have no fear on such a fine ship," she said. "Perhaps we should sing? That would help pass the time."

"Do you know any Spanish songs?"

"What sort of Spanish songs? Ones about love? I know one about a dark-eyed contessa and an Andalusian garden in the moonlight, where she cries for her lost love…"

"Nay!" the boy cried. "Not love. Ones about sea battles."

Bianca laughed. "Very well. I may know one or two like that."

Chapter Seventeen

"Bianca. Bianca, wake up."

Bianca suddenly shot up out of sleep, gasping as she opened her eyes. For an instant, she had no idea where she was. She was still caught in restless dreams. Then she blinked her gritty eyes, glancing around to find herself perched atop a pile of sails. She was covered by half her blanket, the other half tucked around the sleeping boy. He muttered and rolled over without waking, obviously more accustomed to sleeping below decks than she was.

Balthazar stood beside her, gently shaking her shoulder. He gave her a little smile, and she realised that the ship was still. No wind groaned overhead.

And her mouth was dry from the wine and the singing. She had known more songs about the sea than she realised.

"What time is it?" she muttered. "Has the rain ceased?"

"The night is more than half gone," he said. "And it still rains, but the worst of the storm has passed."

"They did say you would see us through it."

"What choice do I have, with such cargo aboard?"

He lifted her from her rough bed, carrying her over to the open hatch. She caught at its edges, pulling herself out as he boosted her up. As soon as she was on the deck, he leaped up behind her.

The rain did still fall, but lightly, a soft, warm shower. There was no heated lightning, no howling wind rushing past the masts. The makeshift mainmast still held.

Balthazar took her hand, leading her to their cabin. One lamp was lit on the table there, proclaiming their safety with its amber glow, casting light over the clutter of papers and books, the blankets folded back on the berth.

Bianca turned to him, studying his face in the half-shadow. He seemed drawn with exhaustion after the long night, his features pale and sharply etched, lines deepened beside his eyes and mouth. He had hastily tied back his wet, tangled hair, and his clothes were soaked through.

Without a word, she reached out and unlaced his shirt, drawing it up and over his head. Then she gently pushed him back into the chair, kneeling at his feet. He went willingly enough, but he watched her cautiously with narrowed eyes.

Bianca just pulled off his boots, encrusted with

water and salt, and tossed them aside. She unfastened his hose, peeling the sodden fabric down his muscled thighs and calves, until he sat before her naked.

She traced the tense, corded muscles of his legs with her fingertips, rubbing at the knots of tension, warming his cold skin under her touch. Slowly, slowly, he relaxed as she caressed him, her lips following her hands along his inner thighs, the flat plane of his hip.

She found an old scar over his ribs, tracing it with the tip of her tongue. He tasted of salt, of rainwater and ale, and that spiciness that was only him. She knew his taste so well now, the lines of his body. She knew just where to kiss, to touch, to make him gasp. She knew how they fit together, how desperately ecstatic his body inside hers made her feel. If only she could know his mind, his soul, too.

As she rose up between his legs, she saw that new knife scar on his shoulder. And she remembered watching him fall to the floor of her tavern, his blood spreading around him. How close she came to losing him before she could even find him again. Before she could find the answers she so desperately craved.

At least, she *had* wanted answers. Revenge. Now she craved something else entirely, craved the hot forgetfulness of sex after the storm.

Craved Balthazar, and the way he made her feel.

He gave a deep groan and caught her by the shoulders, pulling her on to his lap. His lips met hers in a frantic kiss, and she tasted there a need that echoed her own. A need to forget—or mayhap to remember. A need to be together.

His tongue touched hers, and she tasted again the sea, the salt and the bittersweet rain, the dangers of his life. She held on to him as her world tilted and swayed, worse than any ship in a storm. Turning everything upside-down, unrecognisable. Through a red, hot haze of desire, she felt him remove her doublet and hose, her boots and stockings, never breaking their frantic kiss, their connection. That humid blur of breath and lips and quick sighs.

She straddled his lap, wearing only her loose shirt. As she leaned into him, clinging to his shoulders, she felt the friction of the damp cloth against her erect, aching nipples, the press of his smooth, muscled chest on her breasts. Her legs were spread wide over his thighs, and she was open and vulnerable to him as she never had been before.

They were close, so very close—but not close enough. She longed to melt into him, to be a part of him so completely they could never be separated. To feel his breath and heartbeat become hers.

His lips slid away from hers, and her incoherent protest turned to a sharp cry as he took her nipple into his mouth. The moist heat through the fabric was intense, and she moaned as his teeth grazed the too-sensitive flesh. She drove her fingers into his hair, pulling him closer, closer.

"Balthazar!" she whispered against his temple, pressing frantic kisses to his skin, to the pulse that beat there. "I need, need…"

She couldn't even articulate the *needs* that flowed through her, that made her feel as if she would fly out of her skin. She *did* fly, just a bit, as his thumb slipped inside her, pressing just as that one sensitive spot.

She spread her legs even wider, her head falling back as he guided himself into her, his hips thrusting up until she sheathed him completely. An incoherent cry escaped her lips as she raised herself, slowly, enticingly, and plunged back down. He met her thrust for thrust, as perfectly, instinctively choreographed as if they were in the dance.

He kissed her again, their passionate cries and half-spoken love words blending into one. Finally, finally, she felt her climax building inside her, until it exploded. Silver-white light, like lightning, like that magical corona, shimmered behind her eyes. She heard Balthazar cry out her name, felt the warmth of his own climax deep inside of her. For that instant, he was hers, and she was his.

They were truly as one.

Bianca collapsed against his shoulder, her limbs heavy. She wrapped her legs around his hips, holding on tightly as if she feared to fall. As if she feared tumbling into the unknown abyss of the overwhelming passion and never being found again.

She feared she might weep with the overwhelming

force of it all. She closed her eyes, kissing Balthazar's bare shoulder, the edge of his healing scar.

He stood up, still holding her as she clung to him with her arms and legs. She felt him move to the berth, lowering her on to the mattress. She slid over to its very edge, lying on her side as he lay down beside her. He drew the blankets up around them and pulled her back against him, his arm over her waist.

She arched herself into his body, sensing how they fit together now, every curve and angle aligned as if they had been created to be just so. She twined her legs with his, pressing her hand over his to hold him against her. And, at last, they slept.

Balthazar wound one of Bianca's long curls around his finger, watching how the last of the wavering lamplight turned it golden and shimmering. It clung to his skin like a length of the finest Venetian silk.

Bianca sighed in her sleep, her head turning on his shoulder as she burrowed against him. In slumber, she was vulnerable, open to him, to whatever this strange magic was between them. There was none of the caution she built around her like armour in the daylight.

Not that he could blame her for her caution. He was a Grattiano, and she surely remembered all too well what that name meant in Venice. All his father's misdeeds, and Balthazar's own sins, too. She had not seen all he did in the past few years to erase that name, to make a new meaning for it. A new Balthazar Grattiano, here where the closed-in world of Venice had no importance at all.

He didn't know how to make her see that, didn't even know why it seemed so vital that she somehow understand. Balthazar had never put much importance on the opinions of others. It was a waste of time in the end, and a man had to be true to himself, to his own soul—even if it carried him to the very edge of the world.

Yet he found he did care what Bianca Simonetti thought, felt. When they had danced tonight, when he saw her eyes alight with laughter, he wanted to laugh, too. He felt suddenly light and—yes, happy. For that second, he felt happy just to hold her in his arms, to feel her lithe body against his and be with her.

Once, he could have offered her a marble ballroom, a banquet of strawberries and golden Alsatian wine. Velvet gowns, caps of pearls, emeralds for her throat and wrist. He still could give her that, lay it all out at her feet. Yet he sensed those things would never make her smile, not as a dance to sailor's pipes in a crowded ship's hold could.

And he wanted to see her smile again. Wanted it as he craved the freedom of the wide seas, the open sky.

He kissed her bare shoulder, touching the tip of his tongue to each pale freckle scattered there. She tasted sweet, perfect, of rain and wine. She murmured at his kiss, arching back against him.

Balthazar looped a ribbon of kisses, caresses, like

a string of fine pearls along her spine, easing away the bedclothes until she was bare to him. She did not have the fair, pampered white softness of Venetian ladies. She was slim, sun-brown, with a coiled, lean strength to her long legs, her back and arms. Truly, she was beautiful, the most beautiful woman he had ever seen.

But as his tongue traced the groove of her spine, dipping into the hollow of her back, tasting her, feeling her, he wanted to drape her in jewels and furs. To take away all those long, hard years she refused to speak of. The wandering at sea, the husband, the noisy tavern—he wanted to erase all that in luxury and ease.

Not that Bianca would let him. She would surely just laugh at him if she could read his thoughts! He did not understand himself, as he had spent years fleeing those hollow riches, the greed for them, the emptiness.

And in fleeing, he found this moment. This one perfect moment, naked of all those wealthy trappings. Just himself, Balthazar. It was all he could offer her.

Bianca rolled on to her back, smiling up at him as she wound her arms around his neck. "Is it morning?" she whispered.

"Not yet."

"Then what are we wasting time for?"

Why indeed? Time was the one treasure he *did* long for, and it grew shorter and shorter for them. So, he kissed her, a slow, lazy caress that belied that ever-ticking timepiece. He wanted to memorise everything about her, every taste, every sensation.

She seemed to feel just the same. Her legs wrapped around his waist, drawing him closer into her body. She sighed as his lips found the curve of her throat, the line where her shoulder tensed under his touch, and he nipped at her with his teeth. As she gasped, he soothed the sting with his tongue, tracing along the swell of her breast.

With the flat of his palm, he smoothed a gentle stroke over her ribs, balancing her other breast lightly on his palm. She murmured incoherently, her legs tightening around him as if she grew restless, aching. But he refused to rush, not tonight. Not now.

Her skin was taut, warm and alive under his touch. Her heart beat faster and faster, echoing his own need with a pounding, steady rhythm. A drumbeat of life, primitive and undeniable.

He circled her breast, lightly, closer and closer to her nipple, then sliding down again until she moaned. Finally, he gave her what they both craved, rolling the erect nipple between his fingertips as he took her other breast into his mouth.

"Balthazar," she whispered, his name like a touch, a slow stroke. Her back arched as she pressed herself closer into his kiss. He felt her legs open in invitation, the warm heat of her womanhood, but he forced himself to ease away.

Bianca whimpered as he loosed her legs from his hips, but he kissed her lightly on the lips, quieting her. "Shh," he whispered. "Remember—we have time before morning."

She watched him closely as he slid back down her body, leaving a trail of more kisses along her flat belly, the flare of her hips, the top of her thigh.

She braced herself on her elbows, her breath ragged and unsteady as he licked at her inner thighs, at the sensitive hollow behind her knees. And she fell back entirely on to the tumbled blankets as he reached up to part her damp folds.

"Balthazar!" she gasped at the first feather-light touch of his tongue just *there*. "What are…?"

"Shh," he said again, closing his eyes to savour that essence of her, of everything about her. He tasted her again, and the felt the ripples of her response.

When at last he could not stand any more, couldn't bear the intensity of his need for her, he drove himself inside of her. She braced her heels on the edges of the berth, rising up to meet his kiss. They had already had sex, of course, so many times he knew every inch of her body. Every curve and angle, the way she tasted and moved. Yet somehow, as she held on to him and whispered his name, it felt like a new beginning.

It felt like—like a benediction.

Chapter Eighteen

"Blessed be the light of day, and the Holy Cross we say. Blessed be the light of day, and He who keeps the night away."

Bianca opened her eyes at the song from the deck above, the words that signalled the change of watch. There was no patter of rain on the planks over her head, no boom of thunder. All was well now. But for how long?

Balthazar slept soundly next to her, their limbs entangled amid the blankets. She wrapped her arms tighter around him, remembering the lightning and the pounding rain of the night's storms. The way he had seen the *Calypso* and all aboard her safe, pacing the decks long after everyone else took shelter below. And he had carried the ship safely through a terrible hurricane to Santo Domingo, had he not? He always saw them safe.

She might even be coming to believe the tales of Captain Grattiano's magical abilities to come through any storm. To fly across the ocean as if he had wings.

And he most assuredly had magic in the bedchamber. She trembled as she remembered the touch of his tongue on her most secret spot, the way she grew almost insensible with the pleasure of it. No one had ever done that to her before, no one had...

Had ever made her feel that way at all.

No wonder all the women of Venice had been so very in love with him.

She found, much to her shock, that perhaps she *did* trust Balthazar Grattiano after all. She trusted him with this ship, with all the sea. She trusted him with her life, and with her body. What she still could not trust him with, though, was her heart, that heart she had long ago locked away. The heart she feared was now in grave trouble.

Bianca eased herself up in the berth, very slowly so as not to wake Balthazar. She propped herself on her elbow, gazing down at him. Only a small, pink ray of light shone through the porthole, casting a shadowed glow along the harsh, beautiful angles of his face. That new growth of beard roughened his aristocratic features, and the coarse white sheet twisted around his waist made his skin all the darker in contrast.

Her dashing corsair lover.

She smoothed the damp, tangled strands of dark hair back from his brow, and he muttered in his sleep, a frown etching the fine skin.

How many years had she hated him? Hated the thought of him, all he stood for, the privilege and carelessness that had destroyed her young life. As she had struggled her way across Europe, across the ocean, he and his father had taken on the dimensions of demons in her mind.

Now—well, now she was all confusion. Confronted with Balthazar the man, not the demon of memory. A man who awakened such desperate passions that she didn't even know she possessed. She hardly knew where to turn, what to do.

So, just as in Venice, she had run. Run right into the beautiful demon's own lair, into yet more confusion.

Bianca lay back down, Balthazar beside her, so close she felt his steady breath against her skin. She nearly laughed as she stared up at the rough wooden beams. Surely a "demon," one as selfishly pleasure-loving as she had long imagined the Grattianos to be, would have a more luxurious lair than this one! This small space, damp, smelling of salt and tar, open to the noise of the deck. There should be satin cushions, flower petals, rich draperies—soft-skinned women waiting to serve every whim.

So, perhaps he was not such a selfish demon. Not even the spoiled scion of Venetian privilege now. Nor was he a sorcerer of the sea, even if he did show an unwavering instinct for the vicissitudes of the waves. He was…

She knew not what. But it was something she deeply wanted to know.

She felt the touch of his hand on her hip, and shivered as his fingers slid over her stomach, tracing a light pattern on her skin. He kissed her shoulder, the curve of her neck.

"Good morrow to you, *signorina*," he muttered.

"And a fair one it is," Bianca answered. "Sunshine after the storms."

"Storms never last, even the worst ones."

Not the storms out there, anyway. But the private storms of the heart, they went on and on.

He kissed her lips, a deep kiss that tasted of something new, something she could not fathom. But even as she felt her body warm, her fingers and toes tingle, even as everything went all blurry and hot around her, she knew she had to stop. It was morning now, and they could not linger abed. They could not...

Or then again, she thought as he nibbled at her neck, *maybe we could, just for a while.*

But a bell rang above their heads, and the insistent hum of quarrelling voices tore at her sensual spell. She eased away from him, pressing at his shoulders as he tried to kiss her again.

"Don't you have work to do, captain?" she said.

"Aye, work to do here in this bed," he answered, catching her against him as he pressed more kisses to her closed eyes, her cheeks. "Or did I not work hard enough for you last night, *cara*? If you will allow me, I'm sure you'll be most satisfied with my labours today..."

Bianca laughed helplessly as he bore her back down to the mattress, kissing her again and again. She had never seen Balthazar like this before, so very—light. His eyes glowed a bright green as he laughed, too, holding her close to him. He made her feel lighter in turn, as if she could almost float free of all the worries that held her earthbound for too long.

She pushed him away with her foot, still laughing. "Who will stop this ship from running aground, then, if the captain will not leave his cabin?"

"The captain is bound here by a siren," he said. "Aren't all sailors compelled to obey the siren's song? To follow wherever it leads?"

"Even unto doom?" Bianca said. That glow of his eyes, so closely focused only on her, on what passed between them last night, drew her in. As if *he* was the siren, dashing her on the rocks of her own desire! She nearly gave in, until she heard more shouts from above.

She pressed harder, pushing him away with the ball of her foot, and said, "Alas, this poor excuse for a siren is quite exhausted. You do your *work* all too well, Captain Grattiano."

"Very well," he said, with exaggerated resignation. "We will soon reach Vista Linda anyway, and then my only duty will be to you, fair siren."

His only duty? Was there no duty to a family, then? Bianca opened her mouth to ask, but then fell back in a fit of cowardice. She didn't really want to know the answer, not yet.

The truth would come soon enough.

She sat up at the edge of the berth, wrapping the sheet around her as she watched him dress. He fastened his hose, and opened the trunk to search for a clean shirt. As he turned away, she glimpsed red scratches over his shoulders, the marks of her own fingernails on his bronzed skin. She had a sudden flashing memory of clutching him against her, urging him faster in their coupling.

Her cheeks burned, and she had to resist the urge to dive back under the bedclothes. To hide from what had happened between them. From the intensity of how he made her feel.

But she could not hide, could not move backwards. She could only go forwards, to whatever awaited them once the *Calypso* reached land.

"Tell me about this Vista Linda," she said.

Balthazar pulled the shirt over his head, hiding those telltale marks. "It is a small island," he said. "I bought it from a Spaniard who was going back to Madrid. He had an idea of running herds of cattle there, to supply the larger islands. Sadly, he had not the slightest idea of how to run an estancia, how to ship his cargoes out, and it failed."

"And you did not care to take over the cattle scheme?"

Balthazar laughed as he reached for his boots. "I'm far better at sailing than I would be at raising cattle," he answered. "But the island has a pretty prospect. It's a fair spot to rest, to repair the ship and plan the next voyage."

To lodge his paramours? For all Bianca knew, the island could be overrun with women awaiting his return!

Yet strangely, though she could easily picture the Balthazar Grattiano of Venice with an island seraglio, the vision did not fit the man who stood before her now.

"When will we be there?" she asked.

He shrugged. "Today, I thought, but the storm has us off course." He leaned over her, kissing her lips in a sweet, lingering caress. "I will get you there safely, never fear."

Bianca curled her fingers into the soft fabric of his shirt. "I know you will," she whispered. She just wished she knew what would happen once they were there.

He seemed to sense her doubts, and studied her face carefully as if he sought his own answers there. She had none to give him, or herself.

He kissed her again, quickly, and turned away to grab his leather jerkin from the chair. "Come on deck when you're ready," he said. "It grows warm in here."

Bianca leaned back on the berth, teasingly stretching her bare leg. "I thought women were a curse aboard ship. Will I not distract them if I show my face again?"

"You will certainly distract *me*," he growled, his green gaze tracing the length of her naked skin. "But I think the men are all half in love with you after last night. They won't do their work until they see you again, and then they will work twice as hard to impress you."

"Then I will certainly oblige." She waved her foot at him. For an instant, his eyes narrowed and she thought he would carry her back down to the tangled blankets. But he spun around and hurried out the door, slamming it behind him.

Bianca collapsed on to the pillows, feeling the strangest urge to laugh aloud. She tugged the edge of the sheet up over her ridiculous smile, as if there was anyone to see, to wonder at her sudden, uncharacteristic giddiness.

There was assuredly no reason to feel *giddy* at all. She was leagues away from anything she knew, caught in the middle of the ocean with a man whose sensual web tightened ever more around her. She did not really know Balthazar any better than she had so long ago in Venice, though her body so craved his. Needed his, in a way she had never known.

She slowly lowered the sheet, and her gaze met the painted eyes of Signora Grattiano. A ray of morning light fell over her pale visage, her fine brocades and furs, her disapproving frown.

Nay, the lady surely did not frown, merely gazed out at the world with the same patrician resignation as always. Yet it seemed to Bianca she scowled. In the Grattianos' world, a woman like Bianca Simonetti would never be here in Balthazar's life. Oh, she would be good enough for a quick tumble, but not to be a mistress. And never to marry.

Here, though…

Here, she had no idea what her "position" was, or what she wanted it to be. They were all different people here, and bound by none of the old strictures.

Bianca resolutely turned away from Signora Grattiano, sliding off the berth to search for her clothes. Her shirt was stiff with dried saltwater, so she opened Balthazar's trunk to borrow a clean one. She had one of her own, of course, but it seemed a fine excuse to wear his clothes. Be surrounded by the scent of him, just for a bit longer.

As she raised the lid, she glimpsed his bow, carefully slotted along the side of the trunk and cushioned with folded garments. The sunlight played on the polished wood, the inlay of diamond and rose patterns. It was beautiful.

And so deadly. Even unstrung, its arrows tucked away, it fairly vibrated with deceptive menace. Was this, then, the weapon that killed Ermano Grattiano? What terrible thing had led Balthazar, after all those youthful years under his father's evil influence, to kill him?

Was that even what had really happened at all?

The sight of that smooth wood, all graceful lines and curves, only reminded her again how very little she knew.

Did she dare to discover more?

Bianca swiftly extracted a clean shirt, shutting the lid over that bow. If she could only lock away all the past so handily!

She pulled on the soft linen fabric, letting it settle around her nakedness. The sleeves and hem swallowed her, enveloping her in that clean, citrus-saltwater smell of Balthazar's skin. For a moment, she gathered the shirt close, shutting her eyes to inhale deeply, to let all her senses be surrounded only by him.

"What a great fool you are, Bianca Simonetti," she muttered, folding back the sleeves. She put on her hose and doublet, and shoved her feet into her damp boots. She hastily tied her tangled curls up in a scarf, not even glancing in the looking glass. She needed fresh air and work, distraction, before she became as wild-eyed and desperate as all those ladies in Venice.

Bianca hurried out of the cabin, shielding her eyes against the glare of the sun to take in the scene on deck. It was almost as if the storm had never happened at all. The sheltered cove was far behind them, and they were surrounded by the vast blue-green of the sea, the arcing, pale sky overhead. Wind filled the sails, the canvas billowing as they were borne ever further.

Balthazar was high up in the rigging. For a moment, her breath caught at how very far the fall would be should he lose his balance, a long tumble to the waiting water below. But his now-bare feet were nimble and sure as he climbed ever higher, laughing with the sheer exhilaration of freedom, of being one with that sky and the wind.

Had she ever really thought he belonged in those palatial confines of gilt-edged Venice? For she saw now he could belong nowhere but here.

And where did *she* belong? She had no idea. Her tavern was behind her; even if she returned to it one day it would not be the same. Perhaps she had never really planned to go back there at all.

Bianca suddenly noticed that she was standing all agape in the middle of deck, in the way of swabbing and mending. She turned away from Balthazar, from the distant, enticing sound of his laughter, and found a quiet corner where she could sit atop a pile of coiled rope and stare out towards the empty horizon.

Soon enough, something would fill that sky, that space. What would it be? One thing she had learned in her travels, in her wandering life, was that nothing in this land was predictable—and she was never truly prepared for what came her way.

For now, she was adrift on this ship, out of all time. With Balthazar.

She leaned back on her elbows and closed her eyes, inhaling the warm, salty breeze. It was enough. It had to be enough.

At least until fate moved the figures of the dance once again.

Chapter Nineteen

"Land!" The cry came down the next day from the crow's nest, floating like wildfire from man to man along the deck.

Bianca glanced up from the sail she was mending, so caught up in the task, in her own thoughts, that it took her a moment to process the word. *Land.*

She scrambled to her feet, hurrying to join the men gathered at the rail. It was indeed land, or could be. Without a spyglass, it seemed the merest dark ripple in the distance, a break in the endless expanse of sea and sky. Was this, then, their destination? Or merely another port to drift past?

"Is it Vista Linda?" she asked Luis, who stood beside her. "Already? I thought the storm took us off course."

"It could be, Señora Montero," he answered. "We're surely too far north for Puerto Rico."

"The captain works wonders, *señora*!" the ship's boy said excitedly. "Didn't I tell you?"

"You certainly did," Bianca said, remembering the tale of the dancing corona. But could he make a ship fly?

She stood there against the rail as the crew burst into activity behind her, the excited bustle of a ship within sight of home. Bianca knew better than to get in the way. She stood still, watching as the indistinct shore grew closer and closer.

It came into focus, a long sweep of pale golden sand, as the waters shifted into a clear blue-green. At last a joyous cry went up, and the anchors splashed down into the waves.

Bianca found she still could not yet move. She watched, feeling oddly removed from the scene as the ship's boat was lowered to take the first group to shore. This journey was ending. The men were finding their home, a respite from the hard life of the sea.

What would *she* find? She sensed a new voyage just beginning, a new world she could not even fathom.

"Bianca!" she heard Balthazar call. She glanced over her shoulder to find him hurrying along the deck towards her. He had donned a black leather coat, and carried a knapsack slung over his shoulder.

He smiled at her, yet his gaze scanned her face as if puzzled by what he found there. She feared she had no reassurances to offer, not to him or herself. She could only keep moving forwards.

"Come ashore with me?" he said, holding out his hand to her.

Bianca took it, smiling back at him as his fingers closed over hers. "Of course. I'm vastly tired of the smell of your ship, captain."

Balthazar laughed, and caught her around the waist to lower her over the rail to the waiting rope ladder. Her booted feet quickly found the swaying rungs, and she climbed down until Mendoza could help her into the boat. Once it was loaded, they turned towards shore, and whatever waited for her there. She watched the beach approach inexorably, Balthazar and his men pulling on the oars to the tune of a sea chanty.

They were still many yards away when Balthazar leaped out, foaming salt spray casting a splashing mist around his boots. Before Bianca could think what he was about, he reached back and lifted her in his arms again, high above the churning waves.

"Balthazar!" she cried, looping her arms about his neck as she felt the warm water against her skin. "What are you doing? Can you not wait for the boat to reach shore?"

"There is no time for that," he answered. "Can't you feel it?"

"Feel what? That you have gone mad?"

He laughed, swinging her even higher. "The sweet smell of land, *cara*!"

Bianca had to laugh, too; the rough, deep rumble of his laughter moved into her, through her, until it became a part of her own self. She wanted nothing more than to hear him laugh again, to see the flash of that beguiling dimple in his cheek. It was all too rare, like black pearls from the sea. Even in Venice he had been ever solemn, ever watchful. But for the last few days, as the *Calypso* wended its way on its journey, she sensed a new light in him. A gleam in his eyes, a readiness to smile and even laugh.

Was it this place? Did it hold some true magic?

Still clinging to his neck to keep from falling into the surf, Bianca turned her head to examine the shore. It was beautiful indeed, a stretch of pale gold sand sweeping up to a line of palm trees, thick and glossy green. But it was not very different from other places she had seen, other lush and wild islands that seemed to beckon a person closer even as they kept their impenetrable mystery. There were no humans in sight, no living beings at all. Just the wind that stirred among the trees, the crash of the waves against land.

But she could sense something, something ineffable and indescribable in those shimmering sands. In the new spirit she sensed within Balthazar.

Truly, for all the intimacy of their bodies, she knew him not at all. When she thought she had taken his measure at last, he changed on her. He turned, and a new facet presented itself, like a fine emerald.

He emerged from the foam of the waves as they climbed on to that shore. Still cradled in his arms, Bianca tilted back her head to feel the sun's heated caress on her skin. She *did* sense the sweet smell of land, of hot sand and salt wind, of the faint, clean sweetness of flowers and coconuts. Her body vibrated with the sudden, shocking stillness, the lack of the constant roll and creak of a ship.

She opened her eyes to find Balthazar's steady gaze on her. He no longer laughed; a small frown creased his brow, and his eyes were opaque to her now. Yet she sensed he, too, felt that sudden shift between them.

"It is beautiful," she whispered.

"That is why it's called Vista Linda," he said, lowering her slowly to her feet. He held on to her as her boots sank into the damp, soft sand, as she swayed and found her land legs. Even as she steadied herself, he held on to her hand, on to that fragile shimmering connection.

"This is your home, then?" she said. Home—where he stashed that dark-haired lady and her two little sons? Was she soon to encounter them, to face them in all their warm, vital, undeniable reality? What, then, would become of her?

"As much a 'home' as I have," he answered. "It is a refuge of sorts."

Before she could ask him what he sought refuge from, the other men came ashore behind them, running the boat on to the sand. Their shouts and loud, exuberant laughter tore the solitary moment Bianca shared with Balthazar, reminded her there *was* a world outside the golden spell he cast. Outside soft sands and hot sun.

He smiled at her, though his eyes were still unreadable behind their bright sea-glass green. "Come," he said, tightening his clasp on her hand.

Bianca followed him as he led her up the gentle slope of the beach, on to a narrow pathway that led between the swaying palm trees. As they walked along, a curtain of silence seemed to close behind them, blocking out the sunlit shore. It was shady and cool here, with blue-winged butterflies glowing in the underbrush and birds chattering overhead. The smell of tropical flowers, of green, damp, growing things, intensified.

Their boots made almost no sound on the twisting path. Bianca still followed him, despite her trepidation at what lay ahead. Of what awaited her in this enchanted spot.

At last, the thick line of trees broke, and she found they stood on the steep slope of a hill. At its crest was a house, gleaming pure white.

It was not a large dwelling, but long and low with a flat roof and thick stone walls against the island heat. Shutters were fastened over the windows. It seemed silent, deserted, just waiting for a human touch to awaken it to life again.

"Come," Balthazar said, leading her along a new path, this one wider and neatly cleared. As they wound their way closer to the house, she noticed there were smaller dwellings dotted along the terraced hillside, little gardens and pigpens stretching behind each one. They also seemed quiet, yet Bianca thought she heard soft giggles, saw flutterings of cloth behind those doorways.

It was like a tiny piece of Europe set down in a jungle, small and perfect. And so quiet. Her worries of suddenly encountering Balthazar's children faded, but her stomach still felt tight, for she noticed he kept his free hand on the hilt of his dagger.

They reached the stone house, and she saw that the door was thick, bound with stout hinges. Balthazar studied its walls and shuttered windows carefully, his hand tight on hers.

It made her tense, every muscle taut as she listened carefully. All she could hear was the ever-present rush of the wind, the faint gurgle of a far-off stream. She could sense nothing else, no presence but the two of them. Those giggles were surely a dream.

Balthazar gave her a small, tight smile as he released the door latch. "Vista Linda is small and insignificant, not on any charts or maps," he said. "But we have not been here in months and…"

And still Diego Escobar could find it? Or one of those many other enemies a man like Balthazar surely possessed? Bianca shivered, suddenly grateful for that silence, that perfect stillness of this wondrous place.

He ushered her through the door, into his house. Inside, it was still not large—two rooms at the front, a long kitchen at the back, and a loft overhead, reached by a narrow flight of steps.

Yet it had an elegant sturdiness about it, an airy

openness from its whitewashed walls and stone floor, its high ceilings. Its very plainness left room to breathe.

As Bianca gazed around her, she could not help but remember Casa Grattiano. Its cold, cold marble and shining gilt, its satin draperies and wide halls, the suffocating weight of splendour.

There had been days in her life, many of them, when, cold and hungry, she envied that remembered luxury. Yet now, as she saw this house, she knew the palazzo for what it must have been for Balthazar—a prison.

She moved slowly through the silent rooms, a fine layer of sand grinding under her boots as she peeked beneath canvas covers at simple stools and tables, two x-backed chairs. They were sturdy, carved of lustrous tropical woods. There was nothing garish, nothing extraneous.

All was dim and dusty now, but she could see how it would be. How very, very different from his home in Venice it all was.

Bianca unlatched the shutters over one of the windows, throwing them open to let in air and light. Then she turned to see Balthazar still standing in the doorway, his arms crossed over his chest as he watched her coolly.

"I know what this place needs," she said.

"Oh, yes? And what is that?" he answered. "More furniture? Tapestries? Gold plate?"

Bianca laughed. "Nay. It needs a party."

Chapter Twenty

Balthazar strode along the beach, examining the *Calypso* from every angle. Everything had been removed from her decks and cabins before the ship was run ashore, and heaved over with the help of blocks and tackle made fast to the masts. The men were busy scraping and burning off the encrusted seaweed and barnacles. Later they would caulk and replace the rotten planks, applying the pungent mixture of tallow, oil and brimstone. Once she was clean, they could make proper repairs to the mainmast, and the *Calypso* would be her swift, sleek self again.

Just in time to make a run back across the ocean, to European shores before the stormy season. They had been too long in the waters of the New World; Balthazar had business to see to in the Old.

Yet now that he was here, he found himself most reluctant to leave. For the first time in—well, the first time *ever*, he did not feel that relentless desire to push ever forwards. To seek ever new horizons, to never, ever rest.

He noticed things now, like the sparkle of the sun on the sand, the sweet scent of coconuts in the air. The music of strange, bright birds from the cover of the trees.

For the last few days, with Bianca by his side, watching him with her dark eyes, gifting him with her rare smiles, he could somehow slow his restless thoughts to notice all those things. He felt like dancing, even like laughing.

Aye, laughing! All the blasted time. When had that happened before? When had he ever had anything to laugh about?

He could see, just faintly glimpsed behind those solemn brown eyes, that Bianca felt the same. Felt that slow, lazy enchantment weave around them, slowly erasing the ever-present view of the painful past. For just those flashing moments, he forgot who he was, what he had done, forgot who *she* was. He felt only the sensual lure of this place, remembered only that they were a man and a woman. Balthazar and Bianca.

She wanted that spell, too, he could see that. Wanted to laugh and forget, as much as he did. Yet she could not quite let herself. Could not quite let herself be completely free, to share that last small corner of her soul with him.

And that made him hold back, as well. He had hurt so very many people in his life. Would he hurt her, too?

Hurt the one person he found he wanted to keep safe above all others. The one woman he wanted to understand, yet could not read at all.

"Maledetto!" he cursed, kicking at the sand. Women were always a mystery, and Bianca Simonetti the worst of all.

He dragged his loose linen shirt over his head and reached for one of the scraping tools, attacking the encrusted seaweed as if it was his own doubts. His own anger, so thickly grown over his heart it was a part of him now. He worked until his shoulders and back muscles burned, until sweat beaded on his brow. The island sun, a hot white-yellow, crawled overhead, and still he laboured on.

This he understood. This he could master. His ship, this harsh, beautiful land—they were his to command in all things.

Bianca was his to command in nothing. Her body responded when he touched it, but her mind always seemed apart. That would soon change, though. He would make her show him her past, show him why she was here. Why she, out of all the women he had ever known, haunted him.

She was in his territory now. And he would have his answers.

Bianca opened the last of the shutters, leaning out of the window to examine Vista Linda in the late morning light. It seemed more beautiful every time she looked at it, at the expanse of emerald-green and shimmering blue, the tiny clouds like perfect pearls atop a jewel case. It was a shining, quiet haven, where the whole world felt far away.

It could almost be its own world entirely, she thought as she leaned her elbows on the sill. A place where treasure-hungry kingdoms, where grimy, striving human misery, no longer existed. She barely seemed to remember the bustling noise of Santo Domingo, the tavern and her hard work there. And Venice—it was a distant vision indeed, a nightmare that left the merest wisp of dark impression under the sweet light of *now*.

She knew she would have to face it all again one day, when she left this place. But she could not seem to care, not yet. All her anger and hatred, the harshness of life, it burned away, and she just felt lazy and free. Like the flock of bright birds that suddenly took wing from the trees and soared over the roof.

Bianca stretched her arms over her head and went up on tiptoe, savouring that unaccustomed lightness, the soft breeze that floated all around her. She wore no stays or stockings, only her chemise that lay loose against her body. She had tied back her curls with one of Balthazar's head scarves and let it flow down her back.

She twirled around on her toes, once, twice, until she fell dizzily into one of the chairs. Last night, she and Balthazar had uncovered the furniture and made up the large bed in the loft before they had dined on fruit and wine and made love on the crisp, clean sheets. But the house still had that dusty, unused air. That sense of needing to be filled with life again.

Bianca reached for the remains of their supper, munching on a slice of mango as she contemplated the space. Their trunks were stacked on the sand-gritty floor, and the portrait of Balthazar's mother leaned against the empty wall. Balthazar's precious charts were rolled and piled on the table.

Well, if there was one thing she was good at, it was making a cosy space out of anything. She had moved from place to place for years, and it always seemed to fall to the woman to make a room comfortable. Surely she could do that here.

And work would keep her from contemplating too closely exactly *why* she wanted to make things comfortable for Balthazar, in a place that was not her own home.

She found a broom in the corner, and started by sweeping the sand from the stone floor. As she cleared out the grit, she saw that those floors were a lovely coral colour, warm and mellow against the white walls, the simple dark furniture.

She thought again of Balthazar's home in Venice with its vast, rich splendours. This house was so much finer.

Maybe she saw now why Balthazar preferred it so. Why this was his place, this house, this island. She, too, felt its allure. Much like the man himself, she was swiftly finding it quite irresistible.

As she swept the last of the dirt and insects out the

doorway, she heard the strains of a song floating up the hill from the beach where the men were careening the *Calypso*. *"Que hondo! Que hondo! Que hondo es el mar!"* they sang, a song she knew well from her days living aboard ships with Juan Montero.

She smiled, swaying along to the tune. Soon, she found that she was indeed island-mad, singing, dancing with the old broom as her partner. As she danced around the newly swept room, she thought of Balthazar, of how elegantly he had twirled her about the cramped hold. How he had lifted her over the piles of rope as if they performed a stylish volte at the Doge's Palace.

She closed her eyes, imagining herself clad in a velvet gown, her hair piled high with jewelled combs as she danced with Balthazar under the light of a thousand fine wax candles. Under all that marble luxury, watched by envious stares...

When she had been a girl that was everything she had dreamed of. Now what did she want? Revenge? Answers? To possess Balthazar's beautiful body again and again?

She did not even know. But fine gowns and jewels in a palace, that was not it.

She whirled to a halt, breathless and giddy. The exuberant music in her head skidded to a discordant close, and all she could hear were footsteps on the path outside. She turned as Balthazar came to a stop in the doorway, watching her.

He was outlined by the sun, its light gilding his skin and hair to pure gold. He held his shirt in his hand, and his bare chest gleamed with sweat, with tiny flecks of dried seaweed from his careening. His hair was bound back, revealing the sharp, aristocratic angles of his face.

He gave her a crooked little half-smile. "I didn't realise that when you said the house needed a party," he said, "you meant to start today."

Bianca laughed breathlessly, turning away from the powerful distraction of his muscular beauty to lean the broom against the wall. Her lungs felt tight in her chest, her head all blurry and confused. Not an unusual state when Balthazar was near, but here on Vista Linda that heady desire seemed even greater, more undeniable.

"Sweeping floors is not really my idea of a merry time," she said. She faced him again, suddenly wishing she wore more than her old chemise, her dusty bare feet. "But the floor looks better, I think."

"It looks splendid," Balthazar said. He crossed the room in a few long strides, an intent look on his face that she could not escape from even if she wanted to. She could not even look away. He wrapped his arms around her waist, drawing her close to him until she was surrounded by all of his sun-heat, his scent of salt seawater, sweat, sand.

"But you are not meant to be the maidservant here, Bianca," he muttered, kissing her temple, the tip of her cheekbone. His lips gently touched her eyelids, until she closed them with a sigh.

"What *am* I meant to be here?" she whispered, tracing the corded muscles of his back with her fingertips. The damp, warm slickness of his skin.

"Whatever you want," he said. His lips found hers. They knew each other now, the taste and feel of each other, how they fit together, how they moved. She knew his kiss, his touch, yet every time she felt that lightning-quick thrill, that heat and sizzle, it burned her with every caress.

It was intoxicating, almost frightening in its intensity, in the way it overcame her, made her forget all else. He said she could be whatever she wanted—and she wanted to be his lover.

After that...

She felt him ease her back against the wall, their kiss unbroken. Bracing herself to the smooth surface, she wrapped her legs around his hips, drawing him tight into the curve of her body. She felt the iron weight of his erection through his hose, pressed into her womanhood. Their kiss deepened, the whole world turning dark and blurry at the edges, narrowing just to Balthazar's touch on her body.

His mouth left hers, trailing a damp, hot path along her arched neck. He pulled down her loose chemise, baring her shoulders and breasts to his tongue and teeth.

"What *do* you want, Bianca?" he whispered roughly against her nipple.

"This," she gasped. "You."

"Is it really me you want? Or just this." He drew that aching, swollen nipple deep into his mouth.

"I—hmmm." She could hardly remember any words at all when he did such things. She wanted him, of course she did! How could he doubt that after all they had done?

Or did he mean…? Nay, it could not be.

Her nipple slid wetly from his mouth as he drew away, leaving her suddenly cold. Cold, and even more confused than before. He eased his body back from hers, until she stood on her own shaking legs against the wall. She caught only a glimpse of Balthazar's hard face, his forest-green eyes, as he turned from her.

She pulled the folds of her chemise back over her naked shoulders, tying the drawstring tight. Sex between them was easy, right in some mysterious way. Yet now it suddenly felt as if something else came between them. Something new, and complicated.

Yet how could her feelings for Balthazar possibly be any more "complicated" than they already were?

He handed her her boots, which she had set outside the door to dry in the sun. Not speaking, he crouched down beside her, reaching for her foot.

Bemused, Bianca watched as he dusted off her toes with his discarded shirt and slid on first one boot, then the other. He stood, and took her hand in his.

"Come with me," he said.

"Where are we going?"

Balthazar laughed wryly, drawing her towards the

open door, the light of the day. "Bianca, *cara*, for once do not argue with me. Just come."

They walked down the path, past the neglected vegetable gardens, a pack of wild pigs now confined behind a rough fence. Past the other houses, where three giggling native women clad in European gowns shyly watched them go by. Bianca waved at them, and they giggled even more.

Once she and Balthazar reached the base of the hill, he drew her off the narrow path into the trees. It was cooler there, with the brilliant light diffused through the thick leaves. The only sound was the hum of insects, the soft sound of their footsteps.

The pounding of Bianca's heart in her ears.

She thought of his words as she followed him, holding tightly to his hand. Did she want *him*? Did she even know him at all? He had been so many things to her over all these years, a distant, glittering figure of worship. A friend, who had given her a precious, fleeting glimpse beneath the jewelled carapace before they had been so horribly parted. An object of hatred, of all her bitterness. A hardened ship's captain. A skilled lover.

A mystery.

He was surely all those things to her. She was not sure she "wanted" all of that. Yet she much feared she was coming to need it, as she needed water and air.

"Close your eyes," he said.

"What?" she said, startled by the sound of his deep, rough-edged voice in the stillness.

"Close your eyes," he said, glancing back over his shoulder. "Do you trust me?"

Bianca swallowed hard. *Trust* was never an easy matter for her, especially now when she could not even trust herself. "Trust you to do what, Balthazar? To not toss me into a smoking volcano if I close my eyes?"

The very corner of his lips quirked, yet he did not quite smile. "I don't believe there are any volcanoes on Vista Linda."

"Hardly a reassuring answer," she muttered. But she did close her eyes. The dappled sun traced patterns of red and blue on her eyelids, as she felt his hand tighten on hers. He led her forwards, guiding her steps on the uneven pathway.

In the darkness, her other senses were heightened. She felt the gentle caress of the wind on her face, smelled the sweet, fertile green of the trees and flowers. Heard the birds, the hiss of insects—and something else. A faint rustle that grew louder as they walked on. It sounded like the crisp swish of expensive satin. Then she realised what it was. The crash and tumble of running water.

"Open your eyes now," Balthazar said.

And Bianca opened her eyes to a wondrous sight.

They had emerged from the trees into a large clearing, to the edge of a sparkling silvery-blue pool. The swirling waters were fed by the arc of a waterfall pouring over jagged rocks.

"Oh," she breathed. "How beautiful. Is it real?"

He smiled at her, a *real* smile this time. One she saw so rarely. Surely his smile was as beautiful as this place, and it made her throat tighten as if she would cry.

"You have accused me of being a sorcerer before, I think," he said. "But I have no skills to conjure up such a sight."

"It is wondrous indeed."

Balthazar dropped her hand and bent down to pull off his boots. "And it's warm. Come and see."

"You mean, swim in it?"

Obviously that was what he meant, as he divested himself of his hose. As Bianca watched, he dived gracefully into the water, cutting cleanly through the still surface.

He shot back up, slicking his wet hair from his face. "Do you not swim?" he asked.

"I do, a bit," she said. Juan, unlike so many superstitious sailors, had been a swimmer, and made sure she had learned. It had been a long time since she had tried it, though.

"Then come," he said, holding out his hand. He beckoned to her temptingly, the water glimmering like crystal droplets on his naked skin. "I won't let you drown, Bianca *cara*. I promise."

Bianca drew in a deep breath, and laughed. He was an alluring devil, and she could never resist him. She pulled off her chemise and her boots, and dived in after him.

Chapter Twenty-One

As Bianca sank down and down, the warm water closed over her head, surrounding her in silence and that perfect, endless blue. The light above took on a diffuse glow, and the sandy floor was just below her floating-free body.

She thought of an image she had seen once on her mother's tarot cards, a sea goddess clad all in mottled green silk, her long red hair floating around her. As a child Bianca had loved that card, loved to think that such impossible beauty, such serene otherworldliness, existed. Surely such a creature could dwell here, in this watery, solitary paradise.

Her lungs started to ache, and she swam to the surface, breaking through into light and sound again. The song of the birds seemed louder now, the breeze fresher. She felt a touch on her arm, and spun around to find Balthazar standing before her in the water.

And she saw that there were truly magical beings here, gods of the sea.

He was surely too beautiful for her, the unexpected gift of this one moment. But she could make the most of this time. The most of her gift.

She wound her arms around his neck, floating free to wrap her legs tightly about his hips. "It is so glorious here," she whispered. "I never knew such a place could exist, not in real life."

"Nor did I," he said. "Until now."

And he kissed her, kissed her as she longed for him to do. As if he was as hungry for her as she was for him, as if the taste and feel of their bodies entwined was everything. The past was nothing, the future nebulous and insubstantial. Her head fell back as his mouth slid down her throat, over the angle of her collarbones to her breast.

She wove her fingers through his wet hair, pressing his mouth closer and closer to her skin, her aching nipple. She wanted to be so close to him she could not tell where she ended and he began, where they became as one being. As if he read her thoughts, he pulled her body closer to his, resting his face against the erratic beat of her heart.

Without a word, he turned towards the sandy banks of the pool, carrying her with him as they tumbled down to earth, the water lapping at their feet. As he entered her, Bianca closed her eyes tightly, savouring every single sensation, every movement and sound.

The smell of water and sweat on his skin, the heat of the sun on her face. He reached for her hands, pinning them next to her head with their fingers entwined.

They spoke no words at all, but she had never felt so close to another person and she knew she never would again. They were as one, and nothing could ever be the same.

Bianca lazed in the hazy rays of the sun, stretched out on the sandy bank of the pool like an indolent jungle creature with no thought of anything but the warmth, the sweep of the sky above. She closed her eyes, listening to the rush of the waterfall, the soft sound of Balthazar's breath. He lay beside her, his head resting on her shoulder, seemingly asleep, seemingly oblivious to the world around them. Yet she could feel the coiled strength of him under her touch.

She trailed a caress over his shoulder, tracing a light, twisting pattern on his chest. He stretched beneath her fingertips, like the lazy, powerful tiger she imagined him. Even in Venice, even beneath the concealment of his fine clothes, she had seen that barely leashed force within him. The lethal mix of strength and anger that so intrigued her young, sheltered self.

That so intrigued her now.

She yearned to know what was in his mind, his heart. What led him here; what he really wanted. She knew his body, every inch of it. But now she did want more.

Yet in order to have it, Bianca sensed she would

have to do the most frightening thing ever—share her own heart in return.

Her eyes flew open, staring sightlessly up at the pale blue sky, the whirling birds overhead. Her chest felt suddenly tight, her breath trapped in her lungs. As if sensing her sudden tension, Balthazar sat up beside her, her touch trailing away from his shoulder.

"Bianca?" he said quietly, as if he, too, feared to tear the silence of this place. To destroy the fragile peace they had built up so carefully between them.

She turned her head away, watching the eternal ebb and flow of the waterfall rather than look at his face.

"You asked me once what happened in Venice," she said. "Nay, not *asked*. You never ask at all. Perhaps you are a sea god indeed, all-knowing, and have no need of curiosity!"

He laughed, and stretched out beside her again in all his glorious nakedness. "If I were all-knowing, I never would have been caught in that storm in the Mona Passage. I have as much curiosity as anyone. But I have too many secrets of my own to pry into anyone else's."

"I remember how everyone so loved to talk about you in Venice," she said. "To speculate on everything about you."

"Such a vast waste of time. I never did anything the least bit interesting."

"That cannot be true," she said. She rolled on to her side, facing him, her head propped on her palm as she stared down at him. The sun fell over his face in slanted golden bars, his new growth of beard gilded over his taut skin. He gazed up at her with seeming indolence, yet she knew that dark, intent look by now. Behind his elegant carelessness he was always watching, always seeing.

"When I was meant to be getting on with my mending or fetching water," she said, "I listened to the tittle-tattle instead. I doubt you ever had an uninteresting day in your life. There was always some new tale about you."

"And yet you still spoke to me," he said, with an unreadable little smile. "You must have been very brave."

"Or very foolish." Bianca reached out, almost touching his shoulder, yet she could not. Not quite. Her hand fell to the damp sand. "I believed none of the stories I heard. I wanted only to be near you, to listen to you talk to me. To hear of all the wondrous things in your books. But then…"

Her words faded away; she hardly knew what to say. The past had become a silent thing, a hard knot she pressed down and down, so deep inside it had no reality now. Until Balthazar came back into her life.

He seemed to sense some of the dark emotions roiling inside of her as that hard knot unravelled, for he stood up and reached for their clothes lying in discarded heaps by the water. He tossed her chemise to her, and put on his hose. As he fastened them, he sat down near her, yet not so near that she couldn't think.

Bianca pulled the chemise over her head, drawing the thin fabric closer around her like protective armour. "What happened that day in Venice," she said, "that last day, was that your father killed my mother."

She had not meant to say it so baldly, but how else could the words come out? Balthazar's jaw tightened, yet he did not look away from her. Did not turn from the truth. "I feared that was so," he said roughly.

"I thought…"

"You thought I helped him." It was not a question. It was a hard, harsh statement.

"Yes. I was so very frightened! I thought you had used my friendship to distract me, to give your father time for his deed."

Bianca watched him closely, trying to judge his reaction to her words. Whether he believed her or not. Whether that anger that seemed to always lurk just beneath his handsome surface would flare out into the open.

He did not move closer to her, his expression did not alter. But she saw his hands, braced against his thighs, flex, his eyes darken. Balthazar seldom showed his emotions, and being bred in the perilous hothouse of Venice had trained him perfectly in the art of maintaining a marble façade.

Yet Bianca had learned that his eyes always gave him away.

"You thought I would betray you," he said tightly.

"That I would conspire with my father against an innocent young girl."

"I did not know what to think! I was not so 'innocent' that I did not hear the tales of you, of your family. Your father was ruthless, he destroyed everyone who stood in the way of his ambitions. And you…"

"I was a careless debaucher. I wanted only my pleasures."

Bianca swallowed, seeing in her mind that old image: Balthazar stretched out in an open gondola, a beautiful courtesan caressing his face, his chest, as she leaned over to kiss him. "That is what everyone said."

"Yet still you talked to me."

How could she explain to him that she could not help but to talk to him? Some invisible force drew her to his side time after time. "I did not listen then to what everyone said. My mother's friends loved gossip above all else, and you were always a favourite subject. But I did not see how anyone who read the books you did, who talked of such things, could be so very dissipated."

"But I would wager that when my father carried out his foul deed, you remembered every word."

"Aye. And I felt such a fool for ever forgetting. For ever believing you were not a Grattiano, not deep down inside. I was so consumed with anger, with…"

The memory of that blinding, white-hot rage, that fear, washed over her, and she closed her eyes against the force of it. The way it tore away all the years since, and she was that frightened girl again. She spun away from him, wrapping her arms tightly around herself, and hurried to the edge of the pool.

Slowly, the warm, soft water lapping at her feet, the sound of the waterfall over the rocks, soothed her, brought her back to the present. To the woman she was now.

She heard Balthazar rise to his feet, heard him take a step towards her. If he touched her, she feared she would shatter into a hundred pieces. But he did not. He stood there, a few feet behind her, his still, warm presence binding her ever tighter to him. A shimmering, unbreakable bond linking the past, the present.

"That night in Santo Domingo," he said, "when you held the dagger to my throat. You meant to kill me then, to take your revenge."

"I had waited so long to put my mother's spirit to rest," she answered. "Your father stole so much from me; he took away that girl I was, he killed her as sure as he did my mother."

"And then I appeared in your tavern."

Bianca gave a harsh laugh. "What were the odds? It had to be a sign that my revenge was near at last."

"But Diego nearly took that from you."

She closed her eyes, seeing Balthazar lying on the floor, blood seeping from his wound. Just like her poor mother. Blood, death, revenge—an endless, terrible cycle, one that had infected her own heart for too long.

She opened her eyes, staring down at the waters. Those waters were magical indeed. They had washed away the last of that blood, the last of her old anger. They set her free at last.

She turned to Balthazar, smiling at him. "Oh, no. Diego, the poor man, he gave me a great gift that day. Killing you in my tavern would do nothing but destroy my own soul. A soul that is battered and bruised, certainly, but not dead. I thought it was—until I saw you again."

A puzzled frown creased his brow. "What do you mean?"

"What your father did to my mother, to so many other people, was terrible. What he did to you, his own son, was worse. He tried to destroy you, bit by bit every day of your life, to make you the man he was himself. But you did not let him. I could not let him, either."

She walked slowly towards him, holding out her hand until, ever so lightly, her fingers brushed his arm. She felt his muscles tense, yet he did not draw away. She slid her caress down, taking his hand in hers.

"I know now that you were not to blame for your father's crime," she said. "Killing you, hating you, would never bring my mother back. Would never return to me those years I lost. But it *would* take away that last piece of my heart. I couldn't do that. I cannot hate any longer."

Balthazar caught her in his arms, pulling her so close there was not a particle of light between them. She felt his kiss on her hair, her cheek, his arms lifting her from her feet.

"So many people have hated me," he said roughly. "And I never cared at all. Never cared what anyone thought, whether they hated or loved me. It was all the same. But you, Bianca—I never want you to hate me. Even if I deserve it."

Bianca leaned her head back, staring into his eyes. "Nay. I do not hate you."

"I hope you never will, no matter what you discover about me."

She pressed her lips to his, unable to bear more words. More thoughts and regrets. She had poured out so much to him, so many emotions that had been locked tightly inside all these years, that her heart felt wrung out from it. She wanted only to feel. To feel his kiss, his breath and skin and essence, and to know that for this moment they were together. The past gone.

Yet even as they fell together to the grass, their kisses desperate with desire, she couldn't help but remember that drawing. The lady and her children. And she knew that truly she could no longer hate Balthazar, no matter what.

But would she hate herself, for feeling again? For daring to open her bruised heart and let it truly beat again?

Chapter Twenty-Two

"Captain, the crew can't go on like this!" Mauro said. He spoke forcefully, threateningly, but he lingered near the closed cabin door.

Diego glanced up from the charts he was endlessly poring over, scowling at the interruption. "What did you say?"

"I said—the crew won't put up with this much longer. Chasing endlessly around barren islands, no prize in sight. They're saying you're in violation of the agreement, that you should be marooned—"

"*Cabron!*" Diego shouted, bringing his fist down atop the table with such force the empty rum battles clattered. Some of them rolled on to the dirty plank floor with their discarded companions, but he did not notice. These days he noticed naught but his one goal—to find Balthazar Grattiano and make sure the whoreson was truly dead this time.

"This is *my* ship," Diego growled. "And they are my crew. They'll do as they're told!"

"Not if…" Mauro began.

The words strangled to a gurgling noise as Diego lunged across the room, pressing a dagger to the man's jugular. Mauro's eyes bulged.

"I don't want to hear about any poxy *agreements*," Diego said. "We will find Grattiano, wherever he has gone to ground, and then when he is dead there will be prizes aplenty. Enough to make every man here wealthy beyond all his dreams, if they will just show a bit of patience. Or do you think they would prefer to eat their own ears? To be suspended by their testicles from the yardarm?"

Mauro swallowed hard against the blade, and Diego knew that he understood. Diego was a man beyond obsessed, not someone to be argued or gainsaid—or he would indeed carry out every one of those threats.

"I was elected captain," he said, "and we will do things my way. If the men obey, they will be rewarded. If not, they will die horribly and be tossed overboard to feed the fish. *Sí?*"

Mauro nodded carefully above the blade.

"*Muy bueno.*" Diego slowly lowered the dagger, still holding it poised in his hand. "Now go. We have no time to lose."

Mauro fled, the door banging shut behind him, and Diego knew his message was received. They would find Grattiano. What happened after that did not matter.

Diego swung back towards the table, towards all the charts and maps spread out there. A whole ocean for Grattiano to hide in, a myriad of islands. No one had seen him in Havana or Cartegena; he was not headed towards Peru and the mainland coast. That left smaller places, bars of sand and palm trees tucked amid the endless water.

Vista Linda, that mythical spot, was his best guess. Yet he had never seen it; no one even really knew where it was.

He couldn't stop looking, though. Could never cease until they were all dead.

Suddenly infuriated all over again, his head burning with rum, Diego swept the maps off the table. They could tell him nothing at all!

He staggered to his rumpled berth, falling amid the wrinkled, grimy blankets. Surely he was doomed to sail these cursed seas for ever, chasing after a vengeance he could never achieve. The leader of damned men with no hope for revenge.

Above his head, he heard shouts, felt the turn of the ship beneath him. Despite their threats, they would not mutiny. They were too greedy, and Diego had led them to riches enough in the past to earn their brief loyalty. They would steer the *Firebrand* to Grattiano, and after that they could topple off the edge of the earth for all Diego cared. He would happily fall into perdition.

But not just yet. He had to fulfill his one mission,

the one burning purpose that drove his existence. To kill Balthazar Grattiano.

He closed his eyes, falling into a restless, rum-soaked sleep. This was the time he longed for, the time when Esperanza visited him.

As usual, when hazy dreams at last descended on him, she came and sat on the edge of the berth. She wore her Spanish clothes, a garnet-coloured gown and snowy chemise. But her black hair fell free, a glossy curtain to her waist, and her skin was the warm honey colour of her island sun. She gazed down at him, her brown eyes soft and sad.

"You are ill, *mi amor*," she said gently. She stroked his shoulder, yet he did not feel it in his dream. Her touch was for ever beyond him.

"Never fear, Esperanza," he answered. "I won't fail you this time."

"You never failed me," she said, leaning close to him until he could vow he smelled her sweet, white-flower scent. "You swore we would always be together."

"And how did I keep that promise? You are gone!"

She shook her head. "I am here. I'm always here. I try to take care of you, but you make the task so difficult. You just refuse to see."

"See what?" he asked, bewildered. Esperanza liked to speak in riddles, as was the nature of dreams. But he was so tired of never seeing clearly, never really touching her.

"One day, very soon, you will know." She smoothed her touch over his brow, and it felt like a cool breeze through his tangled hair. Clean and soft, pure, in a harsh world.

"You will find the light soon enough," she said. "Don't turn away from it, Diego, I beg you. Don't make what we had disappear for ever."

"Esperanza!" Diego clutched at her hand, but she vanished. All that was left was the darkness of his restless sleep.

And the promise of his vow of revenge.

Chapter Twenty-Three

"Que hondo! Que hondo! Que hondo es el mar!"

Balthazar stretched out in bed, a lazy smile spreading irresistibly over his face as he listened to Bianca singing. Her voice was not one that would be renowned at a royal court, trembling and untrained, but to him it was as sweet as the tropical birds outside. As the waves washing over the sandy shore.

Vista Linda had been a spot of refuge for him ever since he had bought it, an oasis of quiet and beauty in the harsh, dangerous world. Now, with Bianca in his house, it felt like…

Like he imagined a home could be.

He rolled over on the mattress, inhaling deeply of the clean, lemony scent of Bianca's skin lingering in the sheets. Her clothes were draped over the chair, her hairbrush and dish of hairpins on his shaving stand. She had also hung up curtains at the one window in the sleeping loft, pale-coloured cloth that let in the morning light and billowed in the breeze.

He was becoming dangerously addicted to her presence in his house, his life. Addicted to making love to her, feeling her passion rise up to meet his with such eagerness. Addicted to hearing her voice, seeing her smiles. He wanted more of those smiles, more of her laughter, and he feared he would do anything for them.

But Bianca didn't seem to want anything from him. She enjoyed the sex, yet the things other women asked of him—jewels and silks, courtly compliments—she wanted naught of it.

He had no idea what she *did* want. Until she lowered her mask and let him glimpse her heart there by the waterfall, she had been a complete mystery. Yet he could not blame her for her wary concealment, not after what his father had done. Not when Balthazar concealed so much himself.

He frowned and sat up in their bed, wrapping the bedclothes around his waist. He had never felt this way, and it unsettled him. He had seen the way his brother Marc had looked at his wife, how the two of them had shared secret smiles between them, a private language only the two of them understood. Yet Balthazar had never really comprehended, had even felt a bit sorry for them. To love, to care, only meant being vulnerable to pain, to the cruel vagaries of fortune.

He had been alone all his life, and that was for the best. Bianca's presence, the way he had come to rely on her, had crept up on him. Slid inexorably into every crevice of his existence until now, suddenly, he could not imagine being without her.

Not having her in his bed, not being able to talk to her—not hearing her sing in the morning. How had he never realised how dry his life was before?

It was a wonderful, cruel thing. Soon, this time on Vista Linda would end, and he and Bianca would have to face their futures. He had to enjoy her now, and perhaps take advantage of the chance fate gave him, the chance to atone for one small slice of his father's endless sins.

Balthazar washed and dressed quickly, climbing down the narrow staircase from the sleeping loft. Bianca had ceased her singing, but still hummed, sitting in the doorway with a bowl in her lap and a pile of fresh fruit beside her. She peeled and sliced, the sun slanting across her dark hair, revealing the curves and shadows of her body beneath her chemise.

"What was that song?" Balthazar asked.

Bianca glanced back over her shoulder, and gave him one of those beautiful smiles. "Just a sea tune I heard the men singing yesterday," she said. "I'm sorry to wake you with my atrocious singing! Something in the morning breeze just drew it out of me."

"I liked it," he said, going to give her a good-morning kiss. She tasted of mango and lemon, of that green sweetness that was only Bianca.

She laughed. "Then you are as tone deaf as I! There is wine and bread on the table if you're hungry. One of those native women—Rosa?—was baking this morning."

"Mendoza's wife," Balthazar said, pouring out a goblet of wine. He noticed that Bianca had spread a fine cloth over the rough table, and arranged a bunch of bright flowers in a bowl.

Home indeed.

"She seemed very kind, though I could not understand a great deal of what she said."

Balthazar leaned in the doorway behind Bianca, sipping his wine as he lazily studied the way her pinned-up curls lay so enticingly against the nape of her neck. He gave in to the temptation, kissing her just on that soft spot. She shivered and laughed, swatting him away.

"I am working," she said lightly.

He laughed, too, and reached over her shoulder for a slice of orange. "That is a great deal of fruit for two people."

"You did say I could have a party."

"We are having a party *here*?" He peered back into the house, the two small rooms. "How many people are you inviting, *cara*?"

"Not here. Mendoza said he and the crew could cook one of the pigs in a pit on the beach. And Rosa is baking more bread from the flour you brought from Santo Domingo, or at least I think that is what she said. We shall have music, dancing…"

"You *have* been busy this morning. Cleaning, cooking, planning a ball."

"You needn't be disgruntled, Balthazar! I remember a time when you seemed to enjoy a ball beyond all things. Especially a masked ball at the Doge's Palace with Rosina Micelli."

He laughed. "I am not disgruntled! You may do whatever you like. Consider yourself the empress of Vista Linda. I lay my small domain at your feet."

She shot him a puzzled, frowning glance. "Are you certain this largesse is not a guilty offering? Because of what I told you yesterday?"

"Of course I feel guilty for what happened to you," he said quietly. "For what my father did."

"You are not responsible for your father's sins," Bianca answered. She gazed down solemnly at the fruit in her hand, the little dagger. "It took me a long time to realise that. To learn…"

"To learn that I have enough sins of my own?"

She gave him a wry smile. "We all have sins enough to have a heavy burden. We needn't take on the dark deeds of others. Your sins, Balthazar, are probably no greater than those of any other wealthy man. But mine…"

Her voice drifted away, her words blending with the quiet morning.

Balthazar knelt beside her, gently touching her leg through the thin chemise. How warm and sweet she was, so vital and alive. And how far she was from him, yet again.

"What are your sins, Bianca?" he said, gazing up at her face, at the smooth cheek tilted away from him.

She stroked a light caress over his hand, soft as the blue-winged butterflies. "This is a day for a party, remember? A day for us to be young again, to forget all that."

He kissed her fingers, licking away the juice on her skin until he felt her tremble, felt the quickening of her pulse. "Very well," he said. "I did say you were the empress today. We will be young and careless, just as you command."

"And the empress commands that you kiss her," she murmured. "Right now."

"I am your Majesty's servant in all things," he answered, rising up to meet her waiting lips. They were soft, opening in welcome, tasting of fruit and sun, and all the flaming desire between them.

He also tasted something new there—desperation. A deep need to seize the moment, to seize these feelings and never let them go. He felt it, too, and he drew her ever closer, her breasts and legs moulded to his body. Yet even as he reached out to grasp the moment, grasp the very essence of her, it slid away again.

But he had a new resolve. She could not escape him much longer.

He slowly broke away from their kiss, nibbling lightly at her jaw, her cheeks, the bridge of her nose, until she sighed. "If we are going to have a gala ball tonight, your Majesty, there is much work to be done."

"True," she said. "But surely there is still time..." One of her hands trailed over his chest, his hip, but he caught her fingers before they could reach their ultimate goal.

"Nay, I think not," he said. He kissed her fingertips and let her go, let her fall back to her seat on the doorstep. "Later, my empress. After your royal banquet."

Before he could change his mind, could snatch her back into his arms and make love to her right on that doorstep, he walked away. It would be a long day indeed, but hard work digging that fire pit on the beach would be a help, sweating out his uncontrollable desires. He could hardly wait until the night.

As he hurried towards the pathway, he found himself whistling the sea tune Bianca sang. *"Que hondo es el mar..."*

Bianca smoothed her grey skirts, turning about from her perch on the stool to examine herself in the small looking glass. She wished she had something finer, more festive and stylish to wear—something to make Balthazar look at her in fascination.

But the grey was her only gown and would have to do. Besides, if Balthazar ever looked at her any more intently than he already did, she feared she might burst into flames!

She laced up the grey bodice, but left off the matching sleeves, letting her loose white chemise suffice. Once she was content with her garb, she jumped off the chair and opened her trunk, hastily rummaging through the meagre contents. She could already hear the faint strains of music drifting up from the beach as the sun began to set.

She found what she sought, a length of red ribbon, and used it to tie back her loose hair. Then she dug deep beneath folded stockings and chemises to the very bottom, to the heavy bag of coins she hid there. Tucked amid the money was a ring.

She held it up on her palm, the buttery sunlight from the window turning it to pure sparkle. She had never worn it, this ruby surrounded by pearls, yet she had never sold it either. Not even when things seemed most dire.

But neither had she ever taken it out and really looked at it, not since the day Balthazar had hastily pressed it into her hand. Its beauty reminded her too much of those terrible hours, of her cherished friendship gone so very wrong.

Now its blood-red shimmer held only beauty, only the magic of this place. She should attach new memories to it, ones that would erase the old terrors for ever.

Bianca held out her left hand, examining the thin,

worn gold band. Juan Montero had placed it there in their quick ceremony in a Cadiz chapel. He had been older than she, but kind. When they had met in the tavern where she worked as a maid, he thought he found someone young and strong to mend his shirts and wash his stockings. She thought she found someone to take her away from drudgery, from crude men who wrongly thought she was there for anyone's taking.

He married her so she could go with him to the New World, and they were both proved right. They had a good enough marriage, even a friendship of sorts. When he died, and she opened her own tavern in Santo Domingo, she had missed him.

But now she could hardly remember his face. All of that seemed another life entirely, one that had happened to a different woman.

She took off the wedding band and dropped it amid the coins. In its place she put Balthazar's ruby. With that simple act, her heart rose up, as if a weight lifted from it. As if something, old, rusted fetters and chains, were smashed.

Bianca laughed aloud as she slammed the trunk lid shut, and hurried down the stairs from the sleeping loft. Balthazar waited for her in the doorway. He still wore his usual garb of white shirt, high black boots, and black hose and leather jerkin. But he was fresh-shaven, his hair bound back to reveal the fine pearl in his earlobe.

Her escort to the ball at last, after all these years. And it hardly mattered that they were going to a beach to eat fruit and roast pork, to dance on the sand rather than the marble floor of a palace.

He smiled at her, and offered his arm. Bianca slid her hand over his sleeve, and watched as he noticed the ring on her finger. As his green eyes widened just a bit when he remembered.

"You kept it?" he said.

"I could not bring myself to sell it," she answered. "I am glad to have it now, it's so beautiful."

"If you would let me, I would drape you in rubies and pearls of every size," he said. "Emeralds, diamonds…"

"One is enough," Bianca said with a laugh, tugging him with her down the path. "Where would I wear ropes of pearls and emeralds, anyway? To mend sails? Or mayhap to go swimming under the waterfall?"

"To a masque in Venice."

She was caught by the sudden rough solemnity of his voice, and her steps faltered. She glanced over at him. His face was also serious, set in tense lines, yet she did not know why. She could not read his thoughts.

"You are going back to Venice?" she said quietly. "I thought you hated it there. That this, the sea, was your life now."

"A man cannot sail for ever," he answered. "Not when he grows older, when there are things he must face."

Things like a family? Obligations? That lightness

of heart she felt earlier suddenly seemed like a cold lump in her chest. She wanted to know, yet at the same time she didn't want to know at all. Not yet. Not tonight, of all nights.

She made herself smile, and tugged again at his arm. "You are too solemn for this party, Signor Grattiano. And you promised me a dance."

He opened his mouth as if to answer, to argue, but Bianca pressed her finger to his lips. "Tomorrow, you can ask me, tell me, whatever you like. Tonight, I want to dance."

Finally, he nodded, and they continued on their way to the beach. The sailors and their native wives were already gathered there, playing music, laughing, a few of them dancing on the sand. A table was set up with platters of fruit, fish, and bread, and sweet, thick smoke drifted from the open pit where the pig roasted on hot coals.

Beyond the edge of the sapphire-blue water, the sun set amid streaks of orange, red, and purple, catching the whole sky on fire.

It was truly the most beautiful thing Bianca had ever seen. The light, the sea, the music, the soft sand under her feet. Balthazar beside her, sharing it all—it was complete perfection. She stood there, absorbing it all into herself, storing it up against darker days when all this light would be just a sweet memory.

"You said you wanted to dance, *signora*," Balthazar said. His fingers entwined with hers, and he drew her into the midst of all the music and motion. "What is your fancy, then? A pavane, a galliard? The empress may command whatever she likes tonight."

Bianca laughed, twirling around him in allemande, their arms linked. The tropical breeze, the stars just twinkling on above their heads, they were all a part of her and she of them. She and Balthazar were as one now, come what may.

"The empress could command nothing more than what she has right now!" she said, whirling to a giddy halt in front of him. She wrapped her arms around his shoulders, going up on tiptoe to press a soft kiss to his lips.

He lifted her off her feet, spinning her around and around in a delirious kaleidoscope of sand and ocean, sky, smoke—and him.

It was all she could have wanted.

Hours later, the sky was a vast blue-black, dotted with a sliver of moon and a swath of stars, when Bianca collapsed to the sand, the blazing bonfires far behind her. She had danced and danced, drunk fine Spanish wine and eaten fruit and the rich roast pork, and laughed until she thought she could move no more.

She lay down on a soft mound of earth beneath a palm tree, replete and contented. There was still music, but it was slower, quieter, a ballad of home and lost love that gave the party a sweetly melancholy, wine-soaked edge. The men sat around the fires, listening in

silence as they passed around bottles of rum. Mendoza
and his wife had slipped off to their home, but no one
else seemed inclined to leave just yet.

Nor was Bianca, despite the tiredness that soaked
into her very bones. The music was too alluring. She
closed her eyes, listening to the tune, to the ebb and
flow of the waves, the crackle of the fires.

Then she felt a touch on her arm, and opened her
eyes to find Balthazar sitting beside her on the sand. He
leaned back against the base of the tree, his hand sliding
down to clasp hers. His thumb traced the ruby ring.

"You took off your wedding ring," he said.

"Aye. Poor Juan has been dead for more than a year.
I held on to the safety of that ring for too long. It
seemed time to let it go."

"What was he like, your husband?"

Was that an edge of *jealousy* to Balthazar's voice?
She smiled to think it could be so, that *he* could be
jealous of *her*, as she once was of his conquests. But
it was surely only her imagination.

"He was kind," she said. "And good to me, in his
way. He had gone too long without the comforts of a
wife, and was grateful. We were friends, I think."

"Only friends?"

She turned her head to gaze at him in the firelight.
"He was older, and I think never a man with great
passions. Not like you, Signor Grattiano."

He laughed, and slid down to lie beside her. "Ah,
you have discovered my 'great passions', have you?"

"You have never tried to hide them."

He drew her close to him, his arms around her waist as he kissed her neck, the curve of her shoulder where her sleeve slid from her bare skin.

Bianca sighed, curling into him. They lay like that for a long time, wrapped in the warm night as the music faded away and there was only perfect, sweet silence.

Chapter Twenty-Four

A few days after the party, a sudden wave of nausea brought Bianca up off the bed, clutching at her belly. The sick feeling seized her in an irresistible grip, and she grabbed for the wash basin just in time.

Finally emptied of all last night's dinner, she collapsed on to the floor, weak and trembling. Shivering in a cold sweat, and deeply grateful Balthazar was not there to see her. She closed her eyes, listening closely, but the house was quiet. She was alone.

In the days since the dance on the beach, Balthazar had taken to rising early and going to work on the *Calypso*, leaving Bianca to sleep late. Thus he did not know that this was the third day in a row she had woken up ill.

The illness did not last. By noon she could sip some water, eat a little bread, and by nightfall the dizzy nausea was gone.

Bianca sat up slowly, calculating in her mind. Her last courses had been…

In Santo Domingo, just before Balthazar arrived.

"Oh, by St Iago," she whispered, resting her forehead on her knees. She could no longer deny it. She was pregnant. She pressed her hand to her belly. It was still flat, but now she thought she could feel *something* inside, some flutter of life deep within.

"Nay!" she said, her voice catching on a sob. Her life was surely complicated enough—what would a child do to it?

Balthazar's child.

And yet, despite her fear, her cold panic, something else flickered in her heart. Something very like—joy.

It did not last long, though, as she had to be sick into the basin again. When the nausea at last subsided, she was exhausted. She washed her face in the pitcher of fresh water, brushed out her hair, and dressed in a clean chemise. The day was far along now, the sun high in the pale blue sky, and she had no time to lose.

She had put off doing something she dreaded— asking Balthazar about his possible family. About the future. Their time here on Vista Linda was so very perfect, so sweet, she did not want to mar it, to tear its fragile fabric apart. It was easy to just drift along, to swim in the waterfall pool, mend sails, cook, make love.

Now she knew for certain that it was not just herself she had to take care of. If her calculations were right, in just a few months a little new person would make their appearance. And the repairs to the *Calypso* were nearly complete. Balthazar would then surely want to sail away.

She could not stay here and wait for his return like Rosa and the other women, not with a baby coming. Yet she had no idea where she could go, where she could make a new home. A tavern in Santo Domingo was no place for an infant.

And, at the very back of her mind, there was the fearful thought of what had happened to Diego Escobar's wife. Dying alone in childbirth.

Bianca shook her head, forcing away such dark thoughts. They did her no good now. She was strong and healthy. She had to trust the child would be, too. But where would they go, what would they do, once the baby was here?

Suddenly, stowing away on the *Calypso* all those weeks ago seemed even more foolish than it had at the time!

She left the house, intending to go down to the beach and find Balthazar. She didn't have to go that far, though. He was in the overgrown garden, firing arrows from his bow.

The target set beyond the edge of the house bristled with arrows, yet still he raised the bow to his shoulder. He wore just his shirt and hose, his hair bound back with a scarf, his brow glistening with sweat.

His stance was still and unyielding as he took aim, his gaze hard as marble.

She wrapped her arms tightly over her belly, watching as he let the arrow fly. It landed solidly in the middle of the target.

Only then did he turn and see her there. He slowly lowered the bow, running one finger lightly over the beautifully polished wood. He must have read something of her thoughts, for he gave her a wry smile and said, "I have sometimes feared I am like my father."

Bianca stared at him, startled. Once, she too had thought that, had seen them as two parts of the same privileged coin. But having known Balthazar for all these weeks, seen his life now...

She knew that could not be so.

"If you were truly like your father," she said, "you never would have left the riches of Venice. Never would have chosen the life of the sea."

He gave her a crooked half-smile. "Perhaps I came here for more riches? Perhaps the wealth of Venice was not enough for me."

Bianca glanced back at the rough little house, shining white under the bright morning sun. "Then you chose a strange way of going about it."

He laughed, and reached for another arrow, notching it into his bowstring. "True. I came here to make my own fortune, one untainted by anything my father touched."

"But that is not the only reason."

He did not look at her, just raised his bow and sighted it along to the target. The lean muscles of his shoulders and upper arms tensed beneath his shirt.

"Do you possess your mother's gift of fortune-telling?" he said, and released the arrow. It flew straight and true to the centre of the target, right next to the last arrow. "Of knowing the future?"

She shook her head. "If I did, I would have saved myself a great deal of trouble. Sadly, I inherited naught from my mother except my curling hair."

"But still her blood runs in your veins. All kinds of things could be hidden there, just waiting to come out and surprise you when you least expect it."

Bianca walked to the target and pulled out the arrows, holding them up to examine the gleam of the feathers fletching, the sharp tips. "I have none of my mother's magic. Just as you have none of your father's evil. Blood or no, you bear his name—not his soul."

"My soul bears sins as black as any of his." His voice was toneless, flat and quiet, but Bianca knew him better now. She knew the pain of forcing anger and fear down and down, so deep it hardened and became part of a person. A black knot that never went away, until something happened to make it unravel and fly away.

She turned the arrows over in her hand. "Because you killed him," she said softly.

"Aye. Is that not a terrible thing?"

"I don't know," she answered.

"A priest would say so."

"Surely you have noticed by now that I am no priest. I have dark sins to my name, too. I have lied, stolen, fornicated."

"Murdered?"

"I'm sure I would have, if Ermano Grattiano was *my* father." She tossed aside the arrows, moving slowly towards him. At last she stood before him, mere inches away, yet not quite touching. Just close enough that he could see the truth of understanding in her eyes. "Tell me what happened."

He studied her carefully for a moment, as if to decipher whether or not she really wanted to *know*. Then his gaze drifted past her, past the present moment to something only he could see.

"It was not long after you left Venice," he said. "A man had come to the city. Perhaps you remember *Il leone*, the ship's captain who defeated the pirates?"

"Oh, yes! All the ladies were in love with him, he was quite the hero of the hour."

"Were you in love with him, Bianca?" Balthazar said again, with that unreadable little smile.

"I never even saw him. My mother wouldn't let me gawk at processions, and besides…" Besides, she had already been in love then. With Balthazar.

"My father discovered *Il leone* was having an affair with Julietta Bassano. I'm sure you remember her."

Bianca frowned, recalling days and names she thought far behind her. "I never met her, either, but I remember. Your father was desperate to marry her. He thought she was the one destined to give him more sons. That was why he kept wanting his cards read. They told him she would be the one to bring him sons.

Ah, I see now—he tried to kill *Il leone*! And you—you stopped him."

"In a way, yes."

"But how could that be wrong? To defend innocent people from a madman?"

"Ah, you see, *Il leone* was not all he appeared. He came to Venice with a hidden purpose."

Fascinated by this tale he told, Bianca sat down in the shade of a palm tree, working it all out in her mind. Truly, it was better than a scene from the *commedia dell'arte*! "What was it, this secret of his?"

He sat down next to her, carefully laying aside the bow. "He came to Venice specifically to kill Ermano Grattiano."

"Nay!" Bianca gasped.

"Yes. You see, Ermano once killed the mother of *Il leone*. She was Ermano's mistress, and he was her young son's father."

"And thus…"

"My brother, Marc Velazquez. Aye. I suppose Julietta did bring my father a son, just not quite in the way he expected."

"And you had to kill your father to save your brother."

He nodded, watching her solemnly. "I wish I could have saved your mother, too. Saved everyone who was hurt by my father."

Bianca swallowed past the dry knot of tears in her throat. Past this sudden rush of emotions that threat-

ened to engulf her. She went up on her knees beside
him, framing his face in her hands as she gazed down
at him. His eyes were a dark green-gold, wary as he,
too, studied her face. Surely he could not think she
would turn from him after his tale!

Could ever turn from him at all.

"Surely no one was more hurt by your father than
you," she said. "I am wicked enough to believe he got
what he deserved. But you acted in defence of your
brother; you saved who knows how many innocent
lives. Your father killed only out of greed and bad
temper, nothing more. I know *you* could never do that."

He smiled at her. "You do not think me bad
tempered, then?"

She laughed. "I know you wish people to think you
so. And I know you are angry at the ill fortune of being
born a Grattiano. But your ship's crew find you hard, but
fair. They would rather sail under you than any other
captain in the Spanish Main. They would follow you
anywhere."

"And you, Bianca? Would you follow me, even
knowing my bad blood, my dangerous life?"

Bianca thought of the tiny being inside of her, the
child that would share in that "bad blood", that dangerous way of life. "I am here, am I not? I followed
you from Santo Domingo."

"For now, perhaps."

She sat down facing the little house, the wide blue
sky. He was right, of course. They were here now, yet

what would come in the future? Tomorrow and the next day. "Can we not just stay here on Vista Linda?" she said, even as she knew such a fantasy, an eternity of hiding away, could never be.

"For a time, mayhap," he said, then he laughed. "'Tis true I seldom see my family, but I think they might be concerned if I never appeared again."

Bianca closed her eyes at his words. *His family.* Perhaps this was it, then, the truth she had not wanted to face. The bright, hot day suddenly seemed grey and chilly.

"Your family?" she said dully, thinking of his sketch. "You have children?"

"Nay, not that I know of! My brother and his wife, and their children. Two sons and a new baby girl I have not yet seen. They want me to join them at their villa next year, to talk more of Marc's new business schemes."

And, with just those very few words, the light came flooding back. Bianca laughed, feeling suddenly both joyful and foolish in equal measure. He was not married! How could she even have thought he was? Have feared to ask him?

"You mean the business scheme of opening a map-making business?" she said. "Of staying in Europe?"

"You find that amusing, do you? The thought of me minding my cartography shop in Seville or Cadiz?"

"Nay, nay! I just…" Bianca opened her eyes to find him staring at her in puzzlement. Somehow, that made her laugh all the more. She fell into his lap, kissing his face over and over, kissing him as if for the first time.

"Oh, Balthazar," she gasped. "You do like your nephews and your niece, then? You like children?"

He laughed, too, his arms coming around her waist to hold her against him. "I like them well enough."

"And they do not show signs of 'bad Grattiano blood', I am sure."

"They are fine children! Kindhearted and strong, not like their grandfather."

"Nay, they are like their uncle." She kissed him on his lips, long and lingering, feeling that heat and need rise up between them as it always did, undeniable.

She longed to press his hand to her belly, to the "kind, strong" child growing there, to tell him her secret. But an abrupt shout tore into her thoughts, her new hopes.

"Captain!" she heard one of the men call. She fell away from Balthazar, turning to see Luis hurrying up the slope of the hill towards them.

She shielded her eyes from the sun, a sudden buzzing noise in her head shutting out the world, the golden moment dying to cold ashes. Even from this distance she could see the pale strain on Luis's face, the marks of incipient panic and uncertainty.

Not yet knowing what news he brought, she still shivered.

Balthazar stood up, helping her to her feet. His body was taut with that same chilled expectation.

"A ship approaches," Luis panted as he drew alongside them.

"What flag does she fly?" Balthazar asked.

"None, captain."

"No flag?" Bianca said, incredulous. No flag meant only one thing, of course—trouble. She had lived in the islands long enough to know that every man had enemies. Especially a man like Balthazar, with a fortune and a fierce reputation. But these days at Vista Linda, so peaceful, so happy, hidden away from all the greed and harshness of the world, had made her forget that.

Had made her soft and vulnerable, just as she had been as a girl. Back then, she had watched her world explode right before her shocked eyes, and she could do nothing but flee.

Was it all about to happen again?

Bianca stared up at Balthazar's face, that beloved, handsome visage now seemingly carved of granite. Hard, unyielding. She knew she could not flee, could not hide, this time. No matter what happened, what this unknown ship brought, she had to stay with him.

He turned abruptly and snatched up a spyglass that lay by the quiver of arrows. He strode up the slope of the hill, above the house, to the very peak that afforded a view of the harbour below.

Bianca rushed after him, along with Luis. She saw that the men were gathered on the beach, watching the strange ship that lay far out in the water, beyond the reach of the newly re-floated *Calypso*'s guns. Indeed, it flew no flag, bore no identifying marks at all. She could see little of it beyond the darkened wood of its hull, the tangle of its masts.

"Do you know it?" she said.

Balthazar shook his head.

"Perhaps it's damaged and merely seeks safe harbour," Luis suggested.

"No one finds this place unless they seek it," Balthazar growled. "And most know better than to seek it."

Bianca pressed her hand protectively over her belly, watching as a boat, a mere tiny speck, was lowered from the side of the mysterious vessel. It rowed slowly towards shore, borne back and forward again by the waves. A white flag fluttered from the prow.

There were only three men in the boat, but the *Calypso*'s crew tightened into a defensive knot on the beach, swords and daggers at the ready.

"It appears they seek to parley," Bianca said.

A tight, humourless smile touched Balthazar's lips. "Well, we should oblige them, then."

Balthazar stared down at the message in his hand, reading it through twice before peering up at the messengers. They were a grimy lot, toothless, clad in miscellaneous garments and garish jewellery. Their leader, a scarred man who introduced himself as Perez, smiled unpleasantly as he surveyed the length of the beach, the men of the *Calypso* arrayed behind Balthazar.

His avid gaze moved to where Bianca stood with Rosa at the edge of the sand, and he grinned.

Balthazar crushed the message in his grip, his other hand going to the hilt of his dagger. He remembered the satisfying heft of his bow in his grasp, the solid "thunk" of an arrow finding its target. The man's chest would make a fine one.

But, Balthazar reminded himself, this man was not yet the enemy. He was merely the messenger. The bearer of tidings from someone Balthazar thought never to see again.

After Santo Domingo, he would have thought Diego Escobar would go to earth somewhere and rot. He was more persistent, more angry than Balthazar gave him credit for.

And now he sat like a spider on that ship in Balthazar's own harbour, just waiting to spew forth his poison again.

Once, perhaps, Balthazar would not have cared. He would have happily welcomed Diego's revenge, a fitting end to a misspent life. The difficulty was that suddenly life did not feel so "misspent" after all.

He thought of Bianca's face as he told her of what happened with his father, of the quiet understanding, the benediction, he saw in her dark eyes. He thought of kissing her under the waterfall, of her bare skin under his touch. He heard the sound of her laughter as she danced on the beach.

Nay, not so misspent after all. Not now. All these

years, he thought only of himself. But that was done. He had to think of Bianca, of her safety and well-being.

"A duel?" he said. "Your captain dares challenge me to a duel?"

Perez's oily attention snapped back to Balthazar, away from the women, and he grinned. "Just you and him, sword to sword. We *could* fire on your beach, but it would be a shame to ruin such prettiness. Aye, Captain Grattiano?"

And then there was the fact that if that ship came in close enough to fire, the *Calypso*'s guns would blow her out of the water. If she was fully loaded again, that was.

"As you said, this quarrel is between your captain and me," Balthazar said.

Perez shrugged. "*This* quarrel, mayhap."

Balthazar tossed the crumpled message back at his face. "Go back to your ship, and tell your captain I will send word tonight about the location of the duel. I will fight him, but not here."

With that, he spun around and marched away along the beach. There was a commotion as his men bundled the pirate lot back into their boat, but Balthazar did not turn back. He kept going up the slope, towards his house.

A quick patter of footsteps sounded behind him. Bianca laid her hand on his arm, concern and confusion on her face as she gazed up at him.

He did not stop, but he slowed his stride, taking her hand in his.

"What was all that about?" she asked.

"They came from Diego Escobar," he said. "It seems he is now captain of that sorry lot. And he has challenged me to a duel. To the death."

Chapter Twenty-Five

"**I** will meet with Diego here," Balthazar said, pointing to a spot on the map spread out across the table. "It is sparsely inhabited, only a day's sail from Vista Linda, but far enough that he cannot cause mischief here."

"And what then?" Mendoza asked quietly. But Bianca, sitting in the open doorway, heard him well enough.

What then indeed? What would happen after the duel on that deserted island?

"We will head for Santo Domingo to take on our new cargo," Balthazar answered. "Then we will turn towards Spain. It grows late in the year, my brother will be looking for the *Calypso*."

More than the ship, Bianca was certain Marc Velazquez would be watching for his brother, for Balthazar. Did those two little boys in the sketch ask about their uncle? Did they scan the shore for sight of his vessel?

She stared out over the garden, the archery target, but did not see the brilliant sunset, the curling grey smoke of the cooking fires. Instead, she saw herself standing on a strange shore, holding a child's little hand as they strained for a glimpse of an approaching ship.

A ship that might never come.

Balthazar was a strong warrior, Bianca knew that. He was not a man to surrender, not an opponent to be challenged lightly. But he was also a man of honour, where Diego would surely resort to any means, fair or foul, to win. She remembered that glimpse she had of him in Santo Domingo, of his cold, dead eyes.

Diego was truly frozen inside, his soul strangled by the loss of his wife. And she had watched Balthazar come to warm, new life in the past days, just as she had. They had found a brief refuge here on Vista Linda, a healing in its warm pools and golden sands. It was a glorious miracle, one she thought never to see. A moment of happiness, sparkling and perfect.

But happiness left a person vulnerable. Surely Diego would see that, and take the advantage of it.

Yet there was something Diego did not know, and that was the fact that Balthazar was no longer alone. Bianca was a fighter, too, and at last she had something to fight for.

She glanced back at where Balthazar sat with Mendoza and Luis, poring over those charts. Talking intently of the logistics of the voyage, as if that was all there was. Bianca could only think of what would happen when the voyage was over, yet she knew the men would not speak of that, not when she was present.

Suddenly vastly weary, she rose and went to the stairs, climbing up to the sleeping loft. Their voices were only a blur there, a counterpoint to the chatter of the night birds, the distant rush of the sea. She washed her face and untied the scarf from her hair, shaking the tangled curls free over her shoulders as she reached for her comb.

Her belly gave a twinge, a small flutter almost, and she was sharply reminded of all she *did* have to fight for.

"You must be strong, too," she whispered, as she combed out her hair. "We have to all stand together now, against any enemy that comes for us. You are my little warrior."

"Who are you talking to, Bianca?" Balthazar asked, appearing at the top of the stairs.

Bianca stared at him in the wavy reflection of the glass, studying his weary face, the cautious veil drawn back over his gaze. She knew she could not yet tell him of their "little warrior"; he needed all his focus, his strength, for the fight. It had to be her secret, for just a little while longer.

"To myself," she answered, tugging free the last of the tangles.

He gave her a little smile. "I see I left you alone too long, if you feel the need to talk to yourself."

"Indeed you did. I'm sure you won't let it happen

again." She turned to face him, leaning her hips against the edge of the wash stand. "Will you, *mi amor*?"

He sat down on the bed, tugging off his boots. "I would ask you to stay here on the island, but I know that would be futile."

"It would. I am not going to let you escape to Santo Domingo without me."

"Infuriatingly stubborn woman."

"You have yet to see the full extent of my stubbornness, Signor Grattiano." Bianca took the basin of water and went to sit beside him on the bed. As he drew off his shirt, she washed his chest and back, still warm and golden from the hot day.

The bright day, that had suddenly turned so very dark.

She traced the cloth slowly over his shoulders, the lean muscles of his back, the elegant groove of his spine. He slowly relaxed under her ministrations, and she swept aside the fall of his hair to softly kiss the nape of his neck.

"So, Diego is still intent on his goal," she said. "That little scene in Santo Domingo did not deter him."

Balthazar gave a humourless laugh. "Men like him are never 'deterred'," he said. "I knew he would come back eventually."

"Just not quite yet?" Bianca said. "Why could he not just pursue his villainy elsewhere? There is surely more profit in attacking Spanish ships than chasing after you."

"But I am the one he hates, the one he seeks revenge from," Balthazar answered. "And I cannot blame him."

Bianca's hand stilled. "You cannot blame him?"

"He lost the woman he loved beyond all reason, and he holds me responsible for that." He turned to Bianca, running a gentle touch along her bare arm. "If you died…"

"I will not die," she said fiercely. She dropped the cloth, wrapping her hands tightly over his shoulders as if she could hold him to her. Keep him from vanishing for ever. "And neither will you. I feel pity for Diego, but I will not let him win this battle."

"And I won't, either," he answered. He pulled her to him, kissing her fiercely. Bianca kissed him back, savouring the taste and feel of him, the way he smelled of citrus sunshine and sea air, the feel of his body sliding over hers.

"Diego won't take this from me," he muttered against her throat. "No one will, not now."

Bianca fell back on to the bed, drawing him on top of her as their kiss deepened. Their lovemaking had always been intense, needful, yet now there seemed a new edge to it. A desperate, driving desire to touch, feel, be a part of each other. She had to absorb him into her, to memorise every kiss, every touch, and make it integral to herself for ever and ever.

She spread her legs, cradling him in the arc of her body as she ran her fingers along his back, feeling the strong shift of his muscles, the tension of his shoulders. She *was* a part of him, and he of her. Not just their child, not just the joining of their bodies, but something so deep, hidden. Something in the very essence of their souls was the same.

And that would always be so, come what may. But Bianca found she was greedy. She wanted, needed, more, more of him. For a very long time to come. But how could that ever happen, for two people such as them?

Balthazar lay very still, holding Bianca as she slept. He dared not move, dared not even breathe, for fear he would shatter this jewel-like moment.

It would fade soon enough, with the coming of the dawn.

The candles melted low, casting an amber glow over Bianca's body, over her skin and hair. She lay relaxed against him, her legs tangled with his, her curls spilling over her shoulders and the sheets, over his arm. She seemed a part of this island, this place that was the most "home" he had ever known. Free and wild, one with the sun and the sea.

He even suspected he saw her smile more here, and laugh as if she blossomed with the light. Those smiles were truly like emeralds, rare and precious. Balthazar suspected her life had not been an easy one since she had left Venice, despite her reluctance to speak of it. Smiles were not a part of her days, and he cherished them all the more for that.

He wanted her smiles, wanted to see that sudden radiance of her happiness. He wanted more and more of it, of *her*. He wanted, for the first time, a whole lifetime.

Why did such a desire have to come now? he mused as he gently stroked Bianca's cheek with the back of his hand. Now, when he had to face the actions of his past at last? When fate came to his door?

She stirred slowly into wakefulness, rolling over in his arms. Her eyes blinked open, and she stared up at him blankly, as if still caught in her dreams.

One of those soft smiles formed on her lips only to fade away as quickly. "Is it dawn yet?" she murmured.

"Not yet."

"It will be soon enough." She sat up against the pillows, shrugging her hair back over her shoulders. Balthazar rested his head against her naked stomach as she ran caressing fingertips over his face, his chest. Her palm rested over his heartbeat, light and gentle, but weightier than any stone could be.

She truly held his heart, that heart he always thought he did not possess. It was entirely hers; he only wished it could do her some good.

"I know I cannot ask you to abandon this duel," she said. "You would never do so."

"Then you know me well."

"Do I?" She shook her head. "Can anyone really know you, Balthazar Grattiano?"

"You do. You see things, know things, that no other person can. Because no one ever cared to look before."

Her touch moved to his hair, smoothing the tangled strands away from his brow. "You would never stay still long enough for anyone to get a good look."

He laughed. "True enough. I have indeed spent long years wandering across the Atlantic and back, from island to island."

"What have you been seeking in all this wandering?"

He considered this. What had he been seeking, really? "Not what everyone else comes to the New World in search of. Riches, land, fine titles."

"You already had those."

"So I did. When I was a child, my parents always told me those things were all in life. They were my birthright, the only things that mattered at all, and I had to be worthy of them. But they never brought pleasure or satisfaction."

"What did they bring? Anything at all?"

He caught her hand in his, kissing her fingers, the hollow of her palm, the tiny, delicate pulse of life just beneath her wrist. "Only the knowledge that the Grattiano name was a bitter one. That it would be far too easy for me to ruin lives as carelessly as my father did."

"You could never be like your father!"

"Can I not?" He gave a humourless laugh, pressing her hand to his heart again. "Tell that to Diego Escobar. To his wife."

"That was scarcely your fault. It was Diego's, for being so foolish as to refuse to do what was best for his wife, and then blaming someone else for what happened. Yet still you have your own stubborn honour! You will fight this duel even though it makes no sense."

"Perhaps that is why I came to the New World, then."

"To fight?"

"To atone for my Grattiano past. Or maybe to discover who I am beneath all those family trappings. Who can say, really? But all these years, all this searching, somehow I feel it's been leading up to this all along."

Bianca slid down the bed until they lay face to face, wrapping her arms and legs tightly around him. "You truly have a sense of honour that your father was entirely without! I was a fool ever to doubt that, to doubt that you were my friend. You will change what it means to be a Grattiano, and the name will stand for something else now."

"You think I can change the taint of that Grattiano blood? It has been flowing for generations, you know. Cheats and murderers, schemers, liars."

"You've already changed it," she said. Something strange, a quick flash of light, flickered behind her brown eyes. But it was quickly veiled as she kissed him, a quick, desperate embrace. "Just promise me something."

"What? The moon, the sun? Say the word and they are yours."

Bianca laughed, resting her forehead against his shoulder. "I have no need for the moon and sun. But I do have a great need of you. I beg you not to let your honour get the better of you in this duel. Don't let Diego win."

"I promise I will not 'let' Diego win," he said, drawing her closer until there was not even a ray of candlelight between them. Nothing to keep them apart, except what might happen tomorrow. "I will fight like the very devil, knowing you are waiting for me."

She nodded, and kissed him again, opening her legs to draw him against her. Despite that ineffable sense of time fleeing away from them, of moments trickling away with every star that faded in the sky, their love-making was slow. He wanted to memorise the way every inch of her body felt, every sigh and breath.

She arched her head back, and he trailed a slow, sinuous ribbon of kisses along her throat, the curve where her neck met her shoulder, as their bodies moved together in an eternal rhythm. Their fingers twined together against the mattress, her legs around his waist as he felt her breath quicken, her heart pound in her breast, melding with the beat of his.

As the sun rose in the sky, they became truly as one.

Chapter Twenty-Six

Bianca stood on the hot sand of the beach, staring out over the breaking waves. This shore had none of the warm lassitude of Vista Linda, the beautiful play of light and shadows. It was a small, sun-blasted place, barely a dot in the vastness of the sea. Yet this was where all the strands of her life would come together at last, the past and present woven into one great tapestry.

But the future, that was still a blank. She could see the colour just seeping into its edges, woven of the white sand, the hot blue sky, and the boat rowing inexorably towards her.

Out beyond the easy reach of the shore, two ships rode at anchor. The *Calypso*, with most of her crew lined up along the rails, and that strange dark vessel that tore away her idyll at Vista Linda. Only she, Balthazar and Mendoza were ashore now, waiting. Caught in that still, timeless moment.

Balthazar would have made her stay aboard the *Calypso*, she was sure. Yet he knew her well now, and thus knew she would not be dissuaded or forced. She would have found a way to come ashore, even if he had locked her in the cabin!

She had thought nothing could be worse than to stand on that deck and be separated from him by the impassable water, to watch this duel play out from a helpless distance. Now, as that boat drew ever closer, she began to wonder if she had been wrong.

She pressed her hand tight to her belly under the edge of her doublet, forcing away that dizzy, sick feeling. The sure knowledge that so much, that *every-thing*, rode on this one hour.

Balthazar glanced back at her, and gave her a wide smile. He did not seem worried at all. His expression was only calm, faintly interested, as he turned the hilt of his sword in his hand.

He had cast off his doublet and shirt, handing them to Bianca as he did some practice sparring with Mendoza. The sun gleamed on his muscled shoulders, the lean plane of his back. There was strength there as well as indescribable beauty. Bianca remembered his rumoured duels in Venice, all those youthful fights where he always emerged triumphant. She had to have faith that today would be no different. But that sick feeling would not go away.

Bianca stared into his eyes, willing her own strength into him, her own fierce will for him to triumph. For their future to bloom into vivid, solid colour at last. No greys or blacks on the horizon.

Balthazar gave her a nod, as if he read her thoughts, her desperate hopes. "After we leave here, Bianca *cara*," he said, "we should immediately steer a course for Santo Domingo."

"Santo Domingo?"

"Aye, for it is the closest town with a priest. It is past time for a wedding, wouldn't you agree?"

Before Bianca could answer, before she could even form words in her mind, the encroaching boat came to a halt just offshore. Her gaze flew between Balthazar and Diego Escobar, stepping on to the beach swathed in a black cloak, like a crow blotting out the sun. Time, which had slowed to a mere crawl as they waited, sped forth, unstoppable.

She looked back to Balthazar, a million unsaid things crowding her mind, strangling her into frantic silence. She had only seconds to tell him so much, to tell him everything, and she found she could say nothing at all.

But he seemed to know. He handed her his spyglass and pressed her hand in a lingering caress.

"Wait for me," he said. "I will come to you soon, when this is over, and I will expect an answer to my proposal then."

"You needn't wait," Bianca managed to whisper. "You know I will say yes. And yes, and yes! But…"

Balthazar shook his head, and raised her fingers to

his lips for a kiss. "Yes is all I need to hear, Bianca. I think I have been waiting years to hear you say it."

Their hands parted, and he turned away from her to greet his foe. Feeling cold and very alone, as if she was suddenly dropped from the tropical island on to a snowy, solitary plain, Bianca also turned away. She made her way, still numb, to a bare, windy hillock of sand. From there, she could watch the fight through Balthazar's spyglass, yet she would not be so near as to distract him. He needed all his attention for his sword. On defeating his enemy.

Bianca touched the hilt of her own dagger, and wished suddenly that she had his bow and arrows instead. A bow, and Balthazar's skill to use it, so she could save him as he had once saved his own brother.

But she did not. All she could do was watch. And that was maddening!

She thought she felt that flutter deep inside of her, a fleeting reminder that she was not alone. Not really. She pressed her hand to that imagined movement, and whispered, "Never fear, little one. Your papa will be here soon. You're safe."

Resolutely, she thrust away any doubt or fear, and raised the glass to her eye. Balthazar and Diego stood together now on the beach, Diego tossing aside his cloak and shirt. His black hair and beard were longer and wilder than she remembered from that night in the tavern, but the look on his gaunt face was the same. Sorrow, anger, hopelessness.

A man like that truly had naught to lose. Perhaps he even wished for death, but not more than he longed for revenge. That made him dangerous indeed.

Once, perhaps, Balthazar too was such a man. A man eaten up with the demons of his soul. But no longer. Together, they had found an end to such pain and misery, such futile rage. A way forwards at last.

But was it all much, much too late?

Balthazar raised his sword, the sunlight dancing along the polished blade. He assessed his opponent, gazing into his eyes to read that instant before he lunged forwards to attack. Every sense was heightened, every nerve taut. His blood flowed hot and fast in his veins.

Once, when he had been young, he had lived for such moments. For the danger and thrill of the fight, the clash of steel, the coppery tang of blood. It was the only time his anger and despair had an outlet, when he felt free of it at last. When he could let go of thought, of knowledge, and just feel.

Violence could no longer do that for him. Only Bianca could, holding her, making love to her. Looking into her eyes, and knowing she understood.

But he had to fight this one last battle. It was certainly one he had no heart for. When he looked at Diego now, he saw himself as he would be if he lost Bianca—adrift, cast back into that black endlessness of anger. Nay, he had no desire to kill this man, a man he once worked with, sailed with. Yet he knew he had no other choice.

Diego had no choice, either, and Balthazar saw in his eyes that he, too, meant to kill. Meant to see blood shed on this hot sand.

Balthazar finally saw that shift behind Diego's eyes, and Diego lunged forwards, his blade aimed for Balthazar's heart. Balthazar parried, his own sword flashing down to block the advance. The two blades clashed, steel scraping steel in a harsh clatter as they tangled, parted, and attacked again.

Diego was a practised swordsman, and ruthless. His time as a leader of pirates had taught him tricks and feints, but Balthazar managed to stay a step ahead of him. Just barely, though—Diego's fury seemed to grow as the fight went on. His attacks mounted in speed, in viciousness. His blade tip caught Balthazar on the arm before Balthazar could spin away.

The humid saltiness of the breeze turned to blood and sweat, the tang of human emotion. The clash of steel, faster, heavier, drowned out the surf.

Balthazar felt his muscles turning sore and stiff, his reflexes just a shade slower. They both drew more blood, but only cuts and nicks. Enough to give pain, to distract, not enough to end their struggle. The damp sand under their feet was slippery, perilously slowing every movement.

Diego gave an incoherent shout, raising his sword for a thrust to the neck. Balthazar ducked under the attack, dropping on to his free hand to deliver a counter-thrust. His sword cut into Diego's side, sending his opponent crashing to the ground. Yet still Diego fought, redoubling his attacks as if the pain only added fuel to his anger.

As Balthazar struggled to his feet, Diego's sword tip caught him at the edge of his shoulder wound from Santo Domingo. A flame of red-hot agony flashed through him, blinding him for an instant.

He sensed Diego trying to gain his own feet, and Balthazar kicked him back down, pressing his sword to the man's throat.

"Enough of this," Balthazar growled. "Our fight here solves nothing."

"You killed my wife," Diego answered, panting for breath. His eyes burned like coals as he stared up at Balthazar.

"I did not kill your wife," he said. "I tried to help her, but she was ill and there was nothing to be done. You need someone to blame, perchance, and I am the only one you can see. I am heartily sorry she is dead, that you have lost her. But killing me will never bring her back. And I have no desire to kill *you*."

A sudden gust of wind blew around them in the silence. Balthazar's whole body ached, his sweat like poison in his wounds, yet he could not drop his blade. Could not turn away from his opponent.

Balthazar said nothing to Diego that the man could not already know, deep down inside. Yet Diego stared at him as if he spoke an incomprehensible language. The fury still burned, and in a split second he launched himself to his feet with a great, primitive roar. A shout that held within it the fury of a hundred demons flying out of hell.

Balthazar fell back, his sword flashing up to meet Diego's in a clash that reverberated up his arm, into his whole body. He had felt weary, aching, but now his blood ran hot again, and his own anger flared to life.

He could be blamed for many terrible things in the world. He was surely no saint, and never had been. But he had never insulted Diego or harmed his wife. And he would not let the man take away his own future with Bianca.

He would not!

Balthazar went on the attack, meeting each vicious thrust with a flurry of motion. He deflected each blow, answering them with a greater one until at last his sword pierced Diego's shoulder.

The blade slid in and out again in only an instant, yet it was enough to send Diego crashing back to earth. And this time he did not rise again. His life's blood trickled out to blend with the sand beneath him. He stared up at Balthazar, shocked and glazed, until his eyes slid shut and he seemed not to breathe.

Balthazar looked down at him, and suddenly every pain, every ounce of aching weariness flooded back over him. The sadness was so deep and cold, tinged with the bitterness of waste and futility.

Diego had been a good enough man once, a fine navigator, even a friend. That was all gone now.

Balthazar crossed himself and turned away, leaving Diego's second to see to him.

"Balthazar!" he heard Bianca cry, and he saw her running from the hill where she watched the fight. "You're hurt."

She caught him in her arms, frantically examining his bleeding shoulder, the cuts on his arm. "Oh, *mi amor*," she muttered, dabbing at the wounds with her sleeve, her eyes clouded. "I thought you—that you were…"

"Nay," he answered. He gathered her close against him, and every pain receded before the feel of her body in his arms, the sound of her breath, the softness of her hair as the wind brushed it around his neck. She was *here*, and he was alive to hold her. They were together.

It was the loss of just such a feeling that had driven Diego to his doom, and Balthazar intended never to take it for granted. Not for a moment, not ever again.

"It does not matter, these little wounds," he said, kissing her hair. "They are nothing."

"But…"

"Come, let's go back to the *Calypso*," he said, taking her arm and turning her away from Diego. From the ruins of the past, which could hold no fears for them any longer. "I will let you tend my wounds, *cara*, and then I will tell you…"

She glanced up at him, her hand tight on his arm. "Yes, Balthazar? What will you tell me?"

"How very much I look forward to making you my wife."

Chapter Twenty-Seven

Diego slowly opened his eyes, staring up at the cloudless sky above him as his crew rowed him back towards the *Firebrand*. Every roll of the waves was agony, every word he heard like a clap of thunder in his ears. His wounds burned, but not nearly as much as the torment inside of him.

He had failed in his long quest. Not once, but twice. Balthazar Grattiano lived after being stabbed in Santo Domingo; he lived now, walking away after an honourable duel.

Diego remembered the woman running into Grattiano's arms, the dark-haired woman with the sympathetic eyes from the tavern. She held him so tenderly, as if her heart was so very full with love and hope.

Love and hope—had he, Diego, ever known that? He knew he had, with Esperanza, and those emotions were so precious he was willing now to die for them. To kill for them.

Even to live the lawless life of a pirate for them, even as his crimes put love and hope out of his reach for ever.

There was only anger and greed now. Yet still the memory of Grattiano and the woman holding on to each other so desperately haunted him.

He had to find them, to finish his task! He tried to shift on the rough boards of the boat, to shout out for them to cease rowing. But the wound in his side, crudely bandaged and sticky with his blood, sent waves of agony shooting through him. He fell back, staring again at that vast empty sky.

Suddenly, a face appeared between him and the endless hot blue. Esperanza's face, so lovely and young.

She smiled at him, and reached out to touch his cheek. The light caress felt like a sunny breeze, and Diego knew it was all an illusion. A product of pain, mayhap a sign of his approaching end. But he welcomed it all the same, just as he welcomed all those dreams of her.

The illusions were all he had left.

"I failed you again," he whispered.

She shook her head, the ends of her black hair sweeping over his wounded flesh. "You never did. You couldn't."

"But Grattiano still lives."

"Did you not hear his words?" she said. "He was not

to blame for my death. No one was. I was unlucky, but life must end for us all. I only wish we had had more time together."

"We should have had years!" Diego said, feeling that burning anger that had sustained him for so long came rushing back. "Someone must pay for that. I will find him again—"

"Nay." She laid a soft hand on his fevered brow, drawing out all the fury and leaving only weak exhaustion. Defeat. "You must let him go now, and let me go, too. That is all finished."

"Have you come to take me to death, then?" Diego muttered. He felt strangely comforted by the thought that his struggles were ended.

But Esperanza shook her head. "You have another mission here on this earth, one I cannot be a part of."

"What sort of mission? I only know piracy now."

"That was not always so. The man I loved had no villainy in his heart."

"I can't be that man without you! Without your love."

"That isn't true." Her soft touch slipped away, and he could no longer see her face. His vision was hazy, dark at the edges as if night encroached, with all its mysteries and concealments. "I can't help you with your mission now, my love. But I will always be with you."

And she was gone for ever, leaving him all alone on the pitiless sea.

Chapter Twenty-Eight

Bianca stood at her chamber window, staring down at the busy, cobbled street below. It was mid-day, and the citizens of Santo Domingo hurried on their errands. The bells of Santa Maria La Menor rang out above the tangle of shouts and cries. The gossip about Spanish contessas and pirates.

How very strange it felt, to be right back where she had started. It felt as though she had been gone for years, and this was an alien world she had never seen before.

The tavern had been in good hands with Delores, and was tidy and well kept, as prosperous as ever. Bianca thought she saw a flush of disappointment on the maidservant's face when she reappeared, but that vanished into a kind of shy pride as Delores showed her around. It seemed she had devised a new punch recipe that was quite a fine seller, and Señor de

Alameda was a great help to her, despite the end of their relationship in the bedroom. Something to do with the Spanish contessa…

Bianca thought Delores was certainly a better tavern-keeper than she herself could ever be! How happy Delores would be when Bianca left again, this time for good, as Señora Grattiano.

Bianca held out her hand, watching the light reflect on her new emerald ring, placed beside the old ruby. The sunlight turned the stone to the lush green of an island jungle, the green of Balthazar's eyes when he smiled. The green of hope, which she never thought to feel again.

She nearly laughed aloud. There on that tiny deserted island, when she held Balthazar in her arms and knew that he was truly alive, her heart seemed to open wide. That shell she had built up around it so very carefully over the years cracked wide, and she was free. In that moment, she knew joy. And when she said her vows before the altar of Santa Maria, she knew peace.

Where they would go now, what they would do, she had no idea. But for once the uncertainty did not matter. She knew what her future was. It was with Balthazar, and, in a few months, with their child.

She heard the rustle of sheets behind her, and turned to find Balthazar awake and watching her. As soon as they landed at Santo Domingo, he insisted on covering his bandages with his finest velvet doublet and going immediately to the church. Then Bianca insisted he rest.

She smiled at him, at her husband, and went to straighten the bedclothes around him. He took her hands in his, stilling her fussing movements.

"I am not an invalid, Bianca *cara*," he said, drawing her down to sit beside him on the bed.

She touched the edge of his stark white bandage. "Are you not?" she teased. "Perhaps, then, you are exaggerating your wounds so we will all fetch and carry for you."

He laughed, and kissed her as she curled against his unbandaged side. "It would be a fine ruse indeed, for I like having you all to myself. But surely *I* should be fetching for *you*."

He pressed his palm to her abdomen, and she covered his hand with hers. "So, you do know."

"I know. Even if I am a mere man, I know what it signifies when a woman is violently ill in the morning and consumes a hearty meal at noon. I heard you with that basin on the *Calypso* yesterday."

Bianca nodded. "It will pass, when I am further along and the child is bigger. You are not angry?"

"How could I be angry? We will soon be a family, the three of us. But I think…"

He paused, and Bianca frowned. What could he think that he would not speak to her about, after all that had happened? "What do you think, then?"

"If you are not too unwell, I think we should start for Spain as soon as possible. We will be ahead of the stormy season, and you can have the baby there. There are doctors, midwives."

Bianca smiled. He feared for *her*, for their child, and she thought she knew why. Diego Escobar's wife had died in childbirth here in the islands, and she remembered what the raw despair of his grief had driven him to. "I will go with you to Spain, or anywhere you choose. But you needn't fear for my health, or the baby's. We will be well."

"Do you have your mother's gift for prophecy now?" he said, cradling her close.

"Nay, I fear not. The cards are still mere pasteboard to me! Yet I feel all will be well, no matter where we go. And Delores tells me Señor de Alameda would be quite happy to see the last of Captain Grattiano and the *Calypso*. It seems you are well known as a trouble-maker throughout the islands!"

Balthazar laughed. "I fear such a reputation waits for us in Europe, too. Yet they will all find me a changed man."

"How so?"

"I am a respectable married man now, am I not? Aimlessly roving the seas no more. I must seek a new way of life."

"I hope you are not too changed," Bianca protested. "I should hate to no longer recognise my husband!"

"Then we shall not change so very much," he said, carrying her down among the tumbled pillows for a lingering kiss. A kiss that held all the burning promise of passionate years to come. "Signora Grattiano, my love. My wife."

Bianca smiled at the sound of their words, of the knowledge that the past was now truly at rest. All the anger, the pain—it was gone, burned away by the light and warmth of love. A love that would last for all their lives to come.

She did not need her mother's cards to know that. She read the truth of it in Balthazar's kiss.

Epilogue

~~~
⌒⌒⌒⌒⌒⌒
~~~

Cadiz, Three Years Later

"Shh, my dove! Papa is working, we must go in quietly," Bianca said, trying to be stern. Yet she could not help but smile, as little Maria tugged on her hand. Bianca balanced her market basket on her other hip, full of delicacies bought for Balthazar's birthday supper. Under her embroidered velvet gown, just barely visible now, could be seen the slight bump of their second child, due in the summer.

Maria bounced on her little feet, overcome with excitement to be allowed to help prepare for the banquet that night. "And may I have a candied apricot, Mama? And an almond confit?"

Bianca laughed, letting her daughter tug her along the winding, hilly cobblestone street. The city spread below them, all white and dark red in the winter sun.

She nodded to their neighbours as they passed by, Señor Garcia-Marquez the goldsmith, Señora Ortiz the silk merchant. They all smiled as they greeted Maria. Bianca knew her daughter was thought to be overly indulged by her parents, yet no one could resist her shining green eyes and sweet giggles.

"You have no need of confits, Maria *bella*," Bianca said, slightly out of breath by the time they reached the top of the steep lane. The baby certainly grew bigger now! Or perhaps Maria's unflagging energy got the better of her. "You are sweet enough already."

"Mama!" Maria cried. "You promised."

"So I did. Apricots it is, then."

"And may I stay up to watch the dancing?"

"For the first pavane, anyway." The guests would surely dance until dawn, and Bianca knew Maria would fall asleep long before that. Banquets at the Grattiano house were merry affairs indeed, with fine food, wine and music through the warm nights. Especially when there was such an event as a birthday, or a visit from her husband's brother, Señor Velazquez.

Tonight was both, and Bianca felt her heart swell with excitement to almost match Maria's. Even after these years of marriage, a dance with her husband was a great thing to look forward to.

Maria clapped her hands, and dashed towards their front door, her white silk skirts and dark curls swirling. Bianca followed slowly, her proud gaze sweeping over their house.

It was the largest dwelling on the street, set with a fine view of the harbour and the dark red tile roofs of the lower city. It was built of sturdy pale grey stone with one of those same red roofs, red-painted shutters open to the bright day. The white marble doorstep was swept and polished, a painted sign swinging above the door.

Señor Grattiano, the sign read, with an image of an unfurled map. A simple sign, but everyone knew that beyond that door was the finest cartographer in all Europe. Grattiano maps were sought by every ship's owner and captain for their great accuracy, and they paid a fine price for them.

The business prospered and grew daily, as did the Grattiano family.

Bianca followed her daughter into the house, the cool shadows of the marble-floored foyer a relief after the bustle of the market. She handed her basket to a maid-servant and removed her wide-brimmed hat, smoothing her tousled curls back into their gilded net. Despite her warnings to Maria not to disturb her father's work, she heard childish laughter echoing from down the corridor. Balthazar's deep voice answered, and Maria gave a delighted shriek.

Bianca smiled, and followed her daughter's path to the vast, high-ceilinged studio, past the winding staircase leading up to the living chambers and the rich tapestries lining the walls.

The windows were thrown open to let in the light and air, the breeze riffling the stacks of fine nautical charts. Maria sat perched on the edge of the table, chattering to her father and her uncle Marc as the dogs dashed around the floor at their feet. Childish words and masculine laughter blended with the cacophony of barks and the rustle of fine parchment.

It was like the finest music to Bianca's ears, those strains of everyday life in her own home. The delicious sight of her family, her husband and child, told her that at long last she was safe in her very own place. Exactly where she belonged.

Balthazar saw her over Maria's head, his smile widening as he held out his hand to her. She hurried to him, kissing his welcoming lips as their daughter chattered of the fine day behind them, and the even finer evening to come.

* * * * *

Enjoy an extra treat over the page with

SHIPWRECKED AND SEDUCED

A dramatic short story linked to High Seas Stowaway

First published in digital format in
Mills & Boon® Historical UNDONE!

For more short sexy stories in UNDONE!
please go to www.millsandboon.co.uk

Chapter One

〜〜〜

The Spanish Main, 1535

*S*he was going to die.

That sure knowledge should have created panic, tears, screams. But all Maria Gonzales felt was a strange, cold calm. A distance from the whole hellish scene.

The storm raged up suddenly as their ship, the *Santa Theresa,* traversed the Mona Passage, a tempestuous strait between the islands of Hispaniola and Puerto Rico. Black, boiling clouds scudded across the sky, blocking out the light and casting them into abject darkness. Wind howled from astern, shoving their mighty vessel across the waves as if it was a mere handful of kindling.

Rain pounded down; waves broke across the bow, high and strong enough to sweep a man overboard in an instant. The ship pitched and rolled like a child's toy. When the masts, denuded of their sails, snapped, leaving them entirely at the mercy of the sea, Maria knew they were doomed.

She huddled below decks, with Contessa Isabella de Valadez and her other maids, kneeling in the briny water as Father Ignacio prayed.

"Oh, Almighty and merciful God, who hast commissioned Thy angels to guide and protect us…" he cried, his voice high-pitched with panic despite the comforting words. Contessa Isabella's eyes were tightly closed, her soft fingers white as bone on the rosary beads. Her other ladies sobbed, clutching to her velvet cloak, but Maria's eyes were wide open. If these *were* her last moments, she wanted to see everything. See her end coming, death borne on a cold, silvery wave.

All she saw was the cramped hold, barrels of provisions floating in the rising water, splintered masts driving into the ship at angles. Torrents of rain pouring down on them from the cracks overhead. The howling wind drowned out the women's sobs, the priest's prayers, and all she heard was the silence in her own head.

This was not what she had hoped for when she left Seville. Her parents long dead, abandoned by the blacksmith's son she thought she loved, she'd known all that waited for her was a future as a tavern maid. Of scrubbing and fetching, of serving sweaty old men with grasping hands. A black prospect indeed.

But then, like a gift from the Virgin Herself, had come this chance to join the service of Contessa

Isabella. Isabella was going to meet her betrothed, the nephew of His Majesty's governor of the island of Cuba in the New World. A fresh chance, far away from Spain.

Maria had heard frightening tales of the islands, of course. Stories of murderous, heathen natives, bloodthirsty pirates, deadly fevers, strange foods. But surely it could not be worse than her life in Seville! In Havana, she could be someone else entirely.

The voyage went well at first. There was plenty of food, new clothes, a berth to sleep in with the other maids—and no fat old men with pinching hands. Her duties were simple enough—sewing with the contessa, helping her dress in the morning, listening to her read aloud from the lives of the saints. The contessa was young, shy, kindhearted and very, very devout.

And, unlike Maria, very afraid of what awaited her in Havana.

"I wanted so much to be a nun," she confided once to Maria, whispering to her as they strolled the deck. "But my father insisted I marry his choice. What if—oh, what if he hates me? What if I cannot bear to be so far from home?"

Maria thought it did not sound so terrible, being married to the nephew of a royal governor, mistress of her own fine household. A household that was a *real* home, not a rough garret like Maria's former lodging, or even the blacksmith's soot-stained cottage. To possess fine gowns and jewels, and never worry about being hungry.

But she just nodded to Isabella, murmuring sympathetically, and Isabella decided they were confidantes. She began to speak of the future in the islands, of Maria remaining in her household there.

None of that mattered now, with the ship tossing and twisting beneath them. They were all doomed.

Still wrapped in that strange calm, Maria gazed around at the terrified faces. Were they the last thing she would see? The stench of salt water, tar, rotting fish and acrid fear the last smell in her nose?

A cold needle of panic pierced her calm bubble, and she tangled her hands in the soft linen of her chemise. The storm had blown up so suddenly there had been no time to dress. To prepare to meet the saints Isabella loved so much.

I'm only twenty, Maria thought sadly. There should have been so much more to life.

Isabella opened her eyes, meeting Maria's stare. In her brown eyes, the same color and shape as Maria's own, there was no sadness or dread. None of the shrieking terror of the other maids. There was only exultation.

"God is calling to us, Maria," she said, holding out her hand. Her ruby betrothal ring gleamed like fresh blood on her white finger. "Can you not feel it?"

All Maria could feel was the terrible cold of the water. She shivered, and Isabella quickly swung her own velvet cloak around Maria's shoulders. She also removed her necklace, a heavy emerald cross on a gold chain, and looped it around Maria's neck.

"There is nothing to fear," Isabella said. She stood up, clad only in her own white silk chemise, and held up her arms as if to greet a lover.

At that moment, a deafening cracking noise sounded all around them, like a cannon shot. Maria clapped her hands to her ears, screaming as the ship broke up beneath them. All the terror her frozen calm had kept at bay swept over her.

They all plunged into the sea, the stormy waves sucking them down and down, into the black depths.

For an instant she could think of nothing. The water hit her like a hundred swords. But then she heard a voice in her head. Not God or the saints, but her father. A sailor who had died when she was a child.

"Never fear the water, Maria *mia,*" he said, from somewhere deep in her memory. "Work with it—make it your friend. Move through the waves, kicking your legs and moving your arms, like a frog. Let yourself just float free."

Maria wrenched herself free of the heavy cloak, kicking up toward the faint light above her head. She broke free, into the violent world of foamy waves, driving rain, the splintered wreckage of the ship.

The screams of the dying.

Gulping in a deep breath, she kept kicking, kept moving, until she could latch on to a large floating plank. She dragged herself up onto its surface, wrapping her arms tightly around its rough length, and holding on as the sea raged around her.

She felt the emerald cross press against her breastbone. "Help me," she whispered. "Please, I want to live!"

Chapter Two

Carlos de Alameda stalked along the battlements of the fortress of Santo Domingo, staring out at the night-blanketed town. All seemed peaceful now. Deceptively so, for he knew all too well how quickly the wind shifted here in the New World.

The town of Santo Domingo, a bulwark against the untamed jungle at the center of the island of Hispaniola, was built high atop a hill, to give it a natural defensive position against the enemies of Spain. The governor's fortress, the storehouse of the greatest treasure and seat of the royal government, sat at its very highest point. Built of thick gray stone, it was secure behind locked gates and guarded walkways.

But from the battlements, Carlos could see everything. Could see the dark mountains that hid the jungles; could see the river below, its muddy banks holding up the gallows. Empty for now, but surely not for long.

The terrible storm in the Mona Passage had swept all manner of vessels into Santo Domingo's sheltered port, there at the mouth of the Rio Ozama. The waters, purple-black in the night, were packed with a veritable forest of masts. And when the port was this crowded, with all sorts of men, trouble was certain to follow.

When it struck, it would be Carlos's job to fix it. To keep His Majesty's treasure, and the citizens of the town, safe from villains, thieves and liars. The dregs of the sea.

His title was merely that of assistant to Governor de Feuonmayor, but in truth he was much more. The governor was too occupied with building his grand cathedral, Santa Maria La Menor, with making Santo Domingo a beautiful, suitably Spanish city. It was Carlos who was (very) well paid to be King Charles's eyes and ears in the New World. To make sure his subjects were loyal, and the wealth of the New World made it in safety back to Spain.

It was never easy. Never less than dangerous. But he was good at it. And the secrecy of his job made it all the more effective. No one suspected that he, quiet, subdued in dress, always knew what was happening in Hispaniola and all the islands, and the marauders were always caught out in their greed and deceit.

It had not been a simple journey to move from being the son of an ancient, noble, but poor Andalusian family, of a father who was nearly completely disgraced, to this. To being a very wealthy spy, to forging a new life, a new respect for his name, in these rough islands. His mother's brother might have gotten him the assistant's position in the first place, but *he* had made more of it than it ever should have been.

And he had done it with ruthless determination. Soon enough, he would return to Spain in honor, to restore fully his family's estates and make a fine marriage. The Alamedas would rise again, and no New World pirate would stop him.

Yet he had to remain ever vigilant. Especially now, with all the flotsam the storm had driven in.

He stared down over the town, at the houses and taverns lit up in the night. He had gone earlier to Señora Montero's tavern, where all the latest gossip of Santo Domingo could always be heard. The talk was of the storm, of course, of ships lost at sea, of miraculous recoveries. Of the arrival of the near-mythical vessel the *Calypso,* and her legendary Venetian captain, Señor Grattiano.

Carlos did not believe half the tales of Grattiano, of course—legends sprang up like weeds in the fervid humidity of the islands. But as long as he kept the peace, the Venetian captain was welcome to repair his ship in the harbor.

Other vessels, though, were not so welcome. Carlos had ordered extra guards on the storehouses, extra torches along the battlements to keep the dark at bay.

The talk at the tavern was only the usual tonight, but

he was always prepared. He could have stayed longer, could have taken up Señora Montero's maid Delores on her offer of a warm bed. He had bedded Delores before, and she was a pretty, willing woman. A distraction from his job. But somehow, tonight, he could not be distracted.

There had been no word at all on the fate of the ship the *Santa Theresa*. That news only added to the taut sense that something was afoot out there in the darkness. Something was about to happen.

Carlos reached for his spyglass, focusing it on the port below. All afternoon, the decks had been crawling with activity. Now they were silent, as all their crews had come ashore to find comfort and pleasure after the storm's travails.

But one ship, the *Reyezuelo,* still burned torches along its deck. Her captain had not yet been to the fortress to present his credentials. What was happening there?

"Señor de Alameda," a voice said from the doorway.

Carlos turned to see one of the servants watching him timidly. They all knew better than to interrupt his rounds on the battlements, except for matters of great import. "What is it?"

"Governor de Feuonmayor begs that you come down to the great hall, señor. There are some—interesting visitors, and he seeks your assistance."

Carlos nodded shortly. Was this, then, the trouble he was expecting tonight? He set aside his spyglass, following the man down the narrow, torchlit stairs and into the main wing of the fortress.

Despite the fine tapestries on the stone walls, the carved chests and tables from Spain, there was no disguising the martial nature of the building. There were few windows piercing the thick walls, no warm light in the chilly air. No softening feminine laughter. But Carlos liked it well enough. It gave the illusion of strength and security, which served his task better than a fine palace ever could.

And if he sometimes missed that gentle laughter, the scent of flowered perfume—well, that was the price he paid.

He hurried into the grand hall, a vast space hung with the king's standard along with an arsenal of weapons. The hall was sometimes used for receptions and banquets, but tonight the tables and silver-laden buffets were pushed back against the walls. The only people gathered there were the governor and a few of his servants, along with three men clad in sailor's garb.

And a woman, laid out on a stretcher made from canvas sail.

Carlos frowned as he moved closer to the silent group. The woman appeared to be dead. She was very pale, her skin a translucent white against her tangled dark hair. She wore only a stained and torn white chemise—and a heavy emerald cross on a gold chain.

He examined her more closely. That cross was a finely crafted and very expensive piece, and the woman who wore it seemed quite young. Her skin was smooth and unblemished, her brows like wren's wings against her marble brow.

Such a great pity, for one so young and pretty to be gone, he thought. But why was she here?

Then he saw the gentle rise of her breath beneath the tattered chemise, the faint beat of her pulse in the vulnerable hollow at the base of her neck.

"What is this?" Carlos asked, glancing sharply at the governor, the sailors.

Feuonmayor, clad in his fine brocade dressing gown, had obviously just been rousted from his bed and did not quite know what to do. He shrugged. "These men are from the *Reyezuelo*."

Carlos looked to the tallest of the strange men, his brow raised in question. The sailor hastily bowed and said, "We beg your pardon, señor, for interrupting your rest. But we thought we should bring the lady to you at once."

"And just who is the lady?" Carlos asked.

"We don't know. We rode the storm out at anchorage near the island of San Pedro, señor. After the weather cleared, we made for Santo Domingo to make our repairs. That's when we found her."

"Found her?" Carlos said. "What, just floating about in midair?"

"Near that, señor," one of the other sailors said. "She was on the water, holding on to a plank. We hauled her aboard, but she was only awake long enough to tell us she was on the *Santa Theresa* and it went down in the storm."

"The *Santa Theresa?*" Feuonmayor cried. "Alameda, do you think that means…"

Carlos held up his hand for silence, and even the governor obeyed. "Did you find anyone else?"

The sailor shook his head. "She said everyone else was dead."

The governor shook his head sadly. "It was a blessing that even one was saved. Especially if she is…"

His voice trailed away as Carlos frowned, staring down at the pale lady. "We should send word to Havana, to Governor Augusto," he said. He reached out to touch the cross with one fingertip. Her breath stirred beneath him, and he found that she was warm with life. Vibrant with the miracle of her survival on the stormy sea.

Quite against his will, he was moved by the thought of what she must have suffered.

"Surely it *is* her," Feuonmayor murmured. "Look at that jewel."

Carlos nodded, gently lifting the heavy cross to examine its blue-green depths. The lady moaned in her sleep, turning away from him as her tangled brown hair obscured her face. "We should not be too hasty, I think. We must hear her story."

"We knew she was important, señor," the sailor said quickly. "So we brought her to you as soon as we made port. We took the best care of her, I promise you."

"And you will get your reward, never fear," Carlos said. He replaced the cross on her breastbone. Beneath the torn chemise she was very thin, her collarbone and shoulders almost sharp beneath the pale skin. Strange, if she was who they thought. A pampered contessa.

"Summon more servants, and the surgeon," he told Feuonmayor. "She should be taken at once to a chamber and looked after. I am sure Governor Augusto would far prefer to be presented with her alive."

The servants scurried to do his bidding, carrying the lady away as he paid off the sailors and warned the governor and his lackeys to say nothing yet about their new houseguest.

By the time Carlos finished his business and made his way to the woman's chamber, she was dressed in a clean chemise and tucked into bed by the maidservants.

It was one of the fortress's finest rooms, a bower of red and gold hangings usually reserved for visiting grandees. The young woman seemed a bit lost in the midst of the vast bed, but her eyes were open at last. She held a silver goblet tightly between her hands as one of the maids brushed and braided her hair.

She stared down into the dark red depths of the wine, as if she hoped to read something writ there. An answer to some perplexing puzzle.

Carlos knew the feeling very well.

"Señorita," he said gently, slowly approaching the bed. There seemed something delicate about her, as if she was a bird poised to plunge into flight at the slightest sound.

She looked up at him, and he suddenly felt as if *he* was the one pushed off a precipice into open air. Her eyes were large and very dark, almost black in the candlelight, limned in purplish shadows. Shining as purest onyx, they watched him steadily, as if she could read him, his thoughts and motives, while giving nothing away.

It was a look he was wont to give others, quiet and even, and had never received himself. As she watched him, it was almost as if…

As if he stared into a mirror, at the other half of himself.

Then she gazed back down into the wine, and the spell was snapped. Carlos nearly fell back half a step from the force of that connection, but he remained still by sheer force of will. Remained still, and watched her.

"Buenas noches," she whispered, her voice low and rough from all the salt water she must have swallowed.

"The surgeon will soon be here," he said. "I hope you are comfortable in this chamber?"

She glanced up, her gaze taking in the opulent velvet hangings, the tapestries on the walls, the carved bed and chests. "It will suffice for now."

Carlos smiled inwardly, keeping his expression carefully neutral. Ah, so she *must* be a contessa. A fine lady straight from Spain, disdaining the best of the colonies. Or else she was almost as good an actor as himself.

"I am Señor de Alameda, aid to Governor de Feuonmayor," he said. "Please tell me of anything that will add to your comfort—Contessa de Valadez."

One of her brows twitched, but she merely nodded, taking a sip of her wine. "Thank you, señor. All I desire now is sleep."

"Of course." Carlos gestured to the maids, dismissing them. "I hope you will feel up to dining with me tomorrow, contessa. I am sure we have—much to discuss."

She nodded shortly, leaning back against the embroidered bolsters. Carlos gave her another bow before leaving her to her rest.

Sí—they would have much to discuss indeed.

Chapter Three

Maria did not know what had made her say she was Isabella. A fit of madness, perhaps. A brain fever brought on by floating alone on the sea for too long.

No, that was not it. It was that man, that Señor de Alameda, and the force of his dark, steady stare. The polite smile and courtly bow that lay so thinly over a watchful intensity. He had said he was an aide to the governor, but she would wager he was more than that.

Much more.

Maria slid down under the fine bedclothes as the maidservants tucked the linen sheets and velvet counterpane around her. She closed her eyes, drifting in warm lassitude brought on by the wine, by her long voyage and near death. She listened to their soft whispers, like the sound of a dream.

That was yet another reason to be Isabella, even if only for a short while. Maria *liked* being looked after, being waited on and pampered and bowed to. She liked the maids brushing her hair, bringing her spiced wine and cakes. After years of bowing to others, it felt—wondrous.

And having once implied to Señor de Alameda that she was Isabella, she did not want to admit to him she had lied. He didn't look like a man who would easily submit to being deceived.

What harm will it do? she thought, stroking the embroidered edge of the sheet. Isabella was gone, and she would not have minded anyway. She had been kind-hearted. Surely there was no harm in pretending, just for a few days. Just until Maria felt strong and healthy again, until she could devise what to do next.

With her eyes closed, there in the darkness she saw Señor de Alameda's face. He was a handsome man, perhaps the most handsome man she had ever seen. Tall, lean-hipped and wide shouldered beneath his fine, somber black-and-white clothes, not a pale and puffy officiant who spent his whole life signing documents and eating rich food.

He was not old, but not incredibly young either. His clean-shaven face was tinged with bronze by the island sun, all harsh angles of sharp cheekbones and jaw, softened only a fraction by his shoulder-length black hair. His eyes were dark, too, deep-set, burning bright as a night star. Seeing everything.

Nay, he was surely not some mere functionary! Was he perhaps an agent of the Inquisition? Maria had heard terrible whispers that they were everywhere, even in this far outpost of the Spanish Empire. She would have to be very, very careful around him, and play her part well.

It was a good thing she had spent so much time with Isabella on the journey, and studied her manners closely. A woman in Maria's position who wanted to rise in the world, to attend on a fine lady, had to be refined herself. And Maria was a quick student.

She would need all those lessons here, she thought as she drifted into sleep, cradled by the fine, comfortable bed. Particularly around Alameda…

Carlos heard her cries in the night, screams of abject terror. He was a light sleeper, and the contessa's chamber was right next to his—all the better for keeping an eye on her.

He was out of bed in an instant, pausing only to draw a robe over his nakedness and light a candle before hurrying to her room.

Moonlight fell from the narrow window, streaming over the bed. Its rich hangings were drawn back in the warm night, and he saw her tossing and turning in the tangled sheets, her eyes still closed in sleep. She cried out again, her fists flailing as if to fight back the stormy sea.

Carlos rushed to the bed, leaving his candle on the table. "Hush, señorita," he murmured, gently reaching for her. He knew better than to startle awake someone caught in a nightmare. "You are safe now."

At his touch she quieted, but her brow was still

creased. Carlos cradled her close to his chest, rocking her back and forth as he muttered nonsense to her. She curled against him, her head on his shoulder.

She smelled of rose-scented bathwater, of wine and clean linen, but also of salt water and sun, hot, carnal scents that carried the faint memory of all she had suffered. Of the very essence of her.

As she lay so close to him, he felt again how small she was, how slim. And yet she had survived the terrible storm when no one else on her ship had. She must possess great inner strength, he thought, to perform such a feat.

She sighed in his arms, shuddering as if her nightmare still held her in its grip, and she slid even closer to him. Her thin chemise draped from one shoulder, and he saw that not *all* of her was too thin. Her breasts were full and sweet, pale mounds crowned with tempting, strawberry-colored nipples. Soft and round, perfectly designed for a man's touch, for his mouth.

What would she taste like? he wondered, staring down at her bared bosom. What would she feel like against his lips and tongue, her cries turned to heady desire, her pale hands tangled in his hair as she urged him ever closer…

His body hardened at the alluring vision, his blood running suddenly hot in his veins. *Maldición,* but he should have stayed tonight with Delores after all! He had been working too much of late, had been too long without a woman's comforts.

It could not be the lovely contessa who "comforted" him. He laid her gently back against the pillows, drawing her chemise up to cover her breast, her delicate shoulders.

As he tucked the sheets around her, her eyes opened. For an instant, they were distant, unfocused, as if the dream still held her. Then she saw him, and they widened with alarm.

"Oh!" she gasped, clutching at the bedclothes.

"You cried out," he said quietly, drawing the heavy folds of his brocade robe closer over his iron-hard erection. It would never do to alarm her even further. "Were you having a nightmare?"

"I—yes, I think so," she murmured, rubbing her hand over her brow as if to erase the bad images. "I am sorry, I did not mean to wake you."

"I'm a light sleeper," he said. "It serves me well when Santo Domingo is under alarm—or when a lady calls out."

A whisper of a smile touched her lips. They were nearly the same strawberry-red as her nipples, he noticed, then immediately turned his stare away from them.

"You must be close, then," she said. "Or else I must be very loud."

"My chamber is just down the corridor," he answered. He noticed the ewer and goblets the maids had left on the table. "Would you care for some wine, contessa?"

She nodded. "*Gracias,*" she said, watching him as

he went to pour out the wine. "You are close so you can keep watch on your guests?"

He gave her a wary smile. "In a manner of speaking. Santo Domingo can be a most unpredictable place. It is my task to make sure the fortress, and all who inhabit it, are safe."

"A difficult task, indeed. But I have no doubt you are equal to it, señor."

"Such touching faith in someone you just met, contessa."

"Oh, I have tasks of my own. One of them is to observe people. And you, I can tell, would be a formidable foe."

Carlos remembered the men in Spain who had once thought to destroy his father, to ruin the ancient Alameda name. Now it was *their* family names that lay in tatters. He remembered men he had faced in battle, the flash of swords, the clash of steel on steel, the harsh smell of blood.

Then he glanced down at the lady on the bed, who watched him closely with her soft brown eyes.

"I can be a formidable foe, yes," he said. "But I can also be a strong friend. I hope you know, contessa, that I want only to be your friend."

He handed her a goblet, and held his own up in a toast. "To your miraculous rescue, and continued good health."

She sipped at her wine, her gaze at last dropping away. "It was indeed a miraculous rescue," she said.

"I thought surely help would never come, that I would die there alone."

Carlos sat beside her on the bed, far enough that he would not scare her. Would not be tempted to leer at her bosom again. "Was that what you dreamed of tonight? The storm?"

Far from being uneasy at his nearness, she edged even closer. She seemed to take some comfort in not being alone in the depths of the night. "Yes. The thunder, the crash of waves—the terrible sound as the ship broke up. How very cold the water was." She shivered and took another long drink of the wine. "Will I ever forget it?"

"I don't believe we ever entirely forget the bad things that happen to us," he said. "But time will mute them. New, better memories will cover them."

"Have you found it so in your own life?"

"Yes," he lied. "And while you are our guest in Santo Domingo, we shall have to help you start making those new memories."

She laughed suddenly, and he was startled by the bright, rich sound of it, like cathedral bells. Brief as her laughter was, it hinted of a sensual delight beneath. "This fine, comfortable bed is a good start! And the fine company."

She glanced up at him from beneath her lashes, her laughter fading, and for an instant he had the wild fancy she would ask him to join her in that "comfortable" bed. Her gaze slid to his lips, to the bare V of chest revealed by his robe. Heat seemed to follow in the wake of her gaze, a sizzling tension between them.

Then she turned her head away, silently holding out her goblet for more wine. He exchanged it for his own, almost full vessel. He seldom drank much wine—his work required a clear head.

She drank deeply, pressing her lips to the very spot where his had been, and he found his head was anything but clear around *her*.

"Perhaps we could arrange a small banquet," he said tightly.

A ripple of something like alarm passed over her face. "A banquet?"

"Nothing too grand," he said. "Santo Domingo is not like the court at Seville, of course, but the local dignitaries will want the chance to welcome you to the islands. To wear their finest clothes again."

"I have no fine clothes," she murmured. "I fear they would find me—dull."

"When you carry the latest news from Spain? Never." He couldn't help but sense that there was more to her hesitation than lack of gowns, or even ladylike shyness. Most interesting indeed. "And you must not worry about your lost trousseau, contessa. We don't have the most current fashions here, I fear, but we can find something suitable for you. Once you have recovered, of course."

She nodded, her eyelids heavy, and he saw that her goblet was again empty. He reached out to take it from her, and she suddenly clutched at his hand. Her slender fingers were cold.

"You are too kind to me, señor," she whispered.

"You certainly deserve some kindness now, contessa, after your ordeal." He raised her hand to his lips, pressing a kiss to her fingers, her wrist. The skin was white, but it was crisscrossed with cuts and scrapes from the storm. A strange, slight roughness marred her fingertips, the base of her palm. "You must rest now, and recover your health. Can you sleep?"

She nodded, lying back as he smoothed the bed-clothes around her. *"Gracias, Señor de Alameda,"* she whispered, her eyes drifting shut.

Once he was sure she slept quietly, Carlos left the candle burning on the table, returning to his own chamber in the dark. His body was still taut with desire for the contessa, but lust was overlaid with something cooler—suspicion.

The contessa held secrets, he was sure of it. And he would soon find out exactly what they were.

Chapter Four

Maria stared into the wavery looking glass as one of the maids laced up her gown, the words of the page resounding in her head.

Señor de Alameda asks that you dine with him this evening, contessa, if your health permits you.

What could she do but agree? Even if everything in her screamed at her to hide from him. To stay as far from him as possible. Not because he frightened her or repulsed her.

Quite the opposite.

After their long talk last night, wrapped in the warm intimacy of silent darkness, she could not stop thinking about him. Thinking about his deep, gentle voice, his touch, that fleeting glimpse of his muscled chest in the candlelight.

The way he seemed to see so very much when he looked at her. Too much.

It was easy to hide from the servants. She had been one of them for a long time—she knew how their world worked. She merely stayed quiet, maintained a distant, vague mien—not difficult when she was still so very cursed tired. They saw a properly haughty, ladylike noblewoman.

But Maria knew Alameda would not be so easily taken in. He obviously knew the ways of nobility, knew people. It was why she had suspected, nay, *still* suspected him of being a spy. If she wanted to keep up this charade—and she had to, if she wanted to avoid going back to scrubbing tavern floors—she would have to be very, very careful around him.

She had to be strong, to keep from throwing herself at his feet to beg for mercy. Or to keep from leaping into his lap and begging him to kiss her.

Maria frowned at her reflection. Most men she had met were hairy, smelly creatures, grabbing for her with their sweaty fingers. She *never* wanted their kisses! But with Carlos de Alameda, she found herself staring enraptured at his smooth golden skin. Longing to touch that skin, to feel its warmth against her hand, taste it. Be close, ever closer, to him.

"Is the gown not to your liking, contessa?" the maid said.

"I beg your pardon?" Maria said, still far away in her thoughts—with Alameda. She forced herself back to the present, to reality, and really studied herself in the looking glass.

For an instant she did not recognize herself. The gown was finer than anything she had ever worn, dark green velvet embroidered with silver, over a petticoat of silver tissue. The low, square neckline was trimmed with tiny, green-gray beads in a looping, intricate pattern of leaves and flowers.

Her hair, smooth and shining again after being matted and tangled with salt water, was brushed back and bound with a pearl band and sheer silver veil. Isabella's emerald cross was clasped at her throat, a heavy reminder of her dangerous deception.

She touched the necklace, full of wonder at the sight of her new self. She longed to twirl around and around, to grab the maid in an exuberant hug and shout, "I *love* this gown!" But that cross was also a reminder to be always cautious, so she merely nodded.

"It is quite satisfactory," she murmured.

"I'm sure it's quite behind the fashion in Spain," the maid said anxiously.

In Spain, Maria had been too busy keeping her skirt out of the slop water to worry about whether it was in fashion. But she remembered watching fine carriages roll past on the cobbled streets, and craning her neck for a glimpse of their equally fine inhabitants.

"The neckline is lower," she said. "And the sleeves too narrow. But the color is good."

The maid gave her a relieved smile, smoothing a fold of the skirt. "The fabric is from France, contessa. From Señor de Alameda's private store."

"His private store?" Maria examined the beadwork on the bodice. He must be a well-paid spy, then, she mused.

What kind of payment would he receive for handing over a maidservant masquerading as a contessa?

"*Sí*," the maid said. "And he said you are to tell us if you require anything else. I can fetch it for you, contessa."

Maria could tell that the girl was eager for a glimpse into that "private store." Or perhaps Alameda had already made her a gift from it? She was pretty, and he seemed most virile indeed.

She felt a sour pang of jealousy at the thought, and she turned away. "I will need a gown more suitable for the day," she said. "And for the warm weather."

"Of course, contessa," the too-pretty maid said, curtsying.

Maria had no more time to ponder Alameda's sex life, for the page arrived to lead her to supper. Moving at the slow, dignified pace she considered suitable to a contessa, she followed him through the narrow, twisting corridors.

Even though the stone walls were covered by the finest of tapestries, depicting feasts and royal hunts in rich colors, and bright torches burned in ornate sconces, it was obvious that this was a fortress built for defense. Not a fine palace made for luxury and ease. The soles of her new velvet shoes echoed on the cold flagstone floor, the only sound except for the crackle of the torches, the rustle of the page's livery.

But was that a cry she heard from far away? Deep down in secret dungeons? Or was it just the wind from the sea, rushing around the battlements?

She wondered how many prisoners had been led here, frozen with fear. How many had faced the piercing gaze of Señor de Alameda and confessed all, only to be led away to torture and punishment.

"This way, contessa," the page said, his voice making her jump.

Maria laughed nervously. "So many twists and turns! How do you ever remember the way?"

"'Tis easy," the boy said proudly. "Once you've lost your way a time or two, you'll remember."

"I'm sure I never shall," Maria answered. "I will just wander and wander…"

"Then I will just have to mount a search party to find you," Alameda said as they suddenly turned a corner to find him waiting.

"Oh!" Maria gasped, falling back a step. How quickly he always seemed to appear, when she least expected him!

She gazed around at the small chamber. She had half-expected a banquet of sorts, with the governor and his attendants waiting on the contessa. But the table was set only for two, a small expanse draped with fine white damask and placed next to a half-open window. The setting sun, a brilliant swath of pink and orange and gold, gleamed on fine silver plate. Two high-backed chairs, soft with satin cushions, sat at either end.

Somehow, the intimate scene was far more frightening than any etiquette-laden banquet could have been.

Maria stood very still, staring at the small, luxurious table that seemed ringed with traps.

"I hope you are not offended, contessa," Alameda said, all smooth, bland, courtly politeness. "The governor would have liked to dine with you himself, but I feared you would still be too tired after your ordeal. He is organizing an entertainment for next week, so I persuaded him a quiet meal would be best tonight."

"You are most considerate, Señor de Alameda," she answered.

He held out his arm, again clad in black-and-white velvet, and she laid her hand lightly atop it. His muscles coiled under her touch, lean and powerful, and she remembered the way his bare skin had looked beneath that somber fabric.

She swallowed, resolutely facing forward as he escorted her to her seat. She perched carefully on the edge of the cushion, studying the chamber while he took his own chair. Avoiding looking directly at him, at his steady stare, for as long as possible.

It was as finely furnished as the rest of the fortress, with carved Spanish tables and X-backed chairs, the window shuttered and draped with velvet, now looped off to one side with gilt cords. But it was obviously a room meant for work, with a sturdy table piled with documents and small travel chests, valuable leather-bound books. It smelled of vellum, of salt breezes and strange, sweet island flowers.

And of the roasted beef dressed in orange sauce a servant carried in and placed on the table. This was followed by a parade of more fine dishes—vegetables in almond sauce, stewed fish, glazed beef, platters of fruit and tiny sweet cakes.

Maria laughed as Alameda poured a fine golden wine into her jewel-studded goblet. "It appears you were expecting *fifty* guests, señor! I could never eat all of this in a year."

He smiled at her, a beautiful, rare white smile that made her feel terribly warm inside. A warm glow that had naught to do with the wine.

"I was not sure what would tempt your appetite," he said.

She gave him a smile, too, a teasing one. "Do you think I have a delicate appetite?"

"You are too thin, contessa," he said. "Perhaps some fish in rosemary and ginger sauce will appeal to you."

Maria self-consciously slid her too-thin wrists back into her sleeves, staring avidly at the luscious-smelling delicacies the servant was ladling onto her fine plate. "The journey was quite long, and I fear I am not a good sailor," she said, not mentioning the long months *before* the journey of living on bread crusts and rinds of cheese. "This is a most fine repast. Surely as fine as anything to be found in Spain."

"Are you surprised?"

"Perhaps just a bit." She took a nibble of the fish, nearly sighing with pleasure. It had been too long since she had had a meal of any kind, let alone one so wondrously delicious. She had to restrain herself from pouring it all into her mouth.

"We like our pleasures here as well as in Seville," he said, watching her over the rim of his goblet. "Perhaps more so."

Maria glanced out the window, at the town sloping down to the river and the port. In the dying sunlight, the yellow stone and dull red brick of the buildings glowed. The flower-tinged breeze was light and cool.

"Santo Domingo seems a pleasant place," she said. "Not at all lacking in—pleasures."

"I am very glad you think so," he answered. "Governor de Feuonmayor has written to Governor Augusto to inform him of your happy survival. Once he arrives, and your marriage to his nephew secured, you should have many happy years ahead in the New World."

The fruit she had just consumed suddenly tasted like ashes in her mouth. "So suddenly?"

"It will be some time before they can receive the message and respond," he said. "The governor thought it best to inform them at once."

Maria stared down at her plate. How much time, then, would she have as Isabella?

To be with Carlos de Alameda.

"Are you not filled with the joy of anticipation to see your betrothed at last?" he said.

"I do not know him," she answered quietly. "I do not even know his name. Isa—that is, my father only called him 'Señor de Augusto's nephew.'"

"I suppose your family arranged the match with no consultation."

Maria nodded, remembering Isabella's trepidation at the thought of marriage, far deeper than normal maidenly fears. Her ardent desire to be a nun. Well, Isabella was a true bride of Christ now. But Maria had never craved the veil.

Nor had she ever craved marriage, or the lustful touch of a mortal husband's hand. Not until now.

Her gaze slid across the table to where Carlos's hand rested, adorned with a gold-and-sapphire ring on his smallest finger. His fingers were long, elegant, as golden as the rest of him. She imagined them against her bare leg, sliding higher and higher, delicious friction against her skin…

"Are you quite well, contessa?" he asked.

Maria blinked. "I—yes, of course."

"Your cheeks were very pink suddenly."

"It must be the wine."

"Then you should have more," he said, refilling her goblet. "You look quite pretty with pink cheeks."

Maria smiled, absurdly pleased. "The island breeze must be restoring my health."

"I am happy it restores something, then. Mostly it just—takes away."

She gave him a curious glance, but he did not seem

inclined to elaborate. She turned her attention to the room, illuminated now by candelabra the servants lit as the sun sank below the horizon.

"This is quite a fine chamber," she said.

"It is my own library," he answered. "I often dine here alone, but I seldom entertain. The decorations are not grand enough for you, I fear."

"On the contrary," she said. "If you seldom invite people here, I am honored."

She nibbled at a sugar wafer, examining the documents piled on the table with their heavy seals. Surely there was so much secret information concealed there.

"Tell me about Santo Domingo, Señor de Alameda," she said. "How did you come to be here?"

"Why does anyone come here?" he said, pouring more wine for her. "To serve the king. To bring honor to our names."

"And a bit of gold to add luster to that honor?" she teased. Then she nearly clapped her hand to her mouth. A contessa would never *tease* a gentleman! She had imbibed too freely of that fine wine.

But he laughed. "Gold is an honor unto itself."

"Yet do you not find worth in the place itself?" She gestured out the window, toward the town shimmering under the moonlight. "It is so beautiful."

"More beautiful than the palaces of Spain?"

Maria stared at the river, purple-black and mysterious. "The palaces of Spain are not *beautiful*," she murmured. "They are grand but cold. But this—this lives. It is real and warm, and ready for anyone who has the courage to reach out and clasp it. Make it their own."

A place for new beginnings. At least until Governor Augusto and his nephew arrived.

Maria suddenly became aware of the silence in the room, of Alameda's stillness. She stiffened in her seat, slowly turning to face him.

He stared at her with those unreadable eyes, black as the river. He frowned as if he had never seen her before, could not quite fathom who or what she was.

Maria wasn't quite sure herself.

He stood, holding out his hand to her. "Would you care to walk on the battlements, if you are not too tired, contessa?" he said. "There is a fine view of the town from there."

She slid her fingers into his, letting him help her to rise. His touch was so warm and strong on hers, and rather than back away and politely offer his arm, he held her hand as he led her out of the library and back along the winding corridors. They were the same chilly halls as before, a silent, echoing prison, but with him they were somehow transformed. His touch held her aloft, far above the cold stones.

She had never felt *safe* with a man before; men were a foe to hide from. And she knew very well that in truth her life had never been less safe, but for the moment she did not care. She wanted only this one moment with this strong, mysterious, exciting man.

He gave her an enticing smile, helping her up a narrow, twisting flight of stairs. Maria had the sudden, whimsical thought that all the priests were wrong—demons lured unsuspecting humans *up* to hell, not down.

They went through a doorway, emerging into the night itself.

"How glorious," Maria breathed, staring up at the rich, sparkling swath of stars in the dusty-black sky. It seemed the warm, flower-scented breeze brushed them into a shimmering blur. They swept all the way down to the water, touching the roofs, the spire of the fine new cathedral.

She rushed to the crenellations, leaning her elbows on the rough stones as she stared down at the walkways below, enraptured. The flickering lights of the town sparkled, and she could now hear laughter and music. *Life.*

After the terrible storm, the certainty of doom, that life was intoxicating. She wanted to reach out for it, to gather it close to herself and never, ever let it go.

"Be careful!" Carlos said, and she felt his arms around her waist, pulling her back from the rocky edge.

She spun around in his embrace, wrapping her arms tightly around his neck. He, too, seemed part of the night, with his glossy dark hair, his shining eyes. So beautiful and enticing.

She entwined her fingers in his hair, the rough silk of it clinging to her skin. "Surely you see the beauty of it now?" she said.

"I do," he answered hoarsely. "*Diablos al demonio*, but I do!"

And his mouth came down on hers, with the glorious, inevitable force of the waves against the shore. As if their kiss was meant to be since the moment she opened her eyes and saw him standing there across the bedchamber.

She met him with her own fierce ardor, her lips open to the thrust of his tongue. He tasted of wine and spices, of the salt breeze. Of something dark and rich that was him alone. His arms came around her tightly, roughly, and he dragged her up against his lean, hard body. The primitive strength of him sheathed in finest velvet.

Maybe it was all the wine she had drunk, coming so close to death—the tension of her deception. Or maybe it was *him*, the way he felt and looked, the way he smelled so delicious. The secrets in his eyes. An overpowering wave of lust washed over her, making her hot and cold all at once.

She never wanted to let go.

For an instant his arms tensed around her, and she felt a flare of panic that he would push her away. She held on even tighter, pressing her body so tightly to his that nothing could come between them.

He groaned against her mouth, a deep sound of profound longing that reverberated in her own heart.

Through the silvery haze of desire she felt him move her backward until she was pressed against the rough stone wall. Their kiss made everything so blurry, so hot and unreal. So desperate that nothing else mattered. She was not Maria or Isabella—she was just a woman who wanted, needed one man beyond anything.

And he wanted her. She felt it in the press of his erection through her skirts, in the way his hands skimmed roughly over her shoulders, over the bare skin above her bodice.

She moaned as his caress rubbed against her sensitive nipples, as his fingers brushed the swell of her breasts. His touch moved slowly back and forth, stoking the flames of her need ever higher. He seemed to know exactly how to make her writhe, how to touch, kiss, lick....

"Oh!" she cried out as the tip of his tongue found that tiny, sensitive spot just below her ear. His breath was soft, warm against her skin, the rush of it even more intoxicating than the fine wine.

Her head fell back against the wall, her eyes tightly shut as his lips trailed along her throat, the line of her shoulder. In that dark, hot place she felt his hand reach for her skirt, dragging it up and up until his touch brushed her bare leg, just above her gartered stocking.

He lightly skimmed the sensitive skin of her inner thigh, the curve where it met her hip. And, ever so briefly, his knuckle swept over her damp curls.

Maria moaned involuntarily, bracing herself against the wall to wrap her legs around his hips. Her skirts fell back, foaming around them as they twined together.

His lips pressed again to her neck, open, wet, enticing. He licked at the pulse beating in that hollow at its base, the hot rush of life that pounded within her. She had *never* felt so alive before, so full of joy and wonder and sheer need! There would surely be a terrible price later, once cold reality and reason set in, yet it was one she was most willing to pay.

Aye, she was willing to pay anything, if he would just kiss her *there* again.

He bit lightly at the curve of her shoulder, then touched it with the tip of his tongue to soothe the sting. She tightened her legs around him as his kiss slid lower and lower. He tasted the hollow between her breasts, pressed his lips to her heartbeat.

Maria tangled her fingers in his silken hair, arching her back to push herself closer to him. To his oh-so-talented mouth.

But he teased her, leaving a burning-bright ribbon of kisses on her skin. Light, fleeting, his kisses skimmed over the swells of her breast, her shoulders. One hand braced them against the wall, while the other coiled around her naked thigh, holding her wrapped around him.

She cried out, incoherent begging words, until at last he gave her what she longed for. He pulled her bodice down in one smooth movement, and his mouth closed over her aching nipple. Hot and wet, delicious.

That tight core of need inside her tightened, coiling closer and closer until she feared she would faint of it.

"You taste of strawberries," he muttered against her breast. He rested his head against her shoulder, breathing in deeply as if to gain control over himself. Over their insane situation.

But she did not want him to gain control! She wanted him to spin free into chaos with her, to make the very most of this magical moment out of time. This second chance at life.

Her fingers in his hair, she drew him back up to meet her lips, her kiss. She put all she had into that kiss, every fiber of her intense desire for this mysterious man, every shred of the newfound glory of being alive. She tried desperately to weave a glittering net of sexual need so tightly around them that neither of them could escape.

He groaned, his tongue meeting hers with an answering need. A wild desperation, like a primal force unleashed from the tight control she sensed he usually held on his emotions. His caress was rough and needful as it swept over her bare breasts, rolling her nipple between his fingers, plumping and lifting it in his hand. It was frightening, overwhelming…

And so wondrously exhilarating.

Through the enveloping cloud of desire, she felt his touch ease away from her. He lowered her legs back to the floor until she stood again on her own feet, and he tugged her bodice up to cover her bosom.

Maria murmured a protest against his lips, trying to hold on to him, to not let him escape.

But he backed away from their kiss, pressing his finger to her lips. She opened her eyes to find him staring at her. His eyes were very black, opaque, his hair tangled from her touch.

"Shh," he whispered roughly. "We can't do this here."

Before Maria could answer, before she could even begin to think coherently, he seized her hand in his and led her from the battlements.

They went back down the narrow staircase, traversing the same corridors as before. Yet where before Maria had found them cold and forbidding, a lurking prison, now they seemed as warm and inviting as a summer's day. A maze leading her onward, inward, to new wonders. And she was led on that journey by a man who had to be a magician, a sorcerer. For no mortal man could possess such delights, such sensual powers.

And she was under his spell indeed. She had been ever since she first saw him.

Carlos opened a door, gesturing toward it gallantly. His clasp on her hand was light, as if to give her the chance to flee. To not enter that portal, beyond which nothing could be the same.

But Maria knew very well that it was too late to run. Too late to turn back. For good or ill, she sensed that this moment was her destiny, and she had been moving toward it ever since she left Spain.

She stepped through the door.

It was his bedchamber, a slightly smaller version of hers. More books and papers were piled on the tables, showing that he was always working, even in the quiet of the night. The bed and window were draped and covered with black and gold velvet, as if the chamber was swathed in the night itself.

But she scarcely had time to take it all in. He shut the door behind her, a soft click that reverberated with finality. She, they, had made their choice. There was no going back from that moment.

Her heart pounded erratically, the rush of it so loud in her ears that she was sure the whole island must hear it. She closed her eyes as she felt him move behind her, the heat of his body reaching out to curl all around her.

He unlaced the back of her bodice, his touch light and quick as he peeled the rich fabric away. Then he released the fastenings of her overskirt and petticoats, dropping the armor of brocade and velvet from her body until she stood in just her thin chemise and her stockings.

She squeezed her eyes shut even tighter, taut with anticipation, hardly daring to breathe. He removed her headdress, freeing her hair to fall loose down her back. She shivered as he swept the length of it over her shoulder, pressing a kiss to the nape of her neck.

His tongue trailed slowly along the arc of her spine, his hands easing away the last covering of her chemise to make way for his stroking touch. For his kiss. As the linen pooled around her feet, leaving her bare to him, the tip of his tongue pressed to the small of her back, swirling lightly. His fingers trailed over her buttocks, curling over her hip.

One fingertip slid inside her, finding her damp core and pressing hard, and she cried out at the wave of intense pleasure. Intense vulnerability. She tried to step away, but he would not let her. His clasp tightened on her hips, spinning her around to face him.

"Open your eyes," he said hoarsely. "Look at me."

Drawing in a shuddering breath, Maria forced herself to open her eyes. He knelt in front of her, fully dressed, while she was naked but for her stockings and emerald necklace. He stared up at her with those intense dark eyes, holding her in his sorcerer's spell.

As she stared down at him, caught in the web of his sensual power and allure, his touch tightened on her hips. His fingers slid over the soft curve of her buttocks, drawing her closer.

He blew lightly against the curls that hid her wet, aching womanhood, his touch gently nudging her legs apart. Maria sobbed at the intense wave of pleasure, reaching out to clasp his long hair again, to drag him closer. But he eluded her, smiling up at her.

"Have you ever felt like this before?" he said.

"Never," Maria gasped truthfully. She had never even imagined people *could* feel like this, that sex could be so very wondrous.

"Say you're mine," he said softly. "Even if only for tonight, you are completely mine."

"I am—yours." And she always would be. Even if she never saw him again, she would be his, heart and soul.

He lightly licked at her cleft, and she moaned, her head falling back. But he still would not give her all she craved, all she asked for.

"Say my name," he said insistently. "Tell me you want this, want *me*."

"I—I want you," she panted. "Carlos."

And he kissed her *there* at last, his tongue plunging inside her to her very core. Maria's head tossed back and forth as she moaned at the wave of hot sensation. The press of him inside her.

She drove her fingers into his hair, holding them against her as a wave of burning pleasure mounted in her belly. That tense knot, which had wound ever tighter since he had first kissed her on the battlements, unspooled like bright ribbons of sheer joy.

"Carlos!" she cried, trembling from the terrible, wonderful force of it.

He caught her as she collapsed, his arms coming around her to lift her and bear her to his waiting bed. She fell back onto the soft linen sheets, watching avidly as he unfastened his doublet and cast it away. He dragged his shirt over his head, baring his chest to her gaze.

Maria levered herself up on her elbows, panting as she watched him undress. He seemed golden all over, his skin taut over his rippling muscles, shimmering with the heated sweat of desire. A sprinkling of crisp black hair outlined those powerful muscles, the flat brown discs of his nipples, narrowing to a thin line at the band of his hose.

The hose that concealed her greatest desire from her eyes! She sat up, reaching for the lacings, but Carlos caught her hands in his, chuckling hoarsely.

"So impatient," he said, bearing her back down to the bed. "So greedy. Were you not satisfied before, *mi corazon?*"

He kissed the side of her neck, licking and biting, teasing, as she moaned. "I *am* greedy," she whispered, reaching again for his hose. This time he did not stop her. "I want all of you. Everything you can give me."

He swirled his tongue between her breasts. "You should be careful what you wish for. It could easily prove to be far more than you expect."

"I am willing to take that chance." She slid her fingers between the loosened laces, touching the taut, heavy satin of his penis. Her caress slid down its hot, veined length, and she felt it jump under her touch. "Do *you* want *me*, Carlos? Are you mine?"

"Maldicióon," he muttered tightly.

She curled her fingers closer around him. "Say it," she whispered. "Tell me you want me."

"I want you. *Diablo,* but I want you!"

She yanked his hose down, freeing him to her gaze, her touch. He roughly parted her legs wide, driving into her. Deep and fast, to the very core of her.

As he drew away and plunged back into her, his

mouth slammed down on hers, their lips and tongues mimicking the desperate movement of their bodies. Their cries and shouts mingled, their arms and legs a wild tangle on the bed as they tried to get ever closer, to be as one.

That bright pleasure unfurled inside her again, even more intense, more blinding. A shower of sparks, red, blue, white, burning her old self away as she was newborn in his arms.

Above her, his body bent back, taut as a drawn bowstring. *"Querida,"* he cried, thrusting deeply one last time.

Then he collapsed beside her, his head on her shoulder as they shuddered in the last throes of climax. Their legs were entangled, their bodies pressed damply close in the night.

Maria closed her eyes tightly, trying desperately to hold on to it all. Listening to his breath, feeling the press of his kiss against her shoulder. Exhaustion closed over her like a soft, heavy counterpane, weighing her down even as she struggled to hold on to consciousness. To this precious moment.

Carlos was right. She *was* his. And she always would be—even when the terrible day that he discovered her deception came, and all this beauty would be horribly ended. But the memory of his passion would be hers forever.

Nothing could take that away. Even if his passion turned to hatred…

Chapter Five

Carlos lay on his side in the rumpled bed, his head propped on his elbow as he watched the play of the sunrise-light on Isabella's face.

She slept peacefully, a tiny, secret smile on her kiss-reddened lips, as if her dreams were sweet. Her brow was smooth in that serenity of slumber, her hand curled on the pillow palm-up. In sleep, she looked so very young and sweet, free of defenses and secrets.

Free of lies.

He gently touched her hand, uncurling her fingers to examine the pink palm. A ridge of white calluses lay along its base, and there were old, healed cuts along with the fresh wounds of her ordeal at sea. They were the hands of a woman who worked, who scrubbed floors and carried buckets and sliced vegetables, not a lady whose greatest labor was wielding an embroidery needle. Her body, too, was thin and wiry, not soft and pampered, as if she did all that hard work with not enough nourishment.

And she had not been a virgin.

The suspicion that had taken seed when he first met her, the feeling that whoever she was, she was not the Contessa de Valadez, took root and grew. She was an impostor, and as an agent of the king he should clap her in irons at once.

But something stronger supplanted that duty, supplanted all other emotions. He longed to take away all her years of struggle, take away any pain in her past and give her the pampered, luxurious life she deserved.

He raised her hand to his lips, pressing a soft kiss to those calluses, to the pulse that beat so delicately in her wrist. She smelled of rosewater still, and of the salty musk of sex and desire.

When he had invited her to dine with him, making love to her had not been his intention. He'd thought only to ply her with wine, with good food and fine clothes, and slowly peel away the layers of her deception until her true self was revealed. He wanted to know what her game was so he could plan his next move. She was obviously not some typical peasant girl, playing at a crude game of masquerade—she was quieter, cleverer than that. He thought perhaps she could be useful to him.

But as the evening had gone on, he had found that he was the one caught in a web. The flash of her large brown eyes, the curve of her smile, her unabashed sensual delight in her dinner—it had held him utterly spellbound. Enthralled by her in a way he never had been before.

He would find out who she really was, but not by frightening her, not by making her life as hard as it was before she came to Santo Domingo. Just as he was enamored of her, she was not immune to him—he had the scratch marks on his back to prove it. With patience and attention, she would confide in him in her own time.

And then he would know how to act.

He kissed her wrist, nibbling gently at the pulse, the curve of her inner arm. She murmured in her sleep, stirring restlessly against the pillows.

He nipped at the sensitive spot on the inside of her elbow, his caress effortless, pushing the sheets away from her naked body. As his palm smoothed back over her ribs, the weight of her breast, her eyes fluttered open.

"Carlos…" she whispered, her voice rough with sleep.

"Shh," he ordered, cutting off her words with a kiss. Her lips opened beneath his with a soft sigh of welcome, her tongue touching his in the sweetest of good-morning greetings.

Carlos balanced the weight of her soft breast on his palm, his thumb lightly tracing the edge of her sensitive, erect nipple until she moaned against his mouth. Closer and ever closer he moved, feeling the pucker of that strawberry-colored flesh on his skin.

She cried out, and at last he gave her what they both longed for, plucking her nipple between his fingers, rolling it lightly.

His lips tore away from hers, trailing along her arched neck, her shoulder, until they closed over her breast, over the nipple that pouted for his kiss.

He felt her touch in his hair, holding him close against her as her legs fell open beneath him. His body cradled close against hers—they fit so perfectly now, knew each other's every curve and angle. The tip of his penis nudged at her cleft, teasing, making her grow taut with anticipation against him, even as he held himself back.

He kissed her other breast, inhaling deeply of her sweet scent, the roses with the heady musk of desire. Last night had *not* been an aberration, an illusion of the night and the wine. He wanted her, needed her, just as much in the clear light of day.

Her back arched as she pressed herself against his mouth. Her womanhood was open and wet as she slid down his shaft. "Carlos, please, please…" she murmured.

She opened her eyes, her gaze black, unfocused as she stared at him. As he rose up over her, she kissed his jaw, the hollow below his ear, her breath warm and frantic with desire.

"Please, I need you now," she whispered hoarsely. *"Mi querido."*

Carlos groaned, resting his forehead against her

shoulder. *Maldición,* but it would be *he* who babbled all his secrets, not her! He who would be caught. All his years of careful, cold restraint were slipping beyond his grasp, all because of this raw, primitive need for her, and her alone in all the world.

He rolled her onto her stomach so he could not see her eyes, could not drown in them forever, and spread her legs beneath him. He grasped her hips, drawing her up and sliding into her wet, warm passage in one quick thrust. She cried out with the force of pleasure, her back arching up against him, her fists curled tightly into the sheets.

He, too, almost shouted out at the sensation of their joining, the feeling of her against him, tight, clasping him like soft petals as he drew away and plunged forward again. Her hair fell forward, and he kissed the vulnerable nape of her neck, the arch of her spine as he drove into her again.

He felt the heat of her climax, and it made him come, too. An explosion of sparks and fire inside him as he shouted her name over and over in his heart.

She collapsed onto the bed, and he fell beside her, spent, slippery with sweat, drunk with the wondrous pleasure of *her.* Of all they were together. All he wanted to give her.

Whoever she was, he knew that he could never let her go. Never be without her again.

He smoothed her tangled hair back from her face, wrapping the soft strands over his throat and chest. She edged closer, her head against his chest as she drifted back into exhausted, sated sleep.

Carlos gazed down at her, at the two of them entwined—and a plan took form in his mind.

Chapter Six

Maria sat by her chamber window, her fingers automatically plying the needle in and out of the soft linen even as her thoughts were far away. One stitch, then another and another, as she remembered last night. Remembered every single kiss, every touch and caress. Every movement of Carlos's body in hers…

"Ouch!" she cried as the needle pricked her fingertip, drawing blood.

"Contessa!" said one of the maids. "Are you unwell?"

Maria shook her head, staring down at the tiny drop of crimson. "I am fine."

After a morning spent pacing the chamber, a morning after awakening in her own bed, alone, she had seen the maids sewing and thought such a task might distract her. But they were sewing fine shirts for Carlos. And with every stitch, Maria imagined the fabric over his body. Over his smooth, bronzed skin.

The distraction, it seemed, was far worse than the idleness.

She smoothed the shirt over her lap, over the pretty yellow satin of her borrowed gown. Her whole life was merely borrowed now. A stolen idyll, and soon, all too soon, she would have to give it back. The gowns, the fine food, the soft bed—soon they would be only a precious, wondrous memory.

Yet none of it would be as hard to relinquish as Carlos de Alameda.

Maria closed her eyes tightly. In that private darkness she saw his face, the sharp angles of it shadowed in gold by the candlelight of their dinner table. The mysterious smile on his sensual lips, the rich sheen of his long dark hair. The irresistible temptation of his hand reaching for hers. Drawing her into delicious sensual delights she had never before imagined.

She would never forget him, never forget an instant of all they had shared. No matter what the future held, even when she went back to scrubbing floors, she had known love. Known real pleasure. That had to be enough.

Maria opened her eyes, staring down at the snowy-white cloth that would touch him when she could not. When they were gone from each other's lives forever. She forced back a hot, bitter rush of tears. Truly, it was *not* enough! One night could never be enough to quench her passion for him.

But one night was all there was. A message had

been sent to Governor Augusto, and soon he would be here to claim his nephew's bride. She had to be gone by then. Perhaps she could find a ship sailing for another island. Or maybe the Santo Domingo tavern owner Señora Montero, the one Maria had heard the maids whispering about in some wild tale of shootings and pirates, would hire her. She didn't sound terribly choosy.

Before Maria left, though, she had to tell Carlos the truth. No matter how very painful, how coldly frightening the thought was, it had to be done. She owed him that much. And surely, after discovering her lack of a maidenhead last night, he already knew the Contessa de Valadez was not all she should be.

She touched the emerald cross at her throat as she stared out the window, the sunny day all blurry through a glaze of tears.

It was a beautiful island day, the sky a clear bright blue without a cloud in sight, the sunlight all amber-gold. Maria set aside the sewing, going to the half-open portal to see it all more closely. To memorize it in her heart for the moment that this place, like Carlos himself, was gone.

From her high vantage point, she could see the ships in the port, crawling with activity as sailors made repairs, loaded cargoes and prepared for new adventures. The town, too, was crowded with life and motion, with the sounds of bells from the cathedral. The salty-flowery smell of the breeze was warm and sweet.

Once, before she left Spain with Isabella, she had half feared this place would be dangerous and rough, and so would its people. And it *was* rough, but in a way that felt new and alive. Full of wonderful possibilities.

Just like Carlos. Whether he believed it or not, he was a part of this New World.

She leaned on the wide stone windowsill, gazing at the walkways below. They led from the fortress to the town, and were crowded with servants, merchants and sailors going about their business. And just coming up a flight of stairs from one of the storehouses was a solitary figure in black.

Maria's breath caught at the sudden sight of him, and she leaned out even farther, balanced on her palms. His face was somber, preoccupied, as he strode up the walkway, everyone moving swiftly out of his way. But at sight of her a smile spread slowly over his lips.

It made her smile, too, even in the knowledge of what she had to do.

She waved at him. "Good morrow, Señor de Alameda!" she called.

"And good morrow to you, contessa," he answered. His smile widened, tinged with a teasing sensuality that made her shiver. "I hope you had a restful night?"

"Most restful, *gracias*," she said tightly.

"Perhaps you would care to walk with me on the battlements, then?" he said.

Maria nodded. "I will meet you there."

She drew back into the chamber, ignoring the giggling maids as she spun to face the looking glass. Her cheeks were flushed pink just for seeing him again! Her heart pounded frantically with anticipation.

Quickly she smoothed the coronet of braids pinned atop her head and entwined with pearls and yellow ribbons. She smoothed her skirt and, with shaking hands, removed the emerald cross from around her neck and laid it gently on the table.

She dashed out of the room and up the winding stairs she well remembered traversing the night before. If she *had* to part with Carlos, it seemed strangely right that it should be where they had shared their first kiss. Their first embrace.

He was already there, standing by the thick, crenellated wall looking out over the town. The breeze caught at his hair, like a black silk banner in the sunlight. He was perfectly still, ever vigilant over his domain. Ever forbidding.

Her steps faltered at the sight of him, the sight of his stern watchfulness. But then he turned to her, holding out his hand.

She slid her fingers into his clasp, laughing in surprise as he twirled her close to him. He kissed her softly, and she felt his smile against her lips. That rare, beautiful smile.

She sighed and nestled against him, resting her forehead on his chest. Listening to the deep, steady sound of his heartbeat.

"I'm glad your night was *restful,* señora," he said roughly.

Maria laughed again. "I hope yours was the same, señor, for it seems you are up very early indeed."

"There was a great deal of work to be done. While I was—otherwise occupied last night, someone tried to break in to one of the storehouses. There is talk of pirates in the town."

"Pirates?" Maria cried.

"Aye, but never fear. You are safe here in the fortress, and I am sure the villains are long gone from Santo Domingo."

"I *am* certain I'm safe here." Safe with him. But for how long?

"But I fear pirates are the least of my concerns."

"Oh? What could be worse?"

"An elaborate banquet. Governor de Feuonmayor insists on holding one this very night in your honor."

Maria froze. "A—banquet? Tonight?"

"Delicacies have been ordered from every merchant, musicians hired, invitations sent to every corner of Santo Domingo. Everyone is most eager to meet you."

She fell back from him, wrapping her arms tightly around herself to ward off the sudden icy cold.

"What is it, *bella querida?*" he asked. "Do you not feel well enough for a banquet?"

"Nay, I…" She shook her head. *Now.* She had to do it now, before her lies dug her in even deeper. She turned away, hurrying over to the wall so she would not have to look at him while she confessed. One piercing glance from his dark-bright eyes, and the words would strangle in her throat.

She pressed her palms hard to the cold stone. "You must tell the governor to cease going to such trouble for me. I am not worth it. I—I am not what he thinks. What you think."

She heard a faint rustle as he crossed his arms over his chest, but blessedly he did not approach her. He did not have to—she was always acutely aware of his nearness.

"Explain, please," he said, so gentle and quiet. That very quiet was more frightening than any shouted demand.

Maria drew in a deep breath. "I am not Isabella de Valadez."

A long, taut moment of silence spun out between them. "Ah," he said finally, his voice flat and toneless. Cold. "Then, pray tell, señora, who *are* you?"

"I am Maria Gonzales. I was maidservant to the contessa, and we prayed together during the storm. That was when she gave me her necklace. I did not steal it, I promise! I may be a liar, but I have never been a thief."

"Maria. I see. And when you were assumed to be the contessa, why did you not correct everyone?"

Maria swallowed hard. "It seemed a protection of sorts aboard the *Reyezuelo*. I thought if they assumed

I was important I would be left alone. By the time they brought me here, I did not know how to tell the truth."

"And who is Maria Gonzales, in truth?" he said, still in that expressionless tone. He came to her side, standing close yet not touching.

"I am the daughter of a sailor, and my mother died when I was born. Long ago, before I was born, she and Isabella's father—knew each other. The count must have still felt some obligation to her, for when one of Isabella's servants took ill at the last moment he sent for me to take her place. It seemed a God-given chance for a fresh beginning."

"Sent for you from where?" he asked.

"From the tavern where I worked. Before that I kept house for my father, until he died."

Carlos was very still beside her, and she could feel the burning touch of his watchful gaze on her skin. On her very soul.

"I am so sorry!" she cried out, all in a rush. "I never meant to lie to you for so long, but when you talked to me, when you—kissed me…" Her words choked on a sob. "I only wanted to be Isabella for just a while longer. Just to be with you, to imagine what life could be if I was not me, and you were not you. If we were just…"

Suddenly he swept her into his arms, kissing her with a passion and intensity to match hers. A kiss of all the love and desperation they could not put into words.

"I'm sorry, I'm scrry," she sobbed, holding on to

him tightly, her eyes closed. "I will go now, I promise, and you need never…"

"Shh," he murmured, kissing her cheek, her closed eyelids. "Hush now, Maria. I fear I cannot let you leave."

She nodded miserably. "You must arrest me. I know. But I left the necklace. I have stolen nothing."

And much to her shock, he *laughed*. Laughed, and kissed her yet again. "Ah, but you have. You've quite stolen my heart."

"What do you mean?" Maria gasped, trying to step back from him. But he held her fast.

"I mean I am in love with you, no matter if you are Isabella or Maria or any other name, and I cannot let you leave. Not when our betrothal banquet is tonight."

Now she was *certain* she was dreaming! She pulled back from his embrace, staring up into his eyes. He smiled down at her, as if delighted by their whole strange situation. Delighted by her, by life. "What are you talking about?" she said, afraid she was repeating herself horribly.

"Have I failed to mention the fact that Governor Augusto is my uncle, my mother's brother? That you, Maria-Isabella, are my betrothed, sent for from Spain to be my bride? You can hardly leave me now. What is a betrothal banquet without a beautiful wife-to-be?"

"I—you…" she stammered. She pressed her hand to her spinning head.

His expression turned suddenly serious, his dark

eyes intense as he stared down at her, watching her every emotion writ on her face. "And what would my *life* be without you? Empty and cold, just as it was before I found you. Please, Maria. Stay with me. Marry me. Let me make your life as happy as you've made mine. Let me give you—everything."

Maria laughed helplessly. "I—nay, Carlos, I cannot! You deserve too much more than a maid, a liar. You deserve…"

"I don't deserve *you*. But I need you. I need you to stay with me. We are the same—we are meant to be together." He held her hands tightly in his, kissing her fingers, her wrist. The tiny scars on her skin, as if they were the most beautiful marks. He was right, surely. They *were* meant to be together.

And together they could conquer anything. The past, the future. Even the entire New World.

"Then I will marry you," she said, going up on tiptoe and kissing him with all the joy and love in her heart.

He laughed, twirling her off her feet and spinning her around in the golden sunlight that would surely illuminate all their glorious days to come.

* * * * *

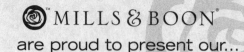

MILLS & BOON

are proud to present our...

Book of the Month

Their Newborn Gift
by Nikki Logan
from Mills & Boon®
Romance

When Lea became accidentally pregnant she
decided that she would go it alone. Rodeo star
Reilly wasn't the sort of man who'd want to
be tied down. But five years later she needs
to tell him her secret…

Mills & Boon® Romance
Available 4th June

Something to say about our
Book of the Month?
Tell us what you think!
millsandboon.co.uk/community

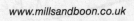

A RUGGED RANCHER...
A TEMPTING TYCOON...
A COMMANDING COP...

These powerful Australian men are
ready to claim their brides!

Available 18th June 2010

2 FREE BOOKS
AND A SURPRISE GIFT

We would like to take this opportunity to thank you for reading th
Mills & Boon® book by offering you the chance to take TWO mor
specially selected books from the Historical series absolutely FREE
We're also making this offer to introduce you to the benefits of th
Mills & Boon® Book Club™—

- **FREE home delivery**
- **FREE gifts and competitions**
- **FREE monthly Newsletter**
- **Exclusive Mills & Boon Book Club offers**
- **Books available before they're in the shops**

Accepting these FREE books and gift places you under no obliga
tion to buy, you may cancel at any time, even after receiving your fre
books. Simply complete your details below and return the entire pag
to the address below. You don't even need a stamp!

YES Please send me 2 free Historical books and a surprise gift.
understand that unless you hear from me, I will receive 4 superb new
books every month for just £3.79 each, postage and packing free.
am under no obligation to purchase any books and may cancel m
subscription at any time. The free books and gift will be mine to kee
in any case.

Ms/Mrs/Miss/Mr _____ Initials _____

Surname _____

Address _____

_____

_____ Postcode _____

E-mail _____

Send this whole page to: Mills & Boon Book Club, Free Book Offer
FREEPOST NAT 10298, Richmond, TW9 1BR